I0745234

THE
BLUE ICE
SHADOW

EBEN BEUKES

The Blue Ice Shadow

Copyright © 2020 by Eben Beukes.

Paperback ISBN: 978-1-952982-71-2
Ebook ISBN: 978-1-952982-72-9

All rights reserved. No part in this book may be produced and transmitted in any form or by any means, electronic, or mechanical, including photocopying, recording, or by any information storage and retrieval system, without permission in writing from the copyright owner.

The views expressed in this work are solely those of the author and do not necessarily reflect the views of the publisher hereby disclaims any responsibility for them.

Published by Golden Ink Media Services   11/27/2020

Golden Ink Media Services
(302) 703-7235
support@goldeninkmediaservices@gmail.com

1
CHAPTER

The man in the linen mask stood motionless as he studied the milling crowd, hooded eyes flickering from face to face until settling on the lone figure in the far corner. The tall blonde man was on the wrong side of fifty but moved with the easy grace of a younger male and when he turned those light green eyes on a well turned ankle passing by, bestowing on its owner that lazy smile, the lady more often than not would experience a flutter of excitement tinged with just a hint of unease. A dangerous man, would be the first impulse, not the sort mother would have deemed suitable.

Yet ...

She would not have been wrong. He was wearing a light grey business suit, no necktie, the dazzling white of the shirt contrasting with the deep golden tan of its wearer. Seated at one of the small cafeteria tables he was stirring a cappuccino as he idly scanned the headlines of a daily newspaper. Sitting with his back to the wall and facing the entrance and the man in the linen mask knew with an old certainty that the owner of that penetrating gaze would have carefully noted the details of every individual in that busy hospital cafeteria. And that the chosen seat wasn't a random act. Old habits die hard.

Harry Dance. And not looking a day older as when their paths had last crossed in that steamy shithole of an African jungle a lifetime ago. Harry who was returning his gaze now, a look of mild puzzlement creasing the corners of the eyes and marking them as those of a man who smiled often. Or spent too much time in the sun.

Shifting his gaze the man in the mask studied the crowd. To his reckoning a pretty regular looking lot for a busy hospital cafeteria at lunchtime. Some patients – one or two heavily bandaged not unlike himself – a few nurses, what looked like visitors buying small gifts before heading off to the wards and a noisy hyperactive gaggle of medical students jostling each other at the service counter. Slowly turning to scan the rest of the room he spotted no-one that would frown at his presence while carefully noting the position of the solitary surveillance camera set high in a corner and covering most of the room.

An all seeing eye recording everything except the magazine rack, just out of sight of the beady black lens he thought. Moving between the crowded tables now, painfully slowly and aware of the looks his pyjamas and dressing gown was getting he suppressed a grimace – that would hurt too much, what with the sutures still fresh and smarting even when opening his mouth for a sip of the ghastly protein drink they insisted he took. The nagging pain in his side from where they took the bone graft.

Approaching Harry's table now and leaning heavily on the hospital issue walking stick, he lurched unsteadily brushing the newspaper from the table. As they both bent down to retrieve the fallen object Harry felt himself go quite cold as a voice from the past whispered *"meet me at the magazine rack..."*

It was the voice of a ghost and staring at the dark eyes behind the slits of that all covering swathe of bandages Harry could be forgiven for seeing a ghost. Carefully reclaiming his chair to finish his coffee Harry scanned the room and, seeing nothing new, nothing to set his nerves on edge, he stood up and strolled over to where the masked man was idly paging through a gossip magazine.

'Hello Mike,' he said softly, picking a periodical at random as he joined the other man with his back to the surveillance camera. 'It *is* Mike, isn't it?'

'For God's sake, Harry, keep your voice down!'

'The CCTV?' Harry said, 'someone watching you?'

Mike Louw, "Mad Mike," as Harry remembered him from their shared past as mercenaries all those years ago, might have had his face altered (not much guesswork there, Harry thought, not with all that bandaging) but the voice was still the same.

'I can't talk now, I'm not supposed to leave my room. If they catch me here talking to you...' There was something in the man's voice, Harry thought, something he had never noticed before, not even in the heat of battle and the cards not falling their way. Fear? Could that be it?

'How did you know I'd be here?' Harry asked as he absently scanned a photo article alleging that everyone in Hollywood slept with everyone else while dressing it up as news. Glancing at a bikini clad ageing star he wondered how much airbrushing had been needed to make the picture halfway presentable.

'I happened to see you walking past my room earlier.'

Harry nodded. That would have been on the fourth floor, Selena up there now and being readied for the surgery. 'What happened to your face?' he asked. At a glance the rest of the man seemed reasonably intact, apart from a slight limp.

About to reply the man stiffened visibly as a young man, a male nurse judging by the uniform, brushed past to claim the table where Harry had been earlier. Harry noticed the whitening of the knuckles on the walking stick, the flicker on nervous eyes. 'I need to talk to you,' Mike whispered, the voice now so low Harry had to lean closer. 'But not here, some place we can be alone.'

'Your room?'

The masked man shook his head, the sudden movement bringing a flash of pain to his gaze, a hand involuntarily reaching up only to fall to his side. 'No! I'm being watched. Savannah forbids me to meet anyone ...'

'*Savannah?!*' Harry couldn't keep the incredulity from his voice, 'You mean ...'

The other man shook his head impatiently, 'Not the military operation from the bush war, this is different, I'll tell you later.' Turning stiffly he stared at the male nurse before lifting his gaze to scan the corridor where a group of white coated medics had just strolled past. Harry replaced the magazine and made a show of glancing at his watch, 'The stairwell next to the elevator on your floor, in five minutes. There's no camera.' And with that Harry left, casually strolling away to head back to the fourth floor where he would wait for Selena's return following her surgery.

No camera in the stairwell, Mike Louw reflected, it was somehow comforting to know that Harry Dance had made that observation almost as a matter of course. But then he had always been a careful man. Seconds later, having paid for the magazine, he headed for the elevators.

The man in the male nurse's uniform watched him go, a frown furrowing his brow. After a moment's hesitation he rose and headed to a wall mounted phone dialling a number from memory. 'Hans? That patient in 405 ...'

There was a moment's delay as the guard manning the security room brought up the relevant data on a computer screen, a curt comment indicating they were on the same page.

'Mr Mike Louw. A Patient of Dr Basson's.'

'Yes, Louw, the one who had the plastic surgery, the man is supposed to stay in his room until they come for him to-morrow.'

'Get to the point.'

'Well, I just saw him down in the kiosk and he was speaking to a visitor, a man.' A note of urgency now in his voice as he sensed the security man's studied indifference. 'It was the way they were talking, soft and not looking at each other, almost as if they're hiding something.'

There was a soft laugh over the line, 'Maybe they're faggots, setting up a contact.'

'Is that what you're going to tell the boss? When it turns out something's wrong, after the clear instructions he gave?'

The line was quiet for a few seconds, the nurse thinking the guard was scanning his screens, trying to pick up the whereabouts of the rogue patient. A moment later his voice, wary now, came back on the line. 'I'm not picking him up at present, hell knows where he's gone. I can't leave here until Ben's back from his break, why don't you go up to his room and check if he's there and get back to me. Take a radio and keep contact. Meanwhile I'll run through the recorded tapes of the last hour and see if I can pick him out. Describe him, what was he wearing?'

With a suppressed oath the nurse tossed the dregs of his coffee carton in the provided trash can and headed for the foyer. *Bloody bunch of lazy shits,* he thought angrily; still, the instructions had been clear: this was one of the special project patients, to be kept away from others until the time came for his transfer to the farm.

The security controller found Harry midway through the previous hour's recorded CCTV footage. A clear shot, good lighting, taken from a camera mounted in a disguised central ceiling dome. After a moment's hesitation he reached for a phone and dialled a number from memory. 'Colonel? Hans here, I'm faxing over a picture of a man we've spotted chatting to our special patient. No details yet but I'm checking with the front desk.'

Standing on the wide veranda luxuriating in the welcome heat of the mid-morning sun, Colonel Jan Ehlers pocketed the cell phone before reluctantly turning to enter the cool darkness of the Halali Lodge's large lounge and head for his office at back. He had been watching the progress of a herd of African buffalo slowly coming into view over the neck of a distant hill and noted with satisfaction that the two tourist groups out on the regular morning safari tour would run into them --- always a thrill for the wide eyed seeker of the big African adventure.

Minutes later he was staring at the picture retrieved from the fax. The image was grainy but there was no mistaking who it was. 'Trouble,' he said softly. 'Big trouble...' Which left him with the daunting decision of what to do with Harry Dance.

It was cold on the landing, the central heating not extending to the stairs. In the old days Harry would have cupped a cigarette, the hot nicotine laced smoke a quantum of comfort against the chill, but those days were over now. Except, the old days had a way of turning up when least expected.

Like now. As he watched the bandaged man carefully shut the door to the stairwell behind him and pause to adjust his eyes to the weaker light, Harry wondered why he bothered with this in the first place, take an interest in whatever trouble Mike Louw found himself in. But then he knew the answer, didn't he? Loyalty. That elusive, invisible, yet all powerful bond between fighting men – *esprit de corps* – some called it. There was a time when this masked stranger with the familiar voice had been under his command, one of his men. How did the Americans phrase it? *Leave no man behind.*

'I think I was seen coming, we don't have much time.' There was a new urgency in the man's voice and Harry nodded, 'Spit it out, Mike; I'm listening.'

'I'm on a police wanted list, Harry. I was working with a special police anti-terrorist unit at Vlakplaas ...'

Vlakplaas. Harry knew the name, the isolated farm where atrocious acts of torture and at times murder was carried out by a rogue police unit, the shocking details laid bare by a subsequent Truth and Reconciliation Commission hearing with the jailing, for life, of the commanding officer. He said nothing, waited for the man to continue.

'It's not just me they're hunting, Harry, there's a lot of us, both police and army, that are wanted and we all know that with the new government the punishment will be quick and harsh. Friends, some whom you know,' – he rolled off a few names – 'put me in touch with *Savannah*, an underground organisation set up to help people like us. People who fought for the dream of a homeland of our own. We were heroes once, Harry; now they want to kill us.'

Savannah. There was that name again. Harry knew with a dread certainty it was going to be a feature of future nightmares and didn't he have enough of those as it was? 'Go on,' he said softly.

'I underwent plastic surgery to my face, here, yesterday. A new I.D. is being created for me and to-morrow I'm being taken to a private game farm, Halali Game Lodge, to recover before being sent overseas.' The two men paused as a door slammed further down the stairwell, relaxing as footsteps receded in the distance. Drawing nearer, Mike Louw continued. 'Many have gone before me, eventually you can even come back if you want and be a free man in your own country again.'

Harry nodded, he could imagine what the trade off would be. It all seemed so wearily familiar, the old snake rearing its hideous head once more.

'...one of the boys was Jannie Smit, remember him? Tall and thin with red hair and ...'

'I remember,' Harry said.

'Well, I knew he had been through this and wanted to know how it all went but he had disappeared, all part of the plan, I guessed. So I contacted his sister who went to school with us, thinking she might just know something.' Here he paused and Harry thought he could sense the tension rising in the man whose voice now had a catch in it.

'She told me Jannie was dead, that his body, his remains, had been found inside a large crocodile killed by game wardens up north one month ago. The animal had been terrorizing the locals down that part of the Umfolozi River.'

'The man had a new face and I.D. How did the police identify him?'

'By his dental records. The thing is they kept it quiet – a big secret – nothing was ever leaked to the press. Linda, that's his sister, only found out because her husband is a cop.'

'Hmm, nasty end.' Harry shrugged, 'Why does this make you nervous?'

'Two things.' Mike Louw said as his eyes searched those of Harry. 'He was dead before the crocodile got him. A bullet to the brain. A professional shot behind the ear.'

'And the second?' Harry asked.

'He had no kidneys,' came the reply, the horror shallow in the man's voice.

There was a sound that had them turn. The male nurse from the kiosk was standing in the doorway, a smile on his lips. 'Ah, there you are, Mr Dance. Your wife is back from surgery, If you'd like to see her now.' The newcomer shared the smile with a silent Mike Louw who mumbled something and eased past to head up the corridor presumably back to his room.

And Harry Dance knew with total certainty that they had been made. Knew that the Death card had once again turned face up.

For he knew there was no way that nurse could have known him as Harry Dance; not when they travelled under the name of Mr and Mrs Harry Dean.

He had been picked up on the CCTV and someone somewhere had looked at some old photos. Someone very well connected and very paranoid.

Someone deadly.

A pile up at the corner of Smith and Marine Parade had the midday traffic slow to a crawl and with an inward sigh Harry eased his sweat soaked back off the seat's backrest and vainly tried to coax more coolness from the car's overtaxed air conditioner. A glance around confirmed that he was pretty much boxed in with no chance of parking and waiting this all out sipping a cold one in one of the many downtown bars.

He had waited until Selena came out of theatre, a brief chat with the attending surgeon confirming that all went well but that it would be several days before they could expect an answer as to the nature of the biopsy.

His wife would be ready for discharge that afternoon. Deciding to return later Harry headed off for a meeting with an old acquaintance, a journalist, whom he hoped to tap for information as to the possible whereabouts of a certain person who was very much unfinished business.

Sitting in the traffic now, watching the rental's temperature gauge slowly climb to just below the point of concern, elevator music on the radio, Harry's thoughts drifted back to the past. He was back in that room with the general, the man who had sent them all to their deaths that night in Luanda when the plastic explosives in his backpack turned out to be a mini-nuke and no-one was supposed to come back. Except Harry did come back and in that room, with the slender cold form of the deadly black mamba slithering down the front of his open shirt, the man's expression one of stark horror as the matt black mouth opened for the strike, he took care of business.

Revenge. A dish best served cold and he, Harry Dance, was actually quite good at that. Took a patient man, of course, often months of relentless pursuit to track that quarry down but, in the end, always worth it.

For Harry knew that until such time as he exacted payment from that one last spectre on his horizon, there would be no peace. No release from the nightmares that had him wake in fright as the faces of the dead flitted by, all eyes on him, silent lips mouthing the same question. Revenge, Harry...You owe us that...

Post Traumatic Stress Disorder the shrink had called it, the one Selena had insisted he see. Seemed there wasn't all that much she could offer in the way of therapy, a matter of dealing with the past, apparently.

Sooner or later every cripple learns to walk in his own way, was how Harry thought of it. Harry's way was to deal with unfinished business.

Revenge.

And the man he was after now, the last on his list, was more than any other the one behind what Harry knew as Lily White. The smiling assassin who had sat in that horror struck Truth and Reconciliation Commission hearing only to say that the secrets of a certain apartheid era project could never be divulged. The Rainbow Nation could not handle that truth...

True, the present trip to South Africa was a long overdue holiday, but Harry saw it as a chance to pick up the spoor again and if Selena knew, she knew her man too well to try and stop him.

He was shaken from his reverie by the sharp bleat of a car horn behind him and as the traffic started moving the music changed ... *take the load of Bennie, put the load on me...*

Memories of an old army favourite. Faces and promises to keep.

2
CHAPTER

As arranged they met with Vusi in the lounge of Durban's Elangeni Hotel at seven that evening. Selena still groggy from the earlier anaesthetic and aware of a dull ache where the breast biopsy had been taken. Vusi asked how she was, a note of concern in his voice and she smiled and squeezed his arm and told him not to worry, the surgeon reckoned it would turn out alright.

Harry waited until they were onto the second round of drinks before asking what Vusi had managed to find out.

'General Meintjes has disappeared off the face of the planet,' came the reply. Nobody has seen him in over a year, in fact ever since the Lily White business hit the news. My contacts figure he's out of the country, probably hiding somewhere in South America.'

The contacts being old comrades from the days of The Struggle, Harry reckoned. The time when Vusi had been a top Umkhonto we Sizwe operative – terrorist in the eyes of the apartheid regime – and Harry one of those hunting him. Men and women who now often held positions of influence and power in the New South Africa and were every bit as eager as Harry and Vusi to bring to justice the architects of the unspeakable crimes against humanity that was a hallmark of the apartheid beast in its death throes.

'Or right here amongst us,' Harry said, 'Hiding in plain sight with a new identity.'

This made the younger man stare at him, a look of wonder in his gaze. 'You know I never thought of that.'

So Harry told him about earlier that day, both Vusi and Selena listening silently to the end.

'Savannah,' Vusi said at length, 'Why pick that name?'

Harry shrugged, 'Why not? Most of the candidates would be from that era, would recall that phase of the war.'

'So it's the old game again,' Selena said softly, 'And we're slap bang in the middle of it.' She had been gazing out the picture windows at the lengthening shadows over the beaches below and the Indian Ocean beyond, the sun all but below the horizon of the land mass behind them that was Africa. Several surfers were still out there, off North Beach and just inside the bobbing buoys of the shark nets, the crowds on Marine Parade thinning now as the sidewalk vendors shut down their stalls to head home.

How beautiful Durban was, she mused, yet how different from the old days – seemingly a lifetime ago – when she came here as a little girl on vacation with her parents. The beaches were all white then, large orange signboards proclaiming them reserved for whites ("Europeans") in both English and Afrikaans. The majority blacks, mainly Zulus, relegated to the role of servants and silent observers. Now it resembled any other city on the east coast of the continent but with modern skyscrapers and a bustling economy – even if much of it was informal – and still the largest and busiest harbour in Africa.

Africa! As always the Dark Continent quickened her pulse, had her senses tingling, made her feel somehow more alive. There was so much happening, the place so much more exciting and, yes, challenging, than she remembered it. How long had it been since they had last lived here? Too many years and it was good to be back.

Even if it was business that brought them back. Unfinished business as Harry called it. With a suppressed sigh she reached for her drink, idly stirring the fruity cocktail with the little umbrella as she gazed at Harry, on the edge of his seat now, in intense conversation with Vusi. Oh Harry, why can't you just let go of this thing? This obsession with killing these men, names only to her but so alive to both the men in her life. What was it Harry had said when they finally got back to the ruins of their home in Marbella, Harry still not recovered physically and emotionally from the ordeal of an Antarctic wasteland, gazing at the blackened embers of what had been their lives? How vividly she still saw it, Harry hardly spared a glance for the ruins of the building, strode straight to the spot where the scattered white marble chips of the driveway was still disturbed. And discoloured. Asked an apprehensive gardener whether that was the spot then kneeling down to softly touch the ground.

She had known, of course, what it was all about. They had never had children, she and Harry, the one empty spot in her life. Perhaps that was why Quinn, "The mighty Quinn" as Harry had affectionately referred to him, was so special to her man. He loved that dog, the big Red Setter his pride and joy. So when he'd straightened up she looked away and pretended not to notice the slight moisture at the corner of an eye, the catch in his voice. "They killed my friend," he'd said softly, "A man's supposed to do something about that…"

Which is when she knew it would be only a matter of time before they found themselves back here once more.

'I have a feeling this business at the hospital earlier might just be connected to Meintjes after all. It's the only lead we have. Louw is due for transfer to this game lodge and I think it might just be a good idea for us to check it out.' He turned to Selena and she knew her man well enough to know she would be the logical one to make a guest appearance at the Halali Game Lodge, said so and even managed to top it with a smile. The operation site was starting to ache and she wondered whether another tequila sunrise would be in order before they went through to dinner, something to wash the painkillers down with and Vusi was quick to summon the waiter.

'I'm already on their radar,' Harry reflected, 'And I doubt whether a disguise would fool them. You, darling, on the other hand, might just pull it off and, as always, Vusi and I would be close by.'

They spent the next twenty minutes discussing the details of the plan: Selena would book a week long stay at the game farm under another assumed name and using one of the many fake passports Harry always seemed to have access to. Before flying out to the farm, she would undergo the necessary radical change of appearance needed to play the role. Meanwhile Harry would look up the sister of the dead man and hopefully get contact details of the policeman she had spoken to.

The plans agreed to and with the prospect of a leisurely meal now quite enticing – Harry was thinking a hot Durban curry with perhaps a nice Cape Shiraz to settle it down – he rose to help Selena out of her deep chair when Vusi spoke. He had been unusually quiet for a while and there was something in his voice that made Harry pause, had him sit down again.

'It's my son,' Vusi said in a low voice. He paused and Harry wondered why he had not noticed the worry in his friend's eyes until now. Of course they knew he had a son – the boy would be a teenager now, Harry reckoned --- and also knew that the boy lived with his mother and that Vusi seldom saw him but the subject was never raised, the black man's personal life a closely guarded secret even from old friends.

'Go on,' Harry prompted.

'He's gone missing,' Vusi said, 'Almost a week now. Joy, his mother, says he went off to a soccer game with a friend and they both disappeared. The police have no clues.' He paused for a moment, Harry suspected to hide the catch in his voice, before going on. 'He's a good boy. He has never done this before...'

Selena had a hand on his arm now, 'We'll find him,' she said with firm conviction and hearing the strength in her voice he knew that was the way it would be. As always she would be the driving force that kept them going.

'I spoke to the police captain in charge, he tells me there has been a number of suspected child kidnappings recently, mainly teenagers, all black boys and all have disappeared without a trace.'

Harry nodded solemnly, 'It's not just a rise in the incidence of runaways? Not that I would suggest ... (he wished he could recall the name of the boy)'

Vusi shook his head, 'The police don't think so, runaways appear on the streets and none of these kids have. The other worry is there has been no ransom notes, no contact at all from kidnappers.'

Harry knew what remained unsaid, knew that Selena would be thinking it too. Could it be a spate of *muti* killings? The country had experienced that before, witchdoctors butchering small children, the *sangomas* using body parts to beef up the potency of their brews. With an effort he suppressed the thought.

'Finding the boy ...'

'Lukas,' Vusi offered.

'Lukas, finding Lukas is now the priority. Vusi, you take the lead on this one but I still feel Selena should make the trip to the game farm as planned. The fact that they identified me that rapidly means, from our own experience, that they'll be coming after us. I want to find them first.'

He rose, offering Selena an arm, a still subdued Vusi following them into the dining room.

It was at five minutes past six the next morning when Colonel Ehlers made the phone call. The number was retrieved from a small notebook kept in his office safe and the delay in making the call was due to difficulty in contacting Mr Heidmann. It had been after midnight when he finally managed to speak to the man who had been attending a dinner party at the Argentinean Embassy. Their discussion had been brief and to the point. 'I suggest you get a mechanic to look into the problem,' the final word from the other man before the line went dead.

So be it, the colonel mused, pretty much what he had figured anyway but it was always better to check with the old man, could have been that he wanted him taken and questioned first, before "fixing the problem." As he dialled the number from the little black book he wondered again about the security of the phone line, the chances of it being tapped. Decided it was unlikely, they had known since the time the previous Savannah client had been disposed of that there was a police interest but were satisfied that the link to the farm had been terminated before the connection could be made. Still, it was prudent to keep to the protocol, for all he knew the other man's line could be compromised.

The man, known to Ehlers only as Muller, answered on the third ring. *Ja?*

Going by the sonorous tone Ehlers figured he had been asleep. He could faintly hear the sounds of bedclothes rustle, make out a sleepy female voice in the background asking who it was and being told to go back to sleep.

'Muller?'

There was a moment's pause on the other side and when the voice came back on the line it was soft, wary. 'Who's this?'

'Mr Brown. We have a small job for you. Two actually.' Without waiting for a reply he went on, 'The usual fee and if it's done by this time tomorrow , there will be a bonus of twenty thousand.'

'Is it local?'

'In Durban. I'll fax the details over.' And with that he replaced the handset on the receiver. From past experience where Muller was involved the results would be swift and final, if sometimes somewhat messy.

Harry Dance's prognosis had suddenly taken a decided turn for the worse. He was humming a tune when he sat down at his desk to type out the details of the hit, the photo of Harry ready to be included. Pity about the doctor, a tame plastic surgeon was hard to come by but Doctor Basson, and his records, were a liability they could not afford to have. Then there was the matter of what to do with Mike Louw, the patient who had been in touch with Harry Dance. Better to bring him in to answer some questions, see how much damage had been done, before finding a final solution for the man who now appeared quite dispensable.

Another task for Muller.

He replaced the phone and swivelled in his chair to gaze out the window, steeped fingers and pensive expression a picture of a man sunk in deep reflection. A barely audible whistle hovered on thin lips as he ran over the plans he had set in motion, searching for a weakness in the strategy. The tune was "my favourite things" from *The Sound of Music*. He loved musicals, saw it no less than five times.

"Raindrops on roses and bright copper kettles ..."

Susan Hetherington smoothed down her tailored nurses' uniform as she took her position behind the reception desk. The white tunic was fresh from the cleaners, crisply ironed with the scarlet shoulder tabs precisely set, the colour bars displaying her specialty qualifications and the silver button indicating her hospital of training were brightly polished as were the small silver nameplate pinned to her left breast, next to the upside down nurse's watch that she had carefully set that morning. The starched nurse's cap was unobtrusively pinned to a neatly bobbed hairstyle and when she had applied the final touches to her makeup minutes earlier in the mirror of the small restroom at back, she noted with satisfaction that she looked good.

It was a matter of professional pride, not like some of the young nurses now coming through the system, all tattoos and body piercings and God only knew what next. Standards were important, especially now, when living in a country that had changed almost unrecognisably in seemingly only a few years. The familiar world of yesterday all but gone now and so many of her class at the old Addington Hospital now either working overseas, working outside the profession or, God forbid, dead.

With a sigh she pulled up the appointments book and neatly arranged the paraphernalia of her desktop. The first appointment was at ten and, as was his practice, Dr Basson had finished his ward rounds minutes earlier and she could now hear him moving about his office as he dictated notes for her to type later.

She was about to get up and tend to a flower arrangement on the coffee table in the patient waiting area when the man appeared in the doorway. Neatly dressed in a lightweight grey suit with a necktie in the colours of the local Sharks rugby franchise, he paused for a moment then turned to close the door leading to the corridor behind him. She was about to protest, ask him to leave it open, when something she saw in his eyes made her hesitate.

They were the palest blue eyes she had ever seen. Washed out, almost colourless and they seemed to see right through her, the way someone would look at an object rather than a person. He was at the desk now and if the eyes were unsettling the smile was downright eerie for there was something infinitely sad about that smile. It didn't go anywhere, not to the eyes, not to the cheeks, just sat there. A parting of the lips more than anything else and when he spoke she found herself startle. 'Is the doctor in?'

It was a surprisingly soft voice, almost gentle and once again with that hint of a deep sadness? With an effort Susan Hetherington pulled herself together, what nonsense was this?! Here they were in the heart of Durban's CBD at nine o' clock on a weekday with fellow nurses and doctors all around down the corridor and she was feeling a chill of foreboding? Please!

'May I help you, sir? We see patients by appointment only.'

'He's in,' the man said. Looking past her at the half open door leading to the surgery. ' I can hear him talking to someone, a patient perhaps?'

'Dictating,' she heard herself say, 'He's dictating letters. I... If you would tell me what I could do for...'

He re-focused his stare on her and even before the man stepped around the desk Susan Hetherington knew there was something terribly wrong. She didn't know what but more than thirty years spent in the kind of environment where life floated past in all its ugliness and hopelessness and finality had gifted her a sixth sense that was all but failsafe.

For Susan Hetherington knew she was about to die. In all those years she had witnessed death many times. In all its ugly forms. But she had never met the Angel of Death, not face to face. Yet she knew, in that last moment of terrible clarity, that Death was in the room, was reaching out to touch her.

In dry air at 68 degrees Fahrenheit sound travels at 1125 feet per second. The muzzle velocity of a standard 115 grein 9 millimetre parabellum bullet fired from a Luger is 1155 feet per second.

Susan Hetherington never heard the shot that killed her.

The sound, when it did arrive a split second later, was little more than the pop of a champagne cork, wisps of acrid smoke drifting through the pores of the bulbous silencer to quickly disperse in the air conditioned atmosphere. Moving quickly the man dragged the nurse's slumped body behind the cover of the reception desk where she would not be seen from the doorway. Then he crossed over to the other room where a startled doctor was halfway to reaching for the phone on his desk.

The first projectile caught him square in the lower chest pulping his heart, the second, arriving before he hit the carpet, a few inches higher and slightly to the left.

Double tap, the trademark of the professional shooter and, Muller noted with detached satisfaction, a quite acceptable four inch grouping.

A quick glance around determined the absence of any surveillance cameras or recording devices, not that he would expect that in a doctor's consulting room but better to make sure. Moving quickly he returned to the reception area to lock the outer door and make sure the body of the nurse behind the desk would not be visible through the frosted glass of the entrance door. Then he went back to the office and closed the door behind him before settling down to the task of sorting through the dead man's files.

It took the better part of twenty minutes to find the files from the list of names he had been provided, fifteen of them in total, easily fitted into the bulky canvas shoulder bag he had brought along. Another four minutes to set the time fuse activated magnesium incendiary device which he placed on top of the pile of residual files scattered about the room.

Setting the fuse for sixty minutes.

In all that time never sparing the slumped form of the man on the floor a single glance, even as he stepped over the steadily growing pool of crimson. He was a professional, no need to check. He too, knew the face of Death.

A quick search produced the office keys from the nurse's purse and as he locked the outer door to the rooms behind him the corridor was still deserted with only subdued everyday noises from the other offices hinting at the presence of routine everyday life.

Minutes later he was seated in the foyer of the Highgate Clinic having selected a chair that gave him a good view of the reception desk. Nine twenty five by his watch, discharge time for the patients going home that day of which a Mrs Selena Dance would most likely be one if his information was correct. Earlier discreet enquiries – it turned out they were family – had revealed that she had been discharged the evening before but was due to return to the surgical ward that morning at nine for removal of a wound drain. As he waited he paged idly through the morning's edition of The Natal Mercury while considering whether a cup of coffee might be a good idea. The kiosk just across the foyer and offering a reasonable view of the desk. Better not, he decided; it was vital that he picked up his quarry when the man came past that desk, there might not be another chance.

So he turned to the sports pages and waited and watched. He was good at waiting and watching.

Fourteen minutes later his patience was rewarded. Harry Dance, looking very much a man of leisure in a light blue linen tropical suit with a navy open necked shirt, escorted his wife into the foyer heading for the elevators that would take them to the car park below the building. They were chatting and Selena, blonde hair brushed back and tied into a bun, had an arm through her husband's and was smiling up at him and walking briskly and even Muller, who normally didn't notice that kind of thing, thought she looked pretty good in those high heeled stilettos she was wearing with such panache.

By the time the lift arrived he was standing right behind them and returned Harry's smile when the pause button was pushed to hold the door open for him and two other latecomers. Standing to the back Muller let the others exit first as they reached the parking level. Hanging back he followed the couple of interest and was relieved to see Harry had parked not far away from his own vehicle.

A white Mercedes with an Avis sticker on the windshield. Standing in the shadows he made a note of the registration before heading to his own vehicle, a tan and cream 1971 Plymouth GTX muscle car he had lovingly restored back to life a few years back. Walking around the back to open the driver's side he paused next to the car's capacious boot to listen for any noise. Satisfied that there was none he climbed behind the wheel and reached for the safety belt.

A cautious man he was always meticulous in his role as an everyday Joe, just another regular guy living a law abiding existence, trying to earn an honest buck. For he knew all to well how easily a well laid plan could go wrong because of a moment's stupidity, or arrogance. A pull over by a traffic cop for a two bit traffic offence could well see him out of pocket to the tune of twenty thousand rands. There was a moment of pleasure as the big V8 started at first turn to quickly settle into that steady slightly irregular rumble of the big block powerhouse which was his only true love in the world he found himself in. Well, beside the wife and kids, of course. So perhaps it wasn't the best choice of vehicle in his line of work, too conspicuous perhaps, but it was a small luxury and the hell with it.

Tilting his head slightly he thought he could hear a slight thud in the back but a glance at his watch showed there was still a good hour to go before the ketamine he had injected the man in the boot with would wear off enough for there to be a problem. Ketamine something he had used before to immobilize those he had to deliver alive and all in all a pretty safe drug.

Developed originally for use on horses and large animals someone had told him, but sure worked well on humans too.

The only worry, a mild one, was the linen mask the item in the boot had wrapped all around his head and face. Could there be a potential airway problem, the man asphyxiate?

Truth be told, he didn't really care. It would be nice if he could drop him off alive so the customer could question him before the problem of disposal would come up. Not that Muller knew anything about the business between the client and the man he had escorted down from his hospital room earlier, the man packed and ready to leave when he arrived and quite willing to accompany him down to the car park, deserted at that early hour, for the travel on to the next phase of a planned journey. Few words between them until they reached the car and the man tried to utter some futile protest as Muller jammed the needle of the prepared syringe into the muscles at the back of the neck and held him down in a wrestling grip until the drug took hold.

Ideally he would have liked to drop him off first at the address he'd been given but there wouldn't have been enough time to get back to the hospital to deal with both the surgeon and Dance.

Dance who was driving now, exiting up the Smith Street ramp and heading down towards Marine Parade, the morning rush hour traffic beginning to drop off and the first signs of holidaymakers in floral shirts and board shorts on the packed sidewalks.

He kept well back, two to three cars between him and the quarry, the big engine hardly turning over, Springbok Radio on the tuner and still doing their breakfast gig. Pleasant warm sun on his arm where it rested on the windowsill. Taking the turn to head up Marine Parade, the sea a bright and glittering blue, he reached for his shades and found a music station that broadcast in English and played country music.

The Elangeni Hotel coming up and slowing down to a crawl as Harry Dance drove up to the main entrance, the doorman stepping up smartly to open the door for Selena. No sign of Dance wanting to get out, waving back at Selena as she stepped through the glass doors where she paused for a moment to chat to a tall black man who gave her a hug before quickly walking across to where Harry Dance was waiting behind the wheel.

Lucky break. His man was heading off somewhere, saving him the hassle of having to find parking, go and scout the hotel to find the room number and plan the next move around that setting. On the move meant he was almost certainly going to get out of the car somewhere and who knows, it might just be a suitable spot for a clean hit.

He'd follow and he'd wait and he'd bide his time.

The only problem was the black man. Who the hell was he and would he pose a problem?

3
CHAPTER

'Is he still with us?'

Vusi's eyes flickered to the rear view mirror as he deftly negotiated an errant delivery van. 'Two tone old model American coupe, keeping a steady fifty yards back.' After a moment he added, 'And making good use of traffic cover. If only the man's ego had let him use a grey Honda Civic we might never have made him.' They had swopped drivers ten minutes earlier, after stopping at a Wimpy for a coffee and to discuss plans for the day. Harry had spotted the car earlier and where it was parked a few cars back, the driver behind the wheel.

'You sure it's a hit?' Vusi asked while patiently waiting for the lights to change.

'Only one way to find out,' Harry grunted and lifted his gaze from what he had been assembling on his lap for the past five minutes, the occasional curse indicating his frustration with the merchandise Vusi had saddled him with. 'Turn left at the next intersection then it's five hundred yards down the road to the quarry turnoff.' He wanted to add "If memory served me right" but reckoned they'd find out soon enough. His only hope was that the place was still as deserted as he remembered it and not covered in squatter's shanties, kids and animals running around.

As they cruised down the rubbish strewn side road Harry again marvelled at how only the main roads, the ones tourists travelled on, were kept under repair. Fifty yards off the beaten track either way and it was pothole city.

Tourism the only game in a town like Durban.

Then they were there and bumping over the uneven dirt track with last night's rain shower masking the depth of the potholes and throwing the two of them about as the car wove its way towards the distant tree line. Harry scanned the surroundings and was satisfied the area was still largely the way he remembered with only a few cars parked in the distance where a soccer game was in progress, the shouts of the kids faint on the light morning breeze. The only other sounds that of the distant hum of city traffic they had left behind with the industrial area they had just come through. No birds which was strange, Harry seemed to remember the baying call of the Hardeha Ibis being a feature of the place.

Maybe they sensed something was about to happen.

'Drop me off here,' he said to Vusi. 'Then drive over to that soccer game and wait for my call.

'How do you know he'll come?'

'He'll come,' Harry said firmly. 'He likely doesn't know exactly where we're staying and no doubt has a deadline if you'll excuse the pun. This might be his only chance before we fly off somewhere.' He was outside of the car now, the tan Plymouth a tiny speck at the corner of his eye, the car parked, waiting.

He watched Vusi drive off then made a show of checking his watch before striding over to the edge of the disused quarry to gaze slowly in all directions, striving for the picture of a man waiting at an agreed rendezvous spot.

Still no movement from the other man, the car stationary with the occasional wisp of vapour from the exhaust. Harry gazed over the expanse of the old quarry, the place much as he remembered it. Grass and small shrubs precariously clinging to the sloping sides with green water and sludge at the bottom and birds sunning themselves on sandbanks or on discarded items of junk and builder's rubbish strewn about. In the distance Harry could make out the half submerged shape of a rusty car wreck. Lifting his gaze he could see the river in the distance, the bridge a low black line on the shimmer dancing off the lazy flow of water and knowing the thundering surf would not be far beyond. The Royal Durban Country Club he reckoned on the other side and straddling those dunes and further on Umhlanga Rocks and the wilderness of Zululand that beckoned.

Adjusting the folded newspaper under his arm he turned to study the car that was now slowly rolling towards him. As always he felt himself go deadly calm, his senses heightened to those of the predator sensing the approach of the prey. He wondered idly if that was how the man behind the wheel was feeling right now.

The Plymouth stopped thirty feet away, Harry motionless as he watched the driver get out and carefully fold his sunglasses away, stowing them in the breast pocket of his shirt. He was wearing a loose fitting khaki bush jacket with the sleeves half rolled up and Harry was relieved to see there was no sign of a long gun. That would have been a problem.

'Mr Jackson?' Harry asked as the other man slowly approached. 'You're five minutes late but I'm glad you could come. Have you got the information?' He had the newspaper clutched in his hands now, striving to create the picture of a man about to do a swap.

Fifteen feet away the man stopped and stared at Harry with what could be a smile or perhaps just a squint as Harry had positioned the sun behind him. He was young, Harry figured mid forties and with a designer stubble and full head of close cropped dark hair handsome in a way favoured by male models. Harry watched in silence as the newcomer moved off to the side, joining Harry near the edge of the quarry but still keeping his distance. Professional, Harry noted with grim satisfaction, the man getting the sun out of his eyes. Harry hated amateurs, considered them far more dangerous as they were so unpredictable.

'Harry Dance?' The voice was unexpectedly soft but with the unmistakeable accent of the northern Afrikaner.

Harry allowed himself a small smile. 'I was expecting someone else but I do believe I recognise you.'

The younger man had both hands by his sides now, hanging loosely, Harry idly wondering whether he was right or left handed. 'Oh?'

'It was a long time ago. The bush war up in Angola, Cuito Cuanavale if I remember correctly. A young Recce sneaked into the Cuban encampment at night and returned at dawn to report the presence of a dozen 120 mm mortars the enemy had brought up. Then capped it by handing over their firing pins to his commanding officer, rendering the mortars useless. Our side got the better of a tough scrap that day.' Harry shook his head at the memory without ever taking his eyes off the younger man's hands. 'I seem to recall him getting the Pro Patria Medal for that feat.'

The man smiled wistfully. 'That was a long time ago,' he said softly. He was glancing around now, confirming that they were alone, before turning his gaze back onto Harry who was standing quite still, watching him.

'You know why I'm here?'

Harry nodded. 'It doesn't have to be this way...'

'Not much call in the New South Africa for old heroes, Harry. Pity no-one told you that.' His hands had moved behind his back, slowly but deliberately and the professional in Harry couldn't help noticing the wide balanced stand as he waited for the move. As always Harry watched the eyes, that's where the sign would come from, seconds before the action and as always he read it right.

'Sorry you didn't make it,' the hitman said as he brought the matt black nine millimetre into view. The motion was almost languid, slow motion even, the man a professional with all the time in the world. The impact of the ejected cartridge cases blew the newspaper clean off Harry's hand that held the bucking forty five, the heavy slugs taking Muller high up on the chest and flinging him backwards all of six feet and he was still airborne as he went over the side of the quarry praecipe, his own pistol following him down in a wide arc of spinning black and gleaming sunlight.

Despite the silencer there was still a report Harry thought would carry a distance and once again he cursed the inaccuracy of the weapon, the heavy Colt never his favourite piece. Stepping up to the edge of the crater he gazed down at where Muller was lying on his back fifty feet below. Gouge marks on the sloping side of the mud walls indicated where he had struck the sides before coming to a rest in a shallow pool of green sludge. Staring hard Harry could not make out any blood on the man's torso and with an inward sigh he raised the gun to take careful aim at the sprawled man's head when Vusi pulled up in a cloud of dust and screeching brakes.

'Get in quickly, Harry, there are cars coming this way, we have to get out of here!' He had the passenger door open and was leaning over imploring Harry to hurry with a waving motion of an arm. With rising agitation he watched Harry slowly lower the gun before stepping away from the edge and getting into the car. Then they were away with spinning wheels spraying mud and both men clinging on as Vusi negotiated the deep water puddles.

Back on the highway Vusi watched Harry disassemble the silenced automatic before stowing it in the glove box and leaning back to gaze out the window at the lush green landscape sliding past. He knew better than to ask what happened, knew that after a kill this hard man that was in so many ways and after all they had been through, still a mystery to him, would be silent and withdrawn for a while.

To his surprise it was Harry who broke the silence after a minute or two. 'I knew him,' he said softly. 'Not that we ever met, but he was a legend in the special forces during the Angolan lot. We all knew him.'

Which, Vusi reflected, as a so-called terrorist at the time and fighting his own war, probably meant he also knew him. No skin off his teeth, let the bastards all kill each other off. Still, Harry was different and it was good to know he still had the skills they had all come to rely on. 'You didn't plan to kill him,' he said. 'He could have walked away.'

'No,' Harry said, 'He couldn't and we both knew it. I might not have wanted to kill him but I did set him up pretty good.'

They drove the rest of the way in silence.

The man lying in the dirty green slime at the bottom of the quarry lay quite motionless for what could have been all of ten minutes. Then, suddenly, an arm moved. Jerkily at first and soon joined by the other as he pushed himself into a sitting position, all the while scanning the edge of the basin he found himself in. In a sea of pain every movement, no matter how small, elicited a grunt of agony as he slowly with clumsy fingers tore off the bullet proof vest worn under his shirt, the Velcro wet and noisy in the action.

Free of the restraining body armour that had saved his life he sank back into the mud while breathing deeply, gathering his strength for the next phase, climbing out of this stinking shithole he was in. Gingerly running an exploring finger over where the vest had absorbed the impact of the heavy slugs he winced as it encountered the two deeply bruised areas. No blood but he reckoned a rib was gone and possibly the collar bone on the left.

Painfully slowly he climbed to his feet, pausing more than once as spasms of nausea mixed with waves of pain, his head spinning before slowly easing off. Jesus he was going to be sore come to-morrow! 'Fuck you, Harry Dance,' he said with feeling as he stumbled towards where he thought a path led up the distant side of the quarry.

Back at the car he stood for a moment, catching his breath that came in painful rasps and listening to the faint but steady hammering coming from the trunk. Idiot! Still, with the sun up high and humidity climbing, it would be like a sauna inside there, especially under those bloody facial bandages. With a sigh he reached for his keys, searching for the one that would open the trunk, let the idiot out. He supposed he could have let him travel up front when he'd collected him from the clinic that morning but then the moron suddenly got cold feet, didn't he? Wanted to go back and make a bloody call, or something. Had to knock him out, didn't he? Well, he thought grimly, the way he felt now it would take very little for him to pop the sucker should there be any more shit.

No matter how well he had been paid to bring him in alive.

4

CHAPTER

Linda Evans was wearing a tracksuit and running shoes when she answered the door on Harry's third push of the bell. Lanky with liquid brown eyes the short cropped blonde hair was tied back by a colourful sweatband and very red painted nails drew attention to slender well manicured fingers. 'Please come inside,' she offered standing aside to let Harry through. She seemed satisfied with his introduction not asking for proof of identity.

'You must excuse my appearance, I've just come back from a ten k run. I'm hoping to do the Comrades Marathon this year.' Lifting scattered books off the couch to create a space for the visitor while blaming the kids who were now at school, she took a chair facing Harry and asked how she could be of help.

'Firstly, thanks again for taking my phone call earlier this morning. I do appreciate you speaking to me about your late brother.'

The young woman, Harry guessed her in the late twenties, shrugged and spread her hands in a gesture of hopelessness. 'I'm just glad someone is looking into the way Jannie... the way he died.' A drop of perspiration escaped from under the headband and she absently wiped it away. 'Is there any news Mr...'

'Dance. Harry Dance.' He had decided against using one of the many aliases he carried ID for, figuring he was bound to meet up with someone who knew him sooner or later anyway. 'The investigation is ongoing and I represent a Special Branch of the National Intelligence Agency that have been asked for help by the police. We are retracing all the steps of the investigation and hence I'm here to ask you a few questions. When was the last time you saw your brother?'

'Two months before he disappeared. He came to see us, my husband was in the army with him, and we had a meal together.'

She went on to describe details of the evening's barbecue and Harry let her finish before pressing on. 'Was there anything different about his manner?'

Linda shrugged, pulling a face, 'He was quieter. We hadn't heard from him in more than a year, didn't know where he was, until he phoned the day before. He had changed his appearance, grown a beard and was wearing glasses with lenses that looked like plain glass to me.' Adding, 'I didn't ask. I knew there had been some trouble and that at one stage the police were looking for him...'

'Did he say anything to your husband?'

'Deon, that's my husband, mentioned later that Jannie seemed agitated and let slip something about a new start somewhere overseas and people that were helping him. He wouldn't say more but promised to be in contact once things had settled. Deon says he couldn't get anything more out of him and at ten that evening he left and the rest I... well, you know...'

She was on her feet now, Harry having accepted the offer of tea and as she busied herself in the kitchen he ambled around the small living room drifting his gaze over the ubiquitous framed family photos – a pigeon pair of flaxen haired pre-schoolers clustered together with mum and a stern looking father before settling on the pictures on the walls. Traditional Afrikaner middle class was the conclusion; the batik of Rembrandt's Laughing Cavalier and Tretchikoff's Dying Swan, prints of Pierneef African landscapes and a croqueted neatly framed reminder, in Afrikaans, that a house is not a home without a mother. Harry wondered what a mother would be without a home but shrugged it off.

Of more interest was a large South African flag, the old orange, white and blue one with the small Union Flag and those of the two Boer Republics at centre. Inscribed in flowing script across the lower section was "Ons vir jou, Suid-Afrika" pledging everlasting allegiance to what could only be the old apartheid regime.

He looked for a family bible but couldn't spot one, probably beside the bedside.

Harry accepted the cup of tea and made appreciative noises about the home made aniseed rusks which were quite delicious. 'You mentioned they were together in the army, does your husband still have contacts in the military?'

As hard as he strove to keep it casual Harry detected the sudden flicker, a note of wariness, behind the depths of her gaze. 'Oh, he left the army years ago, at the time they let Mandela out of prison. Deon said all was lost then anyway and that it was every man for himself in the new South Africa.' Realising she had said more than intended Linda Evans bit her lips and busied herself with replenishing Harry's cup.

'Some of the old units still get together for meetings, you know, chatting about old times, that sort of thing?'

'I don't know about that,' came the answer. 'Deon never talks about it and he's so busy at work now and then the kids... You know.'

Harry said indeed he did and asked her about the policeman she had contacted regarding the death of her brother. A Sergeant Pretorius from the Homicide Division. A contact number followed and Harry looked at his watch and thanked her for the hospitality and promised to let her know once they had more information.

Then he was outside and heading down the garden path to where his car was parked in the shade of a jacaranda tree a short distance away. A big man in a crumpled ill-fitting grey suit was leaning against the hood eating what looked like a meat pie with obvious relish while flicking bits of pastry off his tie. He looked up as Harry approached, eyeing him with no pleasure. Up close now Harry could see that "fat" would be a more accurate description, small lively eyes peering over prominent rosy cheeks while generous jowls spilled over a frayed looking collar that could do with a clean. Scuffed brown Hush Puppies completed the picture.

The casual observer might have ventured "tramp" but Harry knew a cop when he saw one. 'May I help you?' he asked, reaching for his keys.

The fat man, whose name transpired to be Piet Niemand, unfolded his frame from the car and wiped his mouth on a soiled handkerchief. 'Let's take a ride,' he said in a bored tone of voice. 'You drive.'

'What about him?' Harry inclined his head in the direction of the other man sitting behind the wheel of a blue Toyota parked across the street.

'He'll follow.' Niemand waited for Harry to unlock the car before settling into the passenger seat with an audible grunt.

'Where to?' said Harry whose senses were on high alert. Somehow he didn't think the bulge under the fat man's armpit would be ascribed to a medical condition and with a back-up close behind...

'Just drive. Head on down to the beach, we'll talk as we go.' Niemand had produced a stick of chewing gum from somewhere and Harry watched as he unfolded the wrapper, stubby fingers moving with surprising agility.

'What do you want with me?' Harry knew it would be fruitless to ask about the man's credentials. Police would be all that was forthcoming.

The fat man sighed and rummaged through the car's glove box, glancing at the automatic before tossing it back with a snort of disdain. 'Piece of shit. Don't you keep any snacks here? Chocolates, potato chips, any fucking thing?'

'Afraid not.' Following Niemand's directions he pointed the car towards the beachside Golden Mile, the traffic picking up as they approached the first of the traffic lights. A glance at the rear view mirror confirmed that the Toyota was following, keeping a steady distance of several car lengths.

'Harry Dance,' the cop said with a sigh. 'Now where have I heard that name before?' Harry figured Piet Niemand would not be the kind of man to ask a question he didn't already know the answer to. At least not in the kind of quasi friendly atmosphere they now travelled in. He said nothing.

'Let me see. Could it possibly be the same Harry Dance who was involved in that Lily White business a few years back leading to quite a few nasty outcomes for some, I must admit, unsavoury characters? Or could it be the same Harry Dance who was once a prisoner on Robben Island following some shit across the border that to this day is classified under the Official Secrets Act? The same Dance wanted in some circles in connection with a large amount of money apparently missing from some government slush fund?' The baby blue eyes were on Harry now, a look of curiosity mirrored in their depths.

'How did you know I was going to be at that house, just now? Did the woman contact you?'

The fat man laughed, a throaty gurgle that started deep down his guts and floated up to end in an almost musical lilt. 'The bottle blonde housewife? Are you shitting me? She knows nothing. We picked it up on the phone tap when you called her earlier.' The idea seemed to amuse him as another bout of silent laughter had him shake his head. 'That amaze you, Dance? That we sometimes listen in to private conversations? Innocent people and all that shit?'

'May I ask why you are tapping her line?' Entering the top end of Marine Parade now and turning south heading for the main beaches, the sidewalks were filling up with holiday makers patronising the makeshift stalls lining the sea wall.

'Notice anything when you were inside that house, Dance?'

Harry shrugged as he swerved to avoid a death wish cyclist. 'A real Afrikaner family, some relics from the old days. 'He glanced at his passenger, 'Is that what you're hinting after?'

'Very good. The husband is a right wing activist. Ex- AWB. The *Afrikaner Weerstands Beweging,* the resistance movement that played a role in that aborted coup a few years back. Where there was talk of a missing nuclear device ...'

'Cherry Red,' Harry said softly as old memories flooded back. 'Didn't that all fall apart with the death of the leader, Eugene Terreblance? The whole Afrikaner Homeland thing?'

Niemand shook his head, stubbled jowls audibly scraping over his collar. 'Don't you fucking believe it. Anyway, we like to keep tabs on these people and now I'd like to know of your interest in this other business, the killing of Jannie Smit.'

So Harry told him, leaving out the private matter of the search for a certain gentleman Harry had old unfinished business with. Instead spinning the angle of Selena's medical situation that led to the meeting with Mike Louw.

Durban Point Beach coming up now with the old Addington Hospital across the road from where the usual pack of surfers were enjoying the sunbaked waves. 'Turn in here and park over there,' Niemand said indicating the entrance to a paid parking area at the far end of the beach. Harry slotted the car into the indicated spot not failing to notice the proximity of a nearby hot dog stand. The blue Toyota pulled into the vacant slot on Harry's side, the driver, a clean shaven young man whom Harry thought no older than about twenty sat behind the wheel staring out at the sea.

Wafting through Harry's wound down window came the sounds of a distant carousel intermixed with the steady hum of the traffic and the thunderous crash of the surf. Not forgetting the unmistakeable smell of fried onions and sausage. Harry watched as the big man laboriously climbed out of the passenger seat, the car visibly rising on its suspension. 'Let's take a walk,' came the grunt of an invitation as Niemand led the way to the food stall.

His progress was blocked by a wizened black man wearing a dirty white lab coat sporting a barely discernible logo introducing him as a "parking attendant." 'It's ten rand for an hour,' adding, after a moment's hesitation 'boss.'

'Fuck off,' the cop said shouldering the little man aside as he approached the service counter.

'Sorry, boss,' the little man whined. 'I didn't recognise you. My eyes ...' the apology petered out as he sized up the man in the blue Toyota before deciding that avenue didn't look promising either.

Harry watched the big man place his order of two hotdogs and a glazed donut to be washed down with an upsized Coke float. Deciding he might as well join in he ordered a pizza slice with a medium coffee to go. The resigned look on the face of the man behind the serving counter suggested he wasn't harbouring great expectations of being paid long before the softly uttered 'on the house, boss.'

They sat on a graffiti- covered wood slatted bench as the big man worked his way through the snack with the studied attention others might devote to the workplace. The coffee was not bad, decidedly better to Harry's reckoning than the canteen coffee at the police station where the alternate spot for the interview could so easily have been. Stretching his legs out he soaked up the sun as he waited for the cop to stop chewing and gulping and get on with it.

After what seemed a long wait but was probably only minutes, Niemand tossed the remnants of his meal in the general direction of an overflowing trash bin, burped, beat his chest with a clenched fist and turned to Harry with a sigh. 'I like you Dance. I think we might just be of help to each other.' The unexpected bonhomie suggested a response of sorts would be required.

'Oh?' Harry ventured, keeping his voice neutral.

'Sure.' With a grunt the big man straightened up and when he continued there was a different tone to his narrative. 'Jannie Smit was my man,' he said as he stared out to sea. 'He was a wanted right wing terrorist one step ahead of the Truth and Reconciliation Commission and most likely a prison cell to look forward to. I found him first, we nailed him on an unrelated criminal offence and cottoned on to who he really was. His connections to the neo-right underground was what interested me and it wasn't difficult to turn him.'

Seeing the puzzlement in Harry's gaze he went on. 'Have you ever heard the term "Savannah" used outside of its erstwhile military significance?'

'Why don't you fill me in?' Harry said, evading the question.

'It's an underground train, an escape route set up for fugitives from the far right on the run from the law. So secret the public has never heard of it. I got Smit onto that train, he'd already contacted them before he fell into my lap, so it wasn't hard to let it play out.'

'Except,' Harry said, 'Someone found out...'

There was a silence as Niemand studied his hands. 'Someone inside Special Branch,' he said at length adding. 'So until I catch the cunt there's no-one I can rely on. That's where you come in, Dance.'

'What's in it for me?'

The big man stared out to sea, squinting against the bright reflections. Harry was about to repeat the question when he spoke with a hint of weariness. 'I hear you have a good life now, Dance. Over in Spain, I'm told. Fancy house and fast cars, little woman to warm the bed. Would be a pity to lose all that, swop it for a jail cell at Sonderwater.' He turned his gaze on Harry, the eyes watery, surrounding skin pink and puffy and sweating in the building midday heat. 'Look at this.' He handed over a folded manila envelope from an inside pocket.

'An arrest warrant,' Harry said at length, handing it back to Niemand, 'Seems to have my name on it. May I ask why you have it?'

'Someone dobbed you in, Dance. Someone with a direct line to some high placed stooges in the department. Luckily I have a few contacts over there myself, always handy to know what the shits are planning.'

'And your contact intercepted the warrant and now...'

'Not intercepted, Dance, rather *delegated* it my way. As the commissioner always says, we are all one big family in the force. All working towards that same noble goal of justice for all.' Something in his tone suggested that slogan was not likely to be tattooed on his chest, didn't feature in his bedtime prayers.

'And, needless to say, you have not managed to track me down.'

'You're a hard man to find, Dance.'

Harry glanced at his watch, past two and he had things to do before meeting up with Vusi later that day. 'How do I contact you?'

'Here,' he handed over a grubby calling card with what looked like a ketchup smear on a corner, 'Use the mobile number, the work line isn't secure.' Grunting he rose to take off his jacket, placing it on the bench and rolling up his sleeves.

'I have to go,' Harry said, making an effort to get up and being restrained by a ham sized hand with what seemed like the weight of the world's sins behind it 'Sit down, Dance. Tell me about what you've found out so far, where you're heading next.'

It took ten minutes, Harry mentioning the game farm and Selena's planned trip out there. He found it prudent to omit his hopes that the search for Savannah might lead him to his ultimate prey, his old nemesis. When he'd finished Niemand grunted and fished out another stick of gum, the silver wrapper drifting lazily down to the sand. 'Bloody medical tourism. Come for a face lift and do some game viewing on our exclusive resort while you recover. South Africa's answer to sex tourism.' He shook his head in disgust, 'What the fuck will they think of next.'

Harry was about to suggest canned big game hunting but that was hardly news and probably on offer at the Halali Game Lodge as it was. He risked another glance at his watch and this time Niemand let him get up, joining him with a grunt. As they passed the kiosk a pink icing coated donut was placed on the counter ready for the policeman to scoop up in the passing, an apprehensively grinning attendant all but bowing and scraping as the party moved past. Niemand didn't spare him a glance leaving Dance to conclude he was witness to a well rehearsed sequence of events not necessarily falling into the category of running a tab.

Pausing at the cars, Harry fiddling for his keys, Piet Niemand forced down the last of the donut, burped and placed an outstretched hand against the car door preventing Harry from opening it. 'Screw me over on this one, Dance, and I'll make you wish you'd never been born...' It was delivered with a smile, just a little banter between friends. Finally allowed to get in behind the wheel Harry lowered the window to return the smile as his eyes picked up previously unnoticed food and beverage stains on the man's clothing. 'Are you married, Niemand?' he asked with a note of concern.

'Bitch ran off with a vacuum cleaner salesman,' came the grunted reply as Niemand slammed the door shut with more force than strictly necessary.

'Can't imagine why she ever left you,' Harry said as he cranked his neck to reverse the car out of the space before driving away, the looming figure of a scowling cop fading in his rear view mirror.

5
CHAPTER

Cato Manor. Erstwhile dung heap of Durban's Indian population now dung heap to a wider black mass of humanity. Vusi parked the car in the lee of a crumbling building that might once have been painted white or equally might have just started off the colour of despair. Standing motionless for a moment as the pungent smell of overflowing trash cans and open sewers wafted around him he surveyed the gathering of street urchins eyeing him back with equal interest. Vusi knew the score, after all, didn't he grow up in a neighbourhood much like this? Yet it all seemed so distant now but part of him knew that the daily struggle of this ragged yet bright eyed bunch was no different in the New South Africa from what it had been in the days of The Struggle.

Picking out the largest of the bunch, a particularly scruffy looking specimen sporting an expression of sardonic amusement – Vusi had him down for about thirteen – he called him over. *'Kunjani, buti,'* he said in Zulu, the language of his youth as easy on his tongue as if he'd never left. And, in a way, he never had.

Wary now, this well dressed man in the fancy car was clearly not from around there, yet spoke like one of them, the now scowling youngster sidled up.

'What's your name?' Vusi had his wallet out now, aware of young eyes fixed upon it, a low murmur from the rest of the gang hanging back.

'Tsotsi,' came the defiant reply.

Tsotsi, slang for gangster. Vusi let it ride. 'Want to earn some cash, Tsotsi? Let's say fifty rand, half now and the other half when I come back just now and the car's still looking good?'

There was a moment's hesitation, Vusi suspected more for the benefit of the hangers back, but the kid's eyes never left the money on offer and the deal was struck with little more than a nod. And Vusi knew the deal would be kept, wasn't it Harry who always said the only deals worth a damn were the verbal ones, done with the shake of a hand between men of honour?

Another twenty had one of the smaller urchins, delegated by a now businesslike Tsotsi, lead Vusi to the house he was looking for. Joy had given him the address of course, during that telephone conversation a day earlier, but "address" was a relative term when it came to a shanty town.

A short perilous journey dodging rubbish underfoot and snarling chained mongrels darting out from darkened doorways and they were there. Unlike its surrounding neighbours this was a formal dwelling with a small enclosed yard out front, washing on a line at back. There was even an attempt at a garden, hardy gardenias a welcome splash of colour in a sea of drabness. Thanking the youngster with an extra few rand slipped to a broadly smiling face (gratifying to see the gift was accepted with both hands held out, the respectful way he had been taught as a child.)

Vusi opened the rickety gate and stepped onto the porch. Instantly he was greeted by raised voices from inside. One the familiar high pitched voice of a woman the other the deeper voice of an unknown male. An argument of sorts was going on, in a rapid mix of Zulu and English, something about money and rent and responsibility. He was about to knock when there was the sudden, unmistakeable sound of a slap followed by the trailing wail of a woman in despair.

The man, dressed in a soiled white vest with an ill fitting pair of workman's dungarees was standing, fist raised, over the woman who was cowering on a couch, an outstretched arm raised in defence, a pleading look on her face.

'Want to dance with a man?' Vusi said softly, controlling his voice even as the icy feelers of an old familiar rage washed over him. He was standing in the shadows of the doorway now, a silhouette with the light behind him and it took a moment for the man to focus on him.

'Who the fuck are you? What are you doing in my house?' Vusi saw a tall well built black man, late thirties at a guess, manual worker judging by the clothes and work boots. 'I could ask you the same and, if I'm not mistaken, the house belongs to the woman, not you.'

Switching his gaze to the woman on the couch, *his* woman a lifetime ago, Vusi registered the shock on her face, the sudden panic in the widely staring eyes. 'Hello Joy,' he said softly, 'I came as soon as I got the news.' He wanted to add "about Lukas" but, after all those years, what other reason would there be for this meeting?

'Vusi!' she managed with a slight stammer, 'I...I...' His field of vision was suddenly obliterated by a large form stepping into his personal space. 'You come into a man's house and think you can just...' A hand like a shovel pushed Vusi roughly away and towards the door before the woman's scream brought him momentarily to a halt.

"Please, Cyril, don't! He'll kill you! He's not like other men...' The voice trailing off as the man called Cyril advanced upon Vusi who was brushing off dirt stains from the front of his shirt with a hand that was just a little shaky as the old familiar rage welled inside him. 'You're a big man,' he heard a distant voice say, just audible over the rushing blood flow in his ears, 'But you're out of shape. I do this for a living...'

And as the big man lurched forward again, a ham sized fist swinging in a haymaker punch, Vusi stepped inside and raked a heel all the way down a shin with perhaps just a hint of pleasure. And as the big man went down in a howl of pain it was really just a formality to bring a knee up into the broad face with perhaps more force than was strictly necessary. Leaving Vusi, as he stood over the unconscious form, surveying the mess on his trouser leg with a degree of distaste.

'You bastard! You fucking bastard! Look what you've done!' shouted the woman as she knelt next to the slumped form, darting hands hesitant in what she should do, blazing eyes raised to meet those of Vusi who shrugged as he searched for a place to sit. 'You might have me take a look at that nasty bruise on the side of your face, not unlike the one on your upper arm. I think lover boy here got off lightly,' Vusi said in what he hoped was a soothing tone.

'He's a good man, not a bastard like you who disappears for years at a time leaving a woman to look after their child on her own, not knowing whether you're alive or dead...'

Moving aside some magazines Vusi sat down on the couch with a sigh. Part of him thought of explaining to this once familiar stranger that there had been a war, a terrible struggle against a beast called apartheid. That he had been a fighter in that war with a price on his head and a certain unpleasant death if ever caught. That contacting her would only put her, and his son, neither known to the Security Police at that time, in danger. That... But then what was the point? Truth was the war destroyed whatever it was they had and now all that they had in common was their eighteen year old son, Lukas. A son he had not seen in over two years. 'Tell me about what happened to Lukas,' he said at length.

A tear streaked face was raised from where she was still making cooing noises over the slumped form from where gurgling snoring noises were now emanating. 'You bastard! Look at his face! He's not breathing properly, do something!'

'He'll be fine. Try fanning him with a hat if it'll make you feel better.'

Immediately feeling sorry having added the last bit, the old sarcastic Vusi back in the room and not helping. Leaning forward on the edge of the seat to hold out a box of tissues he took on what he hoped was a more placatory tone. 'You have to help me here, Joy, if the boy has been missing for a week already time is of the essence. What can you tell me about the last time you saw him?'

He helped her ease the other man's head onto a pillow and waited patiently as she busied herself carefully wiping away the blood still streaming from a shattered nose. Sensing she was still too upset to be of help Vusi straightened up and wandered off in the direction of where he thought the kid's bedroom might be. He questioned as much to be answered with a grunt and an agitated wave towards the far end of the corridor.

Boys' rooms usually have boys' things. Scattered items of clothing piling out of half closed drawers, shoes tossed carelessly about. Sporting items such as footballs and bats and posters on the walls.

Posters. Standing in the middle of the small faintly sour smelling room Vusi found himself doing a slow traverse as he took in a snapshot of his son's life. What had he expected to see? Posters of action heroes perhaps? Chuck Norris hefting a sawn off shotgun? Or perhaps sporting stars, soccer players (he vaguely remembered Lukas kicking a soccer ball around at some school sports day.)

Video games. Didn't kids nowadays have posters of games, or anime characters?

What Lukas had was posters of humanity's well documented horror stories. Man's unquenchable capacity for torture, racism, exploitation and persecution. The Nazis, death camps, piled on high bodies with smiling Khmer Rouge fighters looking on. Blown up grainy black and white photos of apartheid South Africa, a sea of Black workers in ill fitting overalls holding out their pass books in muted slavery.

And scattered in between the ugly images of mankind's dark side, slogans minted and made famous by a thousand protesting voices. He didn't have to search too hard to find Che' Guevara's bearded image staring down at him.

An activist. His son, his little boy, was an activist.

'It's been like this for almost two years now,' a soft voice said behind him. 'First came the questions at dinner time, questions about you and what you were fighting for and what you believed in. Then, this ...' Her voice faltered and Vusi turned to look at the woman he had once loved. Part of him wanted to reach out, wrap his arms around her and smell the shampoo in her hair and tell her things were going to be alright. But they were way past that now.

'And what did you tell him? What was it we fought for?'

She shrugged, her shoulders jerking in silent sobs as she fumbled for a tissue. 'How could I tell him when I don't know myself?'

Folding her arms as if to ward off a sudden chill in the room she searched his eyes. 'How could I tell him his father fought for freedom and justice and a new life for all when he looks around him, looks at the country where so much blood has flowed, and nothing has changed?'

She was about to go on but Vusi's restraining gesture had her stop. He'd heard it all before, was part of the disillusionment himself and didn't want to hear it all again.

'Where is he now?' he asked. 'Do you think it has something to do with this?' He indicated the wall display.

'Over the past year he has become increasingly withdrawn. He still goes to school, Lukas was always a good student, but he gave up playing sport and his friends never came around any longer. He spent a lot of time on his computer and wouldn't let me see what was on it. At first I thought it was just a phase but lately...' She paused to blow her nose and Vusi had to fight back his mounting impatience. Get to the *point*, woman!

But he knew better than to rush her, instead busied himself searching for signs of the boy's computer, at first glance no sign of a desktop device. Finally, after a few moments of silently watching him pull open drawers and rummaging through a pile of clothes at the bottom of the cupboard, she continued. 'There was this one boy... older, I only saw him here once when I came back early from work and Lukas didn't introduce him. Almost like he didn't want me to see them together...'

'When was this?'

'A week before he disappeared...' Her voice dropped off as she stood still, watching him search the room. 'What are you looking for?'

'His laptop. Does he normally take it with him, to school perhaps?'

Joy shook her head, the movement slow, tired. 'Never. It was always just sitting there, on that desk. A grey HP I think it was. One of those thin new ones with a big screen. Oh, and he had a sticker, a photo, stuck on the lid.'

Vusi straightened up, fixing her with a quizzical look. 'Photo?'

'Yes. A man with dreadlocks and a beard and a colourful knitted cap ... There!' Her followed her indicating finger to a small poster about to become detached from a far corner.

'Jimi Hendrix,' he said thoughtfully. 'Was that the kind of music he listened to?'

She shrugged, 'I know that sometimes, over weekends mainly, he would go down to a cafe of sorts, down by the station somewhere, where he and his friends would listen to music. Sometimes I would hear music coming from his room, modern stuff, you know where they talk rapidly rather than sing?'

'Rap,' Vusi offered, pointing out that no CDs were to be found in the room.

'I think he took them, along with the laptop. There's also some clothes missing. I think he used his school backpack, you can see all the books are there on the desk.'

Vusi nodded. He had seen enough. 'This boy, older boy, he didn't want you to meet; can you describe him?'

'Tall, about your height, but thin and with his hair straightened and tied back in a short pony tail.' She paused, striving to conjure up the image, 'He wore his pants low down at the waist with red sneakers and a tee shirt with a picture of some actor or musician on the front. And one of those wide steel combs stuck in his hair.' She paused, glancing at Vusi with apprehension mirrored on her pinched features. 'Does that help?'

Gangster, Vusi thought. The cool get up and the steel comb, the points no doubt sharpened and a favoured tool of the *"skollie"* he knew all too well. 'Maybe. I'm going to look for this cafe' where the kids go to listen to music, see if I can find this older boy.' Even as he spoke he knew he was being kind to the boy's mother: kids didn't go down to so called cafe's to listen to music any more, if they ever did. No, it would be in search of booze or drugs or girls.

In the lounge Cyril was sitting on the couch, his head tilted back, a blood spattered dishcloth pressed to his nose. Dead eyes watched Vusi as he walked past. At the door he paused, turned to meet the silent gaze of an ex-wife. 'I'll be back,' he said, pulling the door shut. And if Joy thought the message was for her, all the better.

But they were really a gentle warning to lover boy bleeding on the couch.

Outside the heat had notched up a few degrees and the soaked shirt clinging to his back was a reminder of the humidity to come. Slinging his jacket over a shoulder he went back to the car, a smiling Tsotsi coming forward to greet him.

'All safe here, boss!' he beamed as Vusi dug in a pocket for his wallet.

Vusi asked him about the location of clubs or cafe's that teenage schoolboys frequented. Specifically near the local railway station.

'Only *shebeens* down there, boss,' came the instant reply, adding after a moment's hesitation: 'Girls too. Nice ones, I can organise you a special ...?'

Vusi sighed, cutting the would-be pimp short with a weary gesture. 'Take me there and there's another twenty in it for you.'

'Thirty,' came the instant riposte, the youngster's eyes narrowed and calculating.

'Thirty,' Vusi agreed, motioning his young companion to get into the passenger side. He was too tired to argue.

Mama Tembu's turned out to be a ramshackle lean-to indistinguishable from its neighbouring shanties if it was not for the brightly coloured mounted sign sponsored by Coca Cola. Closer inspection hinted at the sign originally belonging to Sammy Pillay, Pawnbrokers, the new name somewhat sloppily painted over the erased lettering, but in the New South Africa people had learned to share. Nobody looked for trouble.

A bench and a few weather beaten chairs lined the outside corrugated wall and four old men sat around a small deal table playing dominoes. Vusi thought he spotted a chicken around a corner but the sun's reflection off the unpainted tin siding was in his eyes and he wasn't sure.

Stepping over the worn threshold he paused for a second to allow his sight to adjust to the sudden darkness. Inside the heat was stifling and as he made his way over to the bar at the far end of the room he was aware of silent stares following his progress.

More colourful signs behind the bar, stickers on the large mirror at back. Soft drinks, beers, different varieties of vodka – whatever tickled one's fancy Mama Tembu could provide and, judging by the body action of the painted beauty sidling up to him, Vusi reckoned the goods on offer would not be limited to liquor only.

'My,' she said running a bright red fingernail down his arm, 'Aren't you a big one?' Her voice was soft and slightly husky and Vusi had to strain to catch the words above the blare from the corner boom box. Not that words would necessarily be needed, normally the message in her eyes would have been enough.

'Thank you, *sisi,* maybe later,' he replied, nodding in the direction of the bar, 'Any chance of a cold beer? And, a cool drink for the boy.'

'I drink beer too!' came the protest from Tsotsi, the youngster drawing himself up to his full height, an expression of indignation on the smooth young face.

'No you don't,' came the firm reply as Vusi took a deep tug from the Carling Black Label stubbie, savouring the ice cold liquid as it coursed its pleasant way down. He was leaning with his back to the bar counter now, surveying the room. Apart from a small dance floor off to the side the place was filled with a variety of different sized tables and an even more diverse collection of seating apparatus, some seats little more than upturned paraffin canisters topped by padded cushions.

Staring down at the dirt floor and the effect the dust was having on his recently polished brogues, he wondered whether the various wood chips and other indeterminate items were possibly the remains of last night's furniture but decided to turn his thoughts to more immediate issues.

'See anyone here you recognise, Tsotsi?'

Sipping his soft drink the kid scowled and nodded sideways at a group of men drinking at a corner table. A card game was in progress, the men slapping the cards down amidst howls of laughter and the clink of bottles as toasts were loudly exchanged. 'Mama Tembu's table,' Tsotsi whispered. 'Those men are local gangsters. Bad men, it is better not to make trouble with them.'

And nobody more likely to know the whereabouts of his son, Vusi reckoned as he wove his way amongst the tables in the direction of the card game. Taking in the other occupants of the room as he passed, two old men half asleep as they gazed unseeingly into their drinks which Vusi recognised as *umkhombuti,* the traditional milky white sorghum beer, something he hadn't thought was still sold in shebeens, the white man's beer having all but taken over. Four or five uniformed schoolkids gathered around a laptop video game, teenagers by the looks of it and probably on their way home from bunking school. Drinks in Styrofoam cups that he reckoned would almost certainly be beer and would be quickly soaked up by the dirt floor should the police decide to stop by, collect their protection money.

Ignoring Tsotsi's insistent tugging at his coattails and the youngster's urgent whispers to come away, Vusi was six feet away from the card players when his way was blocked by a tall muscular young man whose lazy smile Vusi thought was not necessarily friendly. 'Step away, *mon*, issa private game,' came the soft spoken warning, 'Mama, she busy now.'

Pausing in his stride, Vusi looked the man over. Nigerian, he decided, taller than the Southern African tribes and, judging by the dreadlocks and the colours of the sweatshirt, a Rastafarian. The man's bearing quietly confident, a standover man not unlike himself and not someone to take on lightly.

'I would like to speak to Mama Tembu,' he said. 'Pay my respects.'

The Nigerian was about to put a restraining hand to Vusi's chest when a voice from the table stopped him. 'Let him come, he looks interesting.'

Mama Tembu was not quite what Vusi had expected. In Zulu society, as in the rival Xhosa tribal world, it is not unusual to find strong women in positions of power. But this woman was quite light skinned, one of the parents he reckoned must have been a white, also going by the facial features, the somewhat unsettling light grey eyes. Somewhere in her thirties at a guess she wore a sleeveless singlet and both fleshy arms were covered in brightly coloured tattoos. Momentarily taken aback he hesitated.

Noticing Vusi staring at the ink work Mama Tembu smiled, 'You wanna read me or meet me?'

'You look like you've been slapped by a wet *Natal Mercury,*' Vusi replied, referring to a local daily rag. The others visibly stiffened and Vusi felt his neck hairs rise as he sensed the Nigerian bodyguard moving in closer. The moment's awkward silence was broken by a sudden high pitched laugh as the woman thumped the table spilling beer in all directions. After a moment's hesitation the others joined in as a space was made for Vusi at the table.

'Stamped by wet newsprint!' roared Mama Tembu as tears streamed down her cheeks. 'Not the best pick up line I've heard but takes a real man to say it!'

A fresh beer was thrust at Vusi who ran his gaze over the others at the table, concluding these were not the street thugs he was led to believe from Tsotsi's earlier warning, but rather a more upmarket bunch of businessmen of the shady deals variety that had become very much the backbone of the country's thriving informal economy.

Finally composing herself, Mama Tembu looked Vusi over with new interest. 'You're accent's local but something tells me you're not from around here.'

'I've been away, a long time. I have come back to look for my son.'

The woman nodded as she accepted a light for her cigarette from the hovering Nigerian. 'I see. Where do you normally live?'

Vusi told her, explaining in a few short sentences that the boy lived locally with his mother and had disappeared on his way home from school.

'So you live overseas eh?' Mama Tembu repeated thoughtfully, cold eyes showing a flicker of interest. 'Perhaps we could do business, Mr, er...'

'Vusi. Vusi Luwago.' (For a moment he wondered whether that was his real name, last time in Durban he'd been Mkhize. A couple others featured on the selection of passports he liked to travel with.)

He was burning to get to the point but realised patience was needed while he answered a few perfunctory questions as to the nature of his usual business. His inquisitor reflecting that there were definite possibilities for business between them along the nature of "moving" certain merchandise and that perhaps they could discuss things in a bit more detail at some later date. Finally she asked him about Lukas and in a few short sentences he told her all he knew, which he realised was really very little. Wasn't it sad he reflected, that he found it hard to even conjure up the face of his boy? That he had to rely on the recent photograph of a stranger in school uniform he was now showing them to even conjure up a mental picture of his son?

'This uniform,' Mama Tembu said, 'it is the same as those boys over there are wearing. The same blazer and tie.'

'The Dora Makiwane High School,' someone offered. Adding 'Down by the soccer field.'

'Call them over,' she said to the Nigerian who nodded and returned a minute later with a suddenly subdued pack of schoolboys. Turning to Vusi she invited him to put his questions. It turned out several of the boys knew his son. Two were in the same class. None had seen or heard from him since the day he disappeared. Yes, he did come down here sometimes after school but was not part of their circle. Once again the story of the older boy, the one who wore his baseball cap turned around, came up. No name and they had not seen him since either.

Struggling to control his frustration Vusi was about to question them regarding the school, who Lukas' teacher was, when one of the boys, a slightly built youth whose ill fitting uniform suggested a hand me down, mentioned something about other boys having gone missing as well.

Motioning the boy over Vusi made an effort to soften his tone, forcing a smile. 'What do you know about this?'

After a moment's hesitation the boy stammered something about "*muti*" being whispered about the town.

'*Muti...*' Vusi said softly, the word conjuring up ritual killings by witch doctors. The stuff of urban legend but there had been the occasional case ...

'What do we know about children disappearing?' Mama Tembu asked the group. Her voice businesslike now, a steeliness there that explained a lot about her role in that circle. There was a brief discussion amongst the men until one looked up to meet her gaze. 'Young boys, and girls, are forever going missing in the townships, Mama. Often they just run away from home but there have been rumours lately of people offering money for those who would give up a kidney…' A soft murmur followed this statement and Mama Temba held up a hand to instantly quell it.

'And you think maybe some of these children have been taken for their kidneys?'

The man spread his hands, 'Who knows?'

Glancing at the pale features surrounding the cold grey calculating eyes Vusi wondered what aspect of that last statement upset the crime boss most, the fact that children might be plucked off the streets to be butchered for their organs or the fact that a lucrative business was being conducted under her nose without her knowledge or share in the profits.

Rising from the table she turned to Vusi, 'Meet me here at seven to-morrow night and I will have news for you. This is my town, I will find out.'

And with that the meeting was over. Minutes later Vusi emerged into the brightness of the midday heat, pausing to remove his stifling jacket while pondering his next move. Did he trust the woman? Probably not but what other options did he have? Earlier he had considered going to the police but Joy had already done that and for various reasons he was loathe to draw attention to himself.

6

CHAPTER

Unlocking the car and motioning Tsotsi to get in he thought of another option: old contacts in National Intelligence. As quickly he dismissed the thought; Alfred, his old boss, was dead and replaced by people with agendas of their own, mainly ways of enriching themselves. If there really was an organ trafficking racket people high up in positions of power were likely to be involved and getting a kickback.

He would have to do this alone. Driving along, following the boy's instructions and heading back to where they had departed from, another thought struck him. What about the press? A reasonably free press was still part of the South African fabric and the ruling ANC was regularly criticised as well as investigative journalists frequently coming up with salacious details about the latest juicy bit of corruption.

The more he thought about it, the more it seemed the way to go. Momentarily lost in thought he narrowly missed colliding with a cruising Hi Ace taxi, the driver leaning out the window to hurl abuse, the whole encounter possibly aggravated by Tsotsi's middle finger pointing to the sky.

Cursing under his breath as he gunned the stalled engine back into life, Vusi decided to head back to the hotel for a meal and a chance to cool off in the pool. Over a few drinks he'd make some calls, get the name of a journalist that would be able to help and set up a meeting. But first he had to drop off the boy. Noticing the building midday traffic ahead he decided to take a short cut, heading down a side street towards a through road he recalled from earlier when he'd visited the home of his ex-wife. From the corner of his eye he noticed the boy stiffen, 'Don't stop at the robot!'

'What?' Vusi was slowing as the approaching traffic light turned amber and his young companion's sudden agitation momentarily puzzled him. A first thought being that a patrolling cop with an eye out for the young miscreant was amongst the small crowd at the end of the street but, too late, he realised what was about to happen.

A car is hijacked in South Africa on average every six hours. More than sixteen thousand a year. Invariably at gunpoint and with a fatal injury, usually a gunshot, not an all that unusual outcome for the non- savvy motorist.

By the time the car stopped at the red light and the youngster with the AK 47 stepped up to his driver side window, Vusi realised with a sense of grim reality that at least this kid – he couldn't be more than about fourteen – seemed reasonably professional about the whole thing. Lifting his hands off the wheel and raising them he returned the kid's dazzling smile while whispering to Tsotsi through gritted teeth, 'You knew about this hijack spot, didn't you?'

The boy said nothing, just sat there as the doors were yanked open and two youths, still no more than teenagers, closed in, quickly bundling a frightened looking Tsotsi into the back, one following him while the other slid into the front passenger seat.

There was a moment's delay as the kid with the AK 47 struggled to get in the back seat, the barrel of the assault rifle catching awkwardly on the doorsill. Vusi, an old familiar calm enveloping him like a blanket, waited patiently for his new passenger to get it right. Last thing he wanted now was for the kid to panic and shoot him by accident. (How many poor bastards die like that? Shot by an illiterate fourteen year old who barely knows how to operate his four hundred rand pavement special killing tool.) Seeing Vusi's look of apprehension the front seat passenger grinned and lit a cigarette using the car lighter. Vusi wanted to point out the no smoking sticker on the rental's windscreen but couldn't see the point.

'Drive,' came the snapped order, 'turn left and head towards the city.' The voice was deep and raspy for a kid and Vusi thought he smelled marijuana. The light green and none of the handful of pedestrians seemingly in the least interested in what they had just witnessed Vusi did as told while glancing at the sullen face of Tsotsi from the corner of his eye. He wondered how many times the young entrepreneur had sent unsuspecting customers down to that particular spot and what his cut was. A muted "sorry boss" confirmed his suspicions.

Keeping within the speed limit and guided by curt commands and gun prods to his neck Vusi headed down the through road towards what he now realised was the industrial side of inland Durban. There were several traffic lights along the way and now it seemed in order to obey the red signal in their new role as some old friends taking in the sights. Along the way the biggest of the boys, a budding thug somewhat enigmatically called Goodwill, asked Tsotsi what he was doing in the company of the man in the fancy suit whose wallet had moments earlier produced several thousand rand in crisp new one hundred rand notes.

In a muted voice the boy told him, hesitant at first but under the threat of a menacing glare the unfolding tale was accurate enough.

Goodwill seemed to think this over for a minute then pulled out a cell phone and dialled a number. The voice on the other side picked up within four rings and the ensuing conversation was brief and to the point.

'I see,' said Suresh Naidoo softly as he rose from the table where Mama Tembu was still holding court, cackling with glee as she potted another big pool. The Indian walked to the far side of the room, having excused himself with a muttering about business. 'I see,' he said again, as Goodwill finished. Then, still keeping an eye on the gathering at the distant table, he gave instructions. Vusi was to be taken to the warehouse where he would meet them within the hour. 'Pull over a few blocks away and blindfold him, you drive the last bit.'

'What about the boy?'

There was a moment's static on the line as Naidoo thought this over, a fleeting rat-a-tat hinting at the lack of suppressors on the engine of a ageing rust bucket rolling past. 'Does the boy know about the warehouse?'

'No, boss. This is the first time he's been inside a car we've taken.'

'Hmm...' It was tempting to simply drop the kid off, but how much did he know? Especially after bringing the nosy black man to Mama Tembu's. 'Bring him along,' he said, 'Blindfold him too.'

Goodwill's protest about where they supposed to find these blindfolds was cut short as Naidoo pocketed the phone. Idiots! Still, good help was hard to find and with the aid of these young thugs he had built up a nice little trade in the stolen car business. Officially his line of business was the import of Oriental carpets and the odd other sideline best categorized under "import / export," but lately the car theft business had been rather good. The thought made him smile as he carefully adjusted his broad rimmed Panama hat before stepping outside the bar, pausing for a moment as he waited for his driver to open the door of the waiting Jaguar.

Settling back into the plush leather of the air conditioned environment he thought back of how much the business had changed in recent years. In the old days, twenty years ago, stolen cars were quickly disassembled, "chopped," and sold off as spare parts. That was in the days when the police still bothered to try and recover stolen vehicles. Nowadays with a busy city precinct dealing with up to eight murders a day, there was no longer time for such trivia. Your car's stolen? Simply obtain a police claim number then it's off to the insurance company. The car, increasingly sought after expensive models like the Mercedes hijacked a short while ago, were often pre-ordered and quickly re-sprayed and delivered to a client in a far off part of the continent.

Too easy and lucrative. But not as lucrative as the "other business" he was involved in. The business so sensitive not even Mama Tembu, an old associate in crime, knew about.

The business he was now about to attend to.

The warehouse was a disused railway shed surrounded by a large shunting yard overgrown with tall weeds he had purchased many years earlier when he was still considering expanding the family carpet business and needed more storage space. Since then the trains had stopped running as industry had moved to other parts but the building had proved useful in other ways. From a distance the fenced in premises looked deserted and possibly in danger of structural collapse, the only clue as to something unusual the roaming fully grown male ostrich ceaselessly strutting the inside perimeter of the eight foot fence, huge eyes in a tiny bobbing head seemingly missing nothing. Not that it was that unusual a sight in the New South Africa, ostriches in the place of guard dogs. Many a car yard now using the huge birds in that role and for a number of good reasons: they are ever vigilant, quite territorial, aggressive and can easily outrun a human. Above all, they were cheap to feed and hard to poison, the stomach of an ostrich ready to accommodate anything from pebbles to glass to a Coke bottle.

'Hello, Oscar, *my china,*' Goodwill said to the hovering bird as he waited for the heavy gate to swing open. Seconds earlier he had smiled up at the security camera as he pressed the intercom while glancing around for the branch of acacia thornbush that would be somewhere close at hand. Motioning for the car to drive through he waved the dry branch at the animal's head, the long white thorns glistening in the sharp sunlight.

An ostrich's eye is larger than its brain, the only thing the bird is wary of being the acacia thorns and the fear of being blinded. Long neck arched away it hung back, beady eyes never leaving the hand that held the branch. Tossing the branch aside as the gate swung closed behind them Goodwill joined the others in the car as they bumped across the rutted track dodging the deeper mud puddles while heading towards the loading bay of the building where an armed guard with an Alsatian on a leash was watching their approach.

Minutes later, the car now invisible to the outside world as heavy sliding hangar doors creaked shut, they got out to find themselves in a large high ceilinged enclosure, sunlight streaming through several dirty green plastic corrugated roof slats, arc lamps set at intervals along the walls providing extra lighting. Still blindfolded Vusi stood still as he tried to place the sounds and smells of the place while hoping it wouldn't be too long before the foul smelling rag was removed. A scuffle to his left suggested the boy was sharing his predicament. 'You OK, Tsotsi?' he asked, craning his head to where he sensed the boy was.

'I'm sorry, boss,' came the muted reply, the earlier bravado now replaced by the quavering voice of a small boy who suddenly finds himself in a big boy's world.

'Shuddup!' snarled Goodwill as he stepped up to yank the blindfolds off. 'No talking! Come this way!'

Following the lanky frame of the teenage thug Vusi scanned the surroundings, taking in the workshop off to a side, a grease pit and tool laden workbenches reminiscent of a mechanic's workplace, two parked late model luxury cars completing the picture. Currently no-one was working on the cars but Vusi thought he detected the whiff of spray paint in the air which would explain the masking tape adorning the vehicles. Several areas of vaguely outlined paint spots on the cement floor suggested where the cars had been parked while being resprayed. Hustled along by two guards, big blacks who looked like they worked out, Vusi found himself approaching what appeared to be an office space in a far corner. The other two teenagers hung back as Goodwill and the guards, one sporting an AK 47 held casually by his side, ushered the two captives into the glass fronted office, closing the door behind them.

Inside the room was cool, courtesy of an ageing air conditioner humming away in a corner. It was sparsely furnished, a worn wooden desk, several tired looking chairs, a small filing cabinet with a plastic vase on top holding what Vusi wagered were plastic flowers. The calendar on the wall behind the desk featured a broadly smiling deeply tanned bikini girl and, judging by the yellowed edges, Vusi thought it years out of date.

A second door, behind the desk, was opened by a guard who stood aside for Vusi to pass through. Pausing, Vusi took an unresisting Tsotsi by the arm and bundled him ahead and into the room that was brightly lit. A glimpse at the sturdy looking door as it had swung open was enough for Vusi to spot the deadbolt on the inside of the lock and his next move was fast. Too fast for the guard to evade the shoulder lunge at the door slamming him hard against the wall, the other two helpless as the door swung shut and the bolt slid loudly into place.

Ignoring the angry hammering on the other side a crouched Vusi studied the room, only vaguely aware of the boy's widened eyes staring at the thin bladed stiletto flick knife he had sprung from its sheath strapped to his left arm. The knife held lightly in the fingertips of a raised right hand, a classic throwing position.

The room was smaller than the one they had exited from and here there were no skylights, the light coming from several mesh covered sodium lamps set high up in the concrete ceiling. The walls too were concrete with no evidence of any provisions made for ventilation.

No windows. Only another door at the far end which, judging by its solid steel appearance, led to the outside.

A hard room to escape from by Vusi's reckoning. And that was not counting the half dozen large steel barred cages that took up most of the space at the far end of the room.

Each contained a single steel framed cot with thin foam mattress and a slop bucket. Four small faces stared silently at him from inside the wired cages. Terribly young with smooth shiny skins and wide open wary eyes. Vusi knew that when they smiled – if ever they would smile again – large dazzlingly white teeth would be the reward.

All were black. All were boys.

Something else in a corner; several hospital issue baby cots, empty, with a few trinkets scattered about as one would expect in a nursery. Further back what looked like a medicine trolley and a small kitchen.

'What *is* this!?' a shocked Tsotsi whispered as he instinctively edged closer to a still crouched Vusi.

'Another kind of chop shop,' Vusi said softly as the far door slowly swung open to reveal the framed image of a man who was studying them with interest. The brightness of the day was behind him, his face hidden in shadows. There was something in his hand and Vusi knew it would be a gun and that it was pointed at him. 'Welcome. Please don't do anything stupid.' Naidoo lifted the gun, pointed it at a now frozen Tsotsi, 'I'll shoot the boy first...'

Moving slowly Vusi straightened up, the knife clattering on the cement floor with a sharp ping. They watched as the man stepped into the room, shutting the door behind him. Vusi recognised him as one of the men at Mama Tembu's card table.

Motioning them to step away from the door they had just entered Naidoo stooped to retrieve the knife, snapping it shut and pocketing it before unlocking the door to let the others in.

'He took us by surprise, I'll teach him ...' a fiercely scowling muscle growled only to be halted by a curt command from Naidoo.

'Shut up! I'll deal with you later.' Lowering his gun now that the guards were back in the room, he pointed to the cages, 'Put the boy in with the others. The man goes into the one at the end.'

Silent faces watched from behind wire as the orders were carried out in silence. They had seen this before; had been subjected themselves.

Realising the futility of resistance and aware of his responsibility towards the kids in those cages which now included his not too innocent erstwhile henchman, Vusi complied, allowing himself to be patted down, his remaining personal items being placed on the desk. From his new vantage point he had a better view of that desk and all the items that were scattered on them. He was still staring when his view was blocked by a now sombre Indian who studied him with interest.

'Your story earlier at the *shebeen* was of particular interest to me, Mr... Ah...'

'Vusi.'

'Yes. Of course.' The man nodded as he accepted a chair one of the guards had brought up. Vusi remained standing, his face close to the wire, hands in his pockets so the man would not notice the whites of his knuckles as he fought to suppress a deep seated rage. The noise of blood rushing in his ears slowly subsided as Naidoo droned on. '... could not, of course, say anything while Mama was there, but I realised we have a common issue. What pure luck that you decided to visit us here.'

Vusi said nothing. If the man was putting on a suave act it wasn't very convincing.

'So your son has gone missing. What is he, fourteen, sixteen? About the age of our guests in that other cage, would you say?'

Calm now, sensing what was coming, Vusi said nothing.

Naidoo shrugged and busied himself lighting a small black cigarillo, tossing the match. Taking a deep draw he studied Vusi through narrowed eyes. 'I can see I'm going to need some expert help in getting you to tell me how much you know and who, if anyone, you're working with. This little operation,' a sweeping hand indicated their surroundings, 'took a lot of time and effort to set up and is only now starting to pay off. My partners will be keen to meet you.'

Glancing at the faces in the next cage staring silently back at him Vusi realised with a deep sadness that the more things change in Africa, the more they stay the same. He said as much.

'Slavery?' Chuckling softly Naidoo shook his head. 'Nooo... Mr Vusi. Slavery is so old fashioned! In a country with forty percent unemployment slaves can be found everywhere! My business is something much more exotic, innovative you might say.'

Noticing the puzzled look this evoked he studied the glowing tip of the cigarillo before continuing. 'Look at those specimens over there. Do you think anyone will pay money to take them off my hands? No?' Not waiting for an answer he went on, 'but each and every one of them represent something of great value in the marketplace. Something wealthy people are lining up to pay a lot of money for.'

Tiring of the melodrama, Vusi snapped 'Where is my son? Was he here? What is this business you're talking about?' Even as he spoke Vusi finally managed to identify the last of the scattered objects on the desk he had been staring at.

It was a grey HP laptop. Small and new and the sticker on the top was that of a dreadlocked Jimi Hendrix. And as the image and its implications bore into his mind he dully registered the Indian's next words. 'Kidneys, my friend. They have beautiful, lovely, healthy, kidneys...'

It was several hours after dark when the truck pulled up inside the warehouse and Vusi and the others were escorted through the connecting door into the larger work area where they were herded inside the back of the vehicle. A low murmur amongst the huddled ranks of the boys was quickly quelled by a vicious slap or two from the guards whose presence had now been bolstered by two young khaki clad men, both whites, who had driven up in the truck. They spoke Afrikaans to one another and both were armed with pistols. Still angling for a chance to escape Vusi quickly realised these men, unlike the ones he had encountered earlier, were professionals.

While keeping him at gunpoint they quickly and expertly handcuffed the boys using cable ties, also securing the ankles in a way that only hobbling was possible. The other guards helped the boys into the windowless back of the truck where they were made to sit on long benches lining the sides. Studying the sturdy looking vehicle Vusi realised it was an armoured car of the type used by banks and security companies for money transfers.

Once locked in the back there would be little chance of escape.

Then it was his turn. 'Is this the one you phoned about earlier? The one the colonel wants to meet?'

Naidoo nodded. 'Yes. So far he has refused to talk.'

Satisfied that the cable ties securing Vusi's hands behind his back were tight enough, the man the others called Kobus, stepped back. 'Oh he'll talk, alright,' he said with grim satisfaction. 'Once the colonel gets to work he'll sing like a big black canary.'

This amused the other Afrikaner who laughed, 'A bloody *kaffer* budgie!' he said in Afrikaans.

This apparently was very funny – even Vusi knew enough of the language to know the man was referring to the derogatory Afrikaner slang for a housefly. Prodded forwards by the gun at his back Vusi paused next to the man, asked him his name without looking at him.

'What's it to you, *kaffer?*' came the snarled reply.

Vusi shrugged, 'Nothing. It's just that I like to know the names of the men I kill.'

His reward was a painful gun butt to the back of his neck that had him stumble forward where others were ready to help him into the back of the truck. Seconds later the heavy doors slammed shut and they found themselves in utter darkness. Vusi realised that the load bay had been soundproofed, the small observation slots and gunports normally found in these vehicles sealed off. Which meant no fresh air inlets. Wherever they were headed, the journey would have to take less than eight hours max before suffocation took its toll,

He was locked in the back of a security truck modified to transport prisoners in secrecy and about to be taken to some unknown destination with no means of contacting the outside world and the added responsibility of a dozen frightened kids staring back at him with widened eyes, all wondering what fate had in store for them. Knowing it wasn't anything good.

As the truck rumbled off into the night, the ride hard at back as Durban's potholed roads took its toll, he wondered if this was the same journey Lukas had undertaken.

Wondered whether his son was still alive...

Then he thought of Harry Dance and what the hardest man he had ever known would have done under the same circumstances. Well, for one, he thought with a grim sense of humour, there would have been more one liners, more sarcastic jibes at the enemy all calculated to slowly get them angry. For, as Harry always stated, angry and agitated men can be manipulated into making mistakes that much easier. And mistakes is what men like Harry Dance were so good at exploiting.

No mistakes so far but the night was still young. So he did what Harry would have done, moved to the front of the area where the bumps were less pronounced, curled up on the floor at the feet of the startled boys lining the benches, and dropped off to sleep.

7

CHAPTER

'So no guests stay here at the main lodge?'

'No, the lodge closes at midnight with only a receptionist on duty in case of an emergency,' Francois, the young warden – Selena thought him no older than twenty five – said, adding 'and to man the phone. As you have probably already discovered there is no mobile phone cover out here in the bush.'

Motioning to a hovering servant to take the new arrival's luggage down to the cart that would take her to her lodgings, he went on. 'At Halali we offer the genuine African safari experience. Our guests are lodged in tents on the far side of the river, each unit completely private and separated from its nearest neighbour by up to thirty yards. All with a magnificent view of the river and the veldt beyond where the guest can view game grazing at all times.'

'Across the river?' Selena asked as she accepted a complimentary sherry from a broadly smiling waiter whose crisply ironed khaki jacket and tasselled red fez was straight out of a Happy Valley of a long gone Kenya.

'Yes. We have a team of drivers transporting our guests to and fro. All it takes is a phone call to the lodge and we send down a driver to meet you at the river crossing, which you'll be thrilled to see shortly, is by punt, the guests propelling themselves across by means of a suspended pulley system.'

A look on Selena's face had him hasten to add, 'It's all quite safe, you'll see.'

They were standing in the large reception area of the Halali Game Lodge and Selena allowed her gaze to travel over the luxurious trappings of the place. Built on a hilltop overlooking a winding river in the lush green valley thousands of feet below the sprawling single storey structure with its rough hewn stone facade and thatched roof blended with the African landscape as if it had always been there.

Inside the spacious rooms and entertainment areas great care had been taken to recreate an atmosphere of being on safari somewhere in darkest Africa in the nineteen thirties when The Great White Hunter was roaming the plains of the continent. The dining area led to a sunken lounge with giant fireplace at the far end the wall lined with stuffed and mounted hunting trophies, most of the animals magnificent examples of the species even to Selena's untrained eye. The lounge furniture was a mix of fine leather and canvas with scattered animal hides lining the polished teak of the floors.

A large and well stocked bar graced one corner and a handsome young man was propping up the counter while nursing what looked like an invitingly cold beer. Behind the bar a broadly smiling uniformed barman was stacking a fridge from several cartons of assorted beers and soft drinks.

'And the day just gets better and better,' the young man who introduced himself as Jamie Watson exclaimed as Selena accepted the offered handshake.

Introducing Selena as Mrs Dean, Francois added, 'Mr Watson is a photojournalist who is working on an article for National Geographic. He has been with us for a week now and has taken about a million photographs!'

'How lovely!' Selena exclaimed as she extricated her hand. 'You must tell me more later, Mr Watson.'

'Jamie,' he corrected her.

'...Jamie. Now if you'll excuse me I have to freshen up.'

She allowed the guide to whirl her away, aware of the young blonde Adonis' eyes on her back and feeling good knowing that, after all those years, she still had what it takes. Francois was anxious to give her a quick guided tour before taking her to her lodgings and with an obligatory smile she allowed herself to be led through the adjacent entertainment rooms where a few kids were playing table tennis while what appeared to be their mother sat reading in a corner. Francois pointed out a small kiosk where amongst the usual paraphernalia post cards could be purchased, adding apologetically that at present Halali had no internet facilities, something planned for the future.

'At this time of year we don't have many guests, the heat you know and with the rain due any moment the game becomes harder to spot. Most of the guests are at present on the afternoon game drive; we offer that twice daily.'

'Why would the animals be harder to find?'

'In the dry season they have to come to the watering holes which are all close by to our prepared tracks. When it rains there's plenty of puddles in the veldt and they don't come.'

A large snooker table was centre piece in the next, luxuriously appointed, room which, with its leather wainscoting and beautifully framed photographs of famous hunting scenes, had all the appearances of a gentleman's smoking room of the glory days of Empire.

'Lastly but not least, allow me to show you our outdoor area where most of our guests prefer to spend the day at the pool when not out on a safari drive.'

Large sliding glass doors led out to an expansive patio with recliners surrounding a sparkling blue pool and stunning views beyond the low stone wall of the valley below and the green hills beyond.

A handful of guests were sunning themselves at the pool, mainly an older generation and Selena thought she could detect a smattering of German drifting through the open windows. A family group off to one side, one of the small girls waving at her. Selena smiled back at the girl as she stepped out onto the patio, the sun instantly warm and pleasant on her face with the background hum of the cicadas interrupted by the staccato chatter of the birds as they flitted about in search of food scraps on the baking mosaic paving.

'It's beautiful...' she heard herself say, the rising joy in her soul dampened by the sure knowledge that when her native Africa was at its most beautiful it was all too often also at its most treacherous. What was it Harry had called it once, the Janus Continent? Where, in order to survive, people like them needed two faces, one to watch your back.

Harry. Where was he now? Like the man said, there was no mobile phone cover and all she knew was he planned to join her over the next two days, once he had taken care of business back in Durban. And that "business" was the bit that worried her. For she knew with dread certainty that sooner or later Harry's business would put him in the line of fire just that once too often.

It was always a comfort when knowing that Vusi was there covering his back but their friend was called away on a mission of his own now, family business. All she could do in the meantime was settle in and check out the lie of the land as Harry had put it. Find out as much as she could about what really went on behind the scenes of this rich man's playground.

Spy and hope that her man's luck would not desert the both of them.

Minutes later she was seated in the passenger seat of a golf cart, her luggage piled on a back seat, the warden at the wheel as they bumped their way over a rough track heading down to the river. They had passed through the courtyard of a small gated housing complex a few hundred yards downhill from the main lodge and Francois explained this was the quarters of the game wardens as well as some of the other staff. Selena glanced back at the main buildings noting a small wing to one side that suggested living quarters. She questioned him about this and he replied that the section was private lodgings of the owner and his guests would sometimes stay there. No, he didn't think anyone was staying there at present.

Leaving the compound behind – it also housed stables from where guests could embark on guided horseback trips – they were now crossing a vast green plain of knee high green grass and the first of several herds of game came into view. Francois pointed out a small herd of Eland, the giant antelope like statues in their immobility, the only movement steadily chewing jaws and large liquid eyes that gazed at them and through them with little more than idle curiosity. Next up was a scattering of water buffalo their backs gleaming in the sun, the smooth contours broken by strutting white lice birds.

On the distant horizon Selena could make out the shape of three elephants. A male tusker with what appeared to be a female and baby in tow. They were moving languidly through the grass, trunks swaying rhythmically from side to side as they walked, the little one playing catch up in bursts of frenzied activity ignored by its parents.

A tall African man was keeping them company and he waved as they went past. 'That's Silas, their keeper, Francois explained. They're quite tame and the baby was born here on the farm. You can have a ride on the big ones later if you wish, it's just part of the many activities we offer here.

The cart was slowing now as they approached the river and Selena could make out the small floating punt pulled up on the bank. Dense reeds lined the banks of the languidly flowing dark water and she could spot animal tracks in the mud congregating to a shallow pool that was most likely a watering hole.

'What about crocodiles?' she asked as Francois helped her down from the cart.

'There has never been one in this river to our knowledge and we do patrol regularly. This is a tributary of the Umfolozi River which lies about a mile that way.' An outstretched arm pointed in the direction of a distant hill, 'And it's true that there are some there.'

Seeing the question in her eyes he added, 'There's a waterfall downstream – you'll see it on our game drive this afternoon – and that prevents the crocs from getting up here.' He smiled, 'There's nothing to worry about.'

The luggage was loaded onto the punt's platform now followed by the two of them and then Francois was hauling them across the river, demonstrating to his guest how the pulley system worked as they went along. Midway the pull of the river was suddenly strong and the cord like muscles on the young man's forearms rippled and glistened with perspiration. Slightly out of breath he explained that there had been heavy rains and floods recently which explained the plastic milk crates at the landing site they had to step on to access the punt. The crossing took only minutes and Selena found herself being led along a wooden walkway to a tent-like structure a few hundred yards away. From a distance she could see it was suspended on a wooden deck with steps leading up to a small porch and nestling in the shade of a large marula tree right on the river's edge.

Leading off from the walkway, which was bordered by lush thick green kikuyu grass on both side, were side tracks leading off to similar tent structures, all artfully camouflaged by shrubbery and trees so as to be invisible to any neighbours. Then they were at her own quarters and Francois paused in his stride to allow Selena to take in the structure. The spacious wooden deck was set several feet off the ground with the porch facing the river and beyond it the distant lodge. A large olive green tent was erected on the platform, its perpendicular sides featuring rolled up canvas window covers with thick mosquito netting visible behind the openings.

'It's quite...unusual,' Selena managed as she followed the young man up the creaking stairs and into the cool embrace of the tent.

'Our decorators have strived to recreate an atmosphere the way it would have been on safari for the likes of Hemingway and President Rooseveldt all those years ago. All the things you see around you would have been transported on trucks following in the wake of the hunting party accompanied by dozens of servants who would set up accommodation just like this whenever camp was made for a few days.'

If Selena thought it strange that the young Afrikaner would even know about such luminaries as Hemingway and a long dead American president, she kept it to herself. In recent times tourism had become the country's biggest employer and guides such as the young man would have been briefed to an extensive knowledge of their particular field. She reflected on how amazed she was to come across more than one young guide from the Coloured sector who now spoke fluent German in addition to their native Afrikaans and English.

Dragging her thoughts back to the present she let her gaze drift over the lush surroundings as Francois continued his salesman's drone of the tent's trappings. '... well stocked fridge next to the writing table and, if you care to step over here, the bathroom facilities are at the back of this bamboo screen and you will note a full sized bath with hot water on tap as well as leading to a small alcove open to the sky with another shower for those hot summer days.' He pointed out matching washbasins and a screened off flush toilet, all a clever mix of old and new to recreate that living in the bush ambience.

Lastly he indicated the telephone next to the four poster bed adding that it was connected to the lodge reception desk and outside calls could be placed with the help of the receptionist.

'One last thing before I go, it's safe to wander about on this side of the river but please use the phone when you want to come up to the lodge and we'll send a buggy to fetch you. We're always a bit worried that a sudden stampede by the large antelope may cause an injury.'

And with that he was gone leaving Selena to stretch out on the plush mattress and contemplate her next move. The trip by light plane to a nearby dirt landing strip followed by a jarring car ride over farm roads showing signs of recent heavy rains had been tiring and she closed her eyes and let her thoughts drift back to what Harry had told her earlier. Savannah and whatever that meant. So Harry's contact had fingered this place as his next destination following the face altering plastic surgery and Harry was convinced this peaceful tourist paradise would lead him to that last elusive act of a personal vendetta she feared was going to destroy them all.

Situated in wild densely forested countryside on the fringe of the Hluhluwe – Umfolozi National Game Reserve in far northern Zululand, Halali was more than 150 miles from the nearest city which was Durban. An out of the way location to be sure. A very *expensive* spot to hide someone away until the next phase of the identity switch could be organized.

But also a most secure place where prying eyes, and ears, could be kept at bay.

A place Harry thought might just provide him with the next clue as to the whereabouts of the man he had been hunting for so long now.

Soon Harry – she had to remember they were "Mr and Mrs Dean" now – would join her and with that last thought she drifted off in a troubled sleep.

It was three in the morning, dawn still two hours away, when the truck rolled up at the main entrance to Halali Game Lodge. It was expected, the heavy steel gate rolling back silently on well oiled gurneys as the driver pulled up, his co-driver jumping down and entering the gatehouse where the night guard handed him a telephone handset.

'Morning, Colonel,' the co-driver said in Afrikaans as a grunt crackled over the line. 'We have brought in the shipment. All in good shape and no problems.'

'Hmm. No police checks on the road?'

'A traffic cop pulled us over outside Eshowe. Claimed we were speeding but of course we weren't, Jan is always very careful to keep within the limit. This loser wanted a bribe as usual, Jan gave him a hundred bucks and he backed off.'

There was a pause as the man on the other side of the line thought this over. 'The man who was asking about his son, find out who he is yet?'

'No, Colonel, not yet. We have him in the back of the truck with the others as ordered and I guarantee once Jan starts working on him he'll sing like a canary.'

Colonel Ehlers grunted while struggling to light a cigarette, his eyes still blurred from sleep. 'Be careful of this one. Maybe he's just a lost idiot in which case we'll harvest him with the rest and dump him. The worry is that someone might be behind this and that's what I want you to find out.'

'We'll grab a few hours sleep then start on him. Do we see you in the morning?'

'I'll be up later. Make sure you lock them all up securely; and, remember, no noise. Use the ketamine if you have to.'

And with that the line was cut leaving the co-driver, both men had made the journey in the grey overalls of a well known freight company, to climb back into the cab and seconds later the truck began the laborious journey up the hill around the top end of the lodge buildings. Halfway up and on a steep and rock strewn section the driver engaged the four wheel drive and the engine note climbed as the wheels spun and grappled for grip. The co-driver thought he could hear the bodies in the back fall about and even the odd muffled cry as the heavy vehicles swayed and jerked but then the back section had been sound proofed and he put it down to fatigue and an overactive imagination.

Down in the valley they could make out the lights of the lodge and further out the lights of the gate house. The guest quarters on the far side of the hill beyond the river were out of sight.

Ten minutes later they were there, an older warden with a luxuriant beard named Hugo, waiting at the gates to the lions' enclosure, the outer gate already open. Despite the chill of the freshening hilltop breeze he was clad only in a short sleeved khaki shirt with matching short pants and a pair of well worn *veldtskoen* without socks. A Coleman lamp hissed and spluttered on the hood of a parked Land Rover and a set of unflinching reflecting eyes in the darkness off to one side suggested a prowling jackal. Or perhaps a honey badger.

'Where are those bloody lions?' was the first thing the two new arrivals asked as they climbed stiffly from the cab to gratefully accept a mug of hot coffee from a flask produced by Hugo. They were speaking in Afrikaans, the absence of any formal greetings suggesting the three men knew each other well.

'*Moenie worry nie!*' came the reassurance, 'those little beauties are fast asleep!' To confirm this he tapped the barrel of a long gun propped up on the vehicle's front seat. 'I gave them each a little sleeping tablet!' he added to soft knowing laughter from the others.

'Is the Colonel still doing his trick with the lions?'

'Oh *ja*. The tourists love it!'

Then they were back in the truck with Hugo leading the way in the Land Rover. It was a bumpy ride over the open veldt with the long grass scraping audibly on the undercarriage and parting in the yellow beam of the headlights like the wave at the bow of a ship. Halfway across they spotted the lions, three sets of glittering emeralds followed by the familiar yellow brown torsos as the vehicles rolled past. They were lying in a tight bunch, as if seeking refuge from the coolness of the night and showed little interest in the passing party. The driver wondered how long the sedative lasted and his companion thought not all that long but they would be safe while the cargo was being unloaded.

The dull grey aluminium sidings of the building came up next and seconds later they pulled up at the front entrance. Hugo went inside to switch on a generator and a powerful arc lamp bathed the outside area in light. Working swiftly now Jan backed the truck up to the ramp leading up to the doors and Kobus, the co-driver, was ready to help the first of the cargo down.

He was small, no more than ten or twelve – not yet a teenager – and the fact that his hands were shackled behind his back had him hesitate and the warden grabbed him by the collar of his thin shirt and jerked him off the back of the truck and watched dispassionately as he tumbled in a heap onto the ground. The boy fell without a sound and the chain linking him to the next prisoner jerked tight and with a grunt the next boy in line tumbled out, his fall only partially broken by the bony torso beneath.

'*Komaan, kaffer!* Move!'

One hundred yards away and hidden in the darkness, the man lying with the long lens of his night vision camera resting on the lower link of a small break in the fence, stirred and slapped at a sudden sting in his groin. Damn red ants, they were everywhere. When he put his eye to the viewfinder again he could see more shapes being dragged from the truck, four so far by his calculation and all of them children. Judging by their flimsy clothing all were boys.

All were black.

Bowed and shuffling forward black shapes bathed in the eerie green matrix of the infra red viewer punctuated by the occasional flash of white as one of the guards laughed or light reflected off a belt buckle.

And as he watched he filmed, the soft whirr of the Nikon just audible as the viewfinder adjusted to and fro in search of sharp focus in the poor light. Four hours he had been there, lying on a thin rainproof poncho on that hard ground and it wasn't the first night he had been out there, waiting, either. In fact, Jamie Watson mused, it felt like a bloody month but had probably only been four or five nights.

And now finally he had what he had been looking for. The proof that would finally cement his story; the story he had travelled across half the country for not to mention all those months.

He was about to get up, gather his kit for the long trek back downhill to his tent when something made him freeze and quickly re-focus the camera.

A last prisoner was getting out of the truck. This one was not chained to the others but also had his feet secured as well as his hands behind his back with what appeared to be cable ties. One of the guards had climbed into the back of the truck to help him out.

Down onto the ground now and landing on his feet and when he straightened up Jamie could see this was a fully grown man, not a child like the rest.

'This one looks angry enough to catch snakes!' the bearded Hugo guffawed and Vusi felt himself go ice cold. Raising his gaze to take a good look at the man he was momentarily puzzled. For behind the face of this stranger was a voice from the past. A voice once heard never forgotten. And with it memories of a hell camp called Vlakplaas where torture and murder were just two sides of a coin minted in Hades.

There was no mistake. Faces could change – this was the face of a stranger – but a voice was forever.

'Hey, Hugo! This one looks like he wants to take you on!'

With an oath Hugo swung the truncheon hitherto suspended by his side and without a flinch, without the slightest sign of pain, Vusi took the blow and as the tableau froze into a moment of sudden quiet he took one last lingering at the eyes that glared their hatred at him and in that moment all doubt vanished.

It was the same man.

And as he followed the boys inside, all the while fighting the cold rage welling inside him, he knew the game had just taken on a whole new dimension.

As Jamie Watson watched all this he wondered what had just happened and knew that whatever the price, he would have to hear that man's story.

Which meant doing what went against all the rules of journalism. Becoming part of the story...

8

CHAPTER

Mrs Chen carefully set down her teacup and smiled up at the waiter who was quickly at her side to clear away the remains of the morning's breakfast. A tiny Chinese lady of a certain vintage she was dressed in a long sleeved cotton dress with floral pattern and dainty white satin gloves, the whole topped off with a broad brimmed straw hat and large sunglasses that dwarfed the elfin features. The very red lip shade somehow incongruous. She waited for the servant to move off before turning to her companion. 'When do we do this?' she asked in a soft and melodious voice, the English delivered flat and with no trace of an accent.

'At ten this morning, White Paper Fan,' the young man replied as he leaned back in the chair basking in the pleasant warmth of the low winter sun.

'Do not call me that.' Still not looking at him, the tone even and without a hint of reprimand. The young man known as Hilton stiffened but avoided eye contact, instead nodding in muted obeisance. He would have to watch himself, one word from this tiny wizened ageless being could spell disaster for a mere foot soldier. Reminding himself that he was there under the guise of an accompanying son, he excused himself to collect his gear, informing Mrs Chen that he would be calling for her at exactly nine thirty.

It that was OK with her...

She nodded absently as the young man moved off, soft rope soled loafers noiseless over the rough paving of the patio. How well these young men moved she mused, with effortless ease like water running over glistening pebbles. And all of them thin and lithe, just muscle and bone really but then that was the product of a lifetime in the *dojo,* a singular devotion to their art. The art that she and her associates paid handsomely to have at their call, day and night.

Glancing around to take in the fellow guests she wondered whether it had been wise to travel with just the one bodyguard this time, instantly dismissing the thought as ridiculous. A motley bunch of idle soft westerners was all she saw. Typical tourists out for a day of leisure, different languages, bored kids pestering parents, older people mainly. Yet, this was a competitive business she was in and rivals could be lurking. To-night they would be inspecting the merchandise, arrange the transfer details and you never could be sure these pitiful round eyes wouldn't be up to a trick or two.

But this morning there would be a bit of fun. As she got up she was aware of a stiffness in her joints, an ever increasing strain of muscle against gravity and it filled her with sense of the philosophical. At eighty time was beginning to take its toll and soon it would all be over. Nothing like a bit of adrenalin though to get the blood coursing, bring back old memories of the chase. And the kill...

Madame Chen liked to mix business with pleasure.

It was twenty minutes past eleven that morning when Harry Dance finally decided he was lost. He had left Durban more than three hours earlier and using the GPS had managed nicely until it directed him off the highway and onto seemingly endless miles of dirt roads, finally deteriorating into gibberish as if failed to identify any roads from its programming.

The signal on his mobile phone had given out when the road wound behind the first of the tall tree lined hills and he had a dread feeling this was the way it would be from now on. Before leaving the hotel he had left a message for Selena at the Lodge's reception desk, telling her of his expected arrival later that day. All attempts to raise Vusi were unsuccessful. As for a radio station that played music – anything at all really – that wasn't looking promising either.

Twenty miles of bone jarring potholes and treacherous expanses of standing water later and aware of a real need for a coffee he pulled up at a roadside farm store; the only sign of life he had seen in more than an hour. A stone walled and tin roofed affair with a dusty wooden porch that creaked under his tread, Harry was directed to the only phone by a broadly smiling Afrikaner woman who offered him a cup of coffee and a home baked gingerbread cookie which he quickly accepted.

The store smelled faintly of freshly baked bread and while he dialled Vusi's number he took in the surroundings. Tables and diverse items of furniture of all descriptions clustered about the four or five rooms that comprised the shop floor, all laden with local farmer's produce ranging from canned peaches to hand woven sjamboks, the overall effect warm and friendly. Scrubbed wooden floor planks creaked underfoot while farming utensils swung from overhead beams. And hovering within easy hailing distance the ever attendant Mrs Marie Schoeman – the name perched on top of the antique cash register – should the customer require any information as to which of the ladies baked which cake.

Harry fought back memories of a long forgotten childhood on an old Rhodesian farm as he selected a strip of Springbok jerky and smiled back as she coaxed him into purchasing a man sized penknife "to carve it with."

The call to Vusi's mobile was once again fruitless, the voice mail coming through with the same old tune of leave a message and I'll call you back. And as always Harry would leave no message, a fall back security measure. Was there a need for worry? He shrugged off the thought; Vusi was quite able to look after himself and had there been a problem would have got a message through to Harry.

Still, he had work for the man besides wondering whether he had traced his errant son by now.

Pocketing his change he asked Mrs Schoeman about visitors to the Halali Game Lodge.

'Oh, they have only been going for a while now, the new owners, maybe two years. So it's not so well known yet, but I'm sure later, when the cooler weather sets in, more people will come to stay.'

Harry nodded, 'Many overseas visitors?'

'Well,' she hesitated, a frown creasing her brow, 'It's hard to tell but I have noticed a number of foreign looking people drive by lately. Sometimes they stop and come in here to ask directions and I can tell they're from overseas and...'

'And?'

Marie Schoeman shrugged, 'Maybe I'm just being silly, but under the previous ownership – one of the local farmers started the game lodge ten years ago – we got lots of South African families, they used to come in here all the time, and then the new owners put the prices right up, almost to discourage locals from visiting. They also stopped day visitors from coming. The whole place is a bit of a mystery to us locals now.'

'Have you met the new owners?'

Totalling up a few other small items Harry had placed on the counter she shook her head, lips moving silently as she noted down the goods on a ledger, presumably to square with the other ladies later. 'A Mr Heidmann, I believe. A foreigner from South America somewhere. None of us locals have ever met him.'

There was a number of other questions Harry could ask but she was looking at him with suspicion now and he decided it could wait. A last question confirmed that further along the road leading to the game lodge was only a handful of farms, the road eventually deteriorating to a mere track until culminating at the river's edge.

Thanking her Harry headed back to the car aware of searching eyes on his back as he placed his purchases on the back seat and climbed behind the wheel. Pausing for a moment he wondered what he had learned. Nothing he decided and with a shrug set off down the road leading to the lodge.

It was purely on impulse that he drove past the gates of Halali Game Lodge (or was it a subconscious desire to view the river, the spot where a man had been taken by a crocodile not that long ago, the event that started off this increasingly surreal enterprise?) It was twenty past eleven by his watch and warming up pleasantly and visions of a cold beer kept creeping into his consciousness and something made him drive on, the high double fencing of the game farm to his right and the stretching away to be swallowed up by the dense canopy of the forest in the distance.

The terrain was hilly and the road, now increasingly rough and potholed, curved around the base of the larger hills and pools of water testified to the recent heavy rains. Judging by the lack of any fresh vehicle tracks little traffic used the road, Harry had passed the last turnoff to a distant farmhouse some five miles back.

Still the fencing went on and Harry began to marvel at the sheer size of the game park. Then, coming around a sharp bend, he encountered a broad irregular ditch running across the track. At a guess a gully eroded by floodwaters and a quick inspection confirmed it would take a four wheel drive vehicle to proceed any further.

He would have to turn back. Getting out of the car Harry stretched and glanced around. Thick undergrowth all around and a small hill to his right, the fence dropping off to the far side. Curious to glean a better view of the lie of the land, he took a pair of binoculars from the glove box and, shedding his jacket, climbed the hill. The grass was wet and slippery and Harry wished he had the foresight to wear more suitable shoes than the smooth soled loafers now struggling for traction. Sweating slightly and somewhat out of breath he reached the top and was gazing at the valley below. Nestled between steep rocky outcrops a glistening creek wove its way over partially submerged fallen tree trunks and large rocks, the sounds of the fast flowing water just faintly audible.

Harry was about to focus his attention on the landscape further along the track he had been following when something caught his attention. It was a flash of light. Just a moment's image on the retina but from across the valley, away from the water, and nothing that nature would conjure up.

Instinctively he was down on his stomach and raising the binoculars. There it was again and as the images came into focus he could clearly make out a party of three, two men and what looked like a woman, or was it a young girl? The glint was off the barrel of a rifle and bringing the powerful glasses into sharp focus Harry could make out the game farm's logo on the shoulder patch of what had to be one of the employees from the lodge. The other was a young man who moved with the kind of easy languor of the quietly confident and Harry thought he would be one to watch in a tight corner. Shifting his point of focus he was surprised to note that the third party was in fact a tiny Chinese female. To their rear and a hundred yards away he could make out the shape of a vehicle parked in the shadows of a large mopane tree.

The man with the rifle was setting up a folding chair for the lady and the young man was assembling some object he had taken from a large canvas bag. All three cast frequent glances in the direction of upstream where the gorge narrowed to a dark passage between large boulders.

Shifting his position slightly Harry was able to focus the binoculars onto that darkened patch of earth. At first he saw nothing and then there was the slightest of movements in the shadows and Harry found his pulse quickening as he finally saw what had reared its head.

It was a lion. A magnificently maned beast and Harry could see the shape of figures in the background and not far away from the king of the jungle.

But this was an old king. A king whose time had passed and with the jackals gathering. Judging by the yellowed teeth and battle scarred head as the animal rolled back its head to emit a deep throated roar, Harry reckoned at least twenty even thirty years old. And when it rose from the shadows, goaded to its feet by the four or five drivers – Harry thought they brandished long handled cattle prods – it limped and there was something wrong with one front plate sized paw and then it was into the sunlight that danced off its mane like fire on old gold.

The killing field had been well selected. With the merciless tormentors at his back the only way the old beast could go was to follow the river, enter the open stretch of low grass that now separated it from the hunter.

For that was what Harry was now witness to; as sickening a piece of canned hunting as ever there had been. The young man had assembled his weapon, a crossbow by the look of it and was glancing questioningly at the professional hunter who was now talking into a two way radio, presumably with someone in the chase party. After a moment's hesitation the man lowered the radio and motioned the young man forward while expertly slotting a bullet into the rifle's breech. Just in case the would-be assassin's nerve failed at the moment of truth. Filled with a sudden deep sadness Harry wanted to do something, shout something but he knew the lion was doomed, himself nothing but a spectator in a ghastly dance of death.

Hyenas, he thought grimly. Hyenas were the fate of old lions, the ones that had lost control of the pride and been forced out on their own only to be hunted down and torn limb from limb by the relentless cowardly predators.

And now he was witnessing the human hyena in action. Trophy hunting; the unspeakable in pursuit of the uneatable. How it sickened him. For all the blood on his hands Harry had never killed for sport and certainly never when the odds had been so stacked in favour of the hunter.

He wondered how they had transported the old animal to that site, thought it must have been by truck and most likely doped, the beast only now recovering but not to its full, albeit weakened strength. Wouldn't do to have a guest mauled or, God forbid, killed!

The lion, aware of danger ahead, paused. Ignoring the pack of tormentors at its back it was staring straight ahead, neck craned forward, frame crouched in sad parody of a happier time when a powerful fearsome charge would have been the sure outcome of this confrontation.

But that was a long time ago and Harry watched in silent horror as the young man rose from the waist high grass twenty yards away and took careful aim. Man and lion stared at each other for what seemed an eternity then a twelve inch metal bolt of whispering death flashed across open ground and a king died. The only sound, floating across the valley a split second later, a low growl as a huge yellow body sank into the African grass one last time.

Unable to tear his gaze away as he fought a sudden cold rage Harry watched at the old lady made her way to where the beast had fallen, impatiently waving away the efforts of the professional hunter who wanted to first confirm the kill. Then she was kneeling at the side of the lion and he watched as she carefully placed an exploring finger where the bolt had struck home, only to bring it to her parted lips.

And Harry saw the look on that face and knew he was staring at the real killer and suppressed a shudder. Death by proxy, how many times had he been in those sights? Was this one of those times? Instinctively he knew this was no ordinary hunting party, this was something else. But what? And how did this odd Chinese couple fit in with what was happening at Halali Lodge?

He was about to rise, return to the car, when something new caught his eye. A slight movement, halfway up the opposite rise of the gorge and further down the river. Taking up his prone position again Harry refocused the binoculars and it took him only a moment to find the other man where he was lying half hidden behind a low salt bush. Young, Harry thought, wearing camouflage gear and handling a telephoto lens he was now restoring to a rucksack. He watched as the man retreated keeping low and using the ground cover before disappearing from view.

Interesting. More so knowing that as surely as he had spotted the mysterious stranger he himself had been spotted and no doubt photographed.

A sudden feeling of indescribable loneliness came over him as he turned on his back, his gaze drifting over the distant green clad hills. What are you doing here, Harry? Jagged flashes of all his yesterdays came and went. The years on Robben Island, a political prisoner rubbing shoulders with Nelson Mandela, the Cherry Red affair and the hunt for the missing mini nuke that led to the life of an arms dealer in sunny Spain. Then the events that in an instant destroyed the life he had built for them, taking him all the way down to the icy hell of Antarctica and the quest for the Holy Grail that was Lily White. And the one constant linking all that a handful of apartheid era politicians and generals that were still, after all these years, weighing down on his soul.

What is it you want, Harry? Is it revenge? Is it the knowledge that there's still one man out there that needs to pay? Pay for the destruction of your home and things dear, for crimes against humanity that never quite came to light during the Truth and Reconciliation hearings? Or is it a road to perdition you're on, Harry; penance for the evil *you* have done?

Your wife is tired, Harry. Selena is putting on a brave face but how long can she carry on? Vusi is tired, wants to re-connect with family, settle down. How long before it's over, Harry...?

Wishing that he was still smoking he cupped his hands behind his head and thought of the Israeli death squad that had hunted and killed the perpetrators behind the Munich Olympics massacre all those years ago. Thought about how, after a never ending nightmare of killings and counter killings the team had simply decided that enough was enough. That one man, one team, can never set right all the wrongs of the world.

Cherry Red. A time when, wounded and helpless, he had stared into the fathomless eyes of a stone killer waiting for the stiletto to come towards him. And had opened his eyes to see the man walk away. *No mas...no mass...*

Walk away. Walk away...

Then a cloud drifted over the face of the sun and a shadow fell across that place. The distant sound of the river faded into the background and where birds had been singing there was only the silence. Harry turned icy cold and a shiver of an ancient fear stirred inside him. Here on this peaceful hillside he was face to face with eternity and he suddenly realized his own insignificance in the grand scheme of things.

Time stood still as he lay there as if turned to stone, hardly daring to breathe, and then the sound of the river gradually came back to him as a small breeze stirred the long grass. With a trembling hand he took out his handkerchief and wiped the beads of sweat from his brow. Then he sat up and breathed in the sweet clear air of Africa and after a while he felt better. What is it, Harry old boy, a voice said inside him, could it be post traumatic stress disorder after all these years? *You* of all people? Iron Harry, Harry the Angel? The thought made him smile wryly. Whatever it was, it was time to get all this over with now. He owed that to himself and, above all, he owed that to his wife and his partner.

Raising the binoculars he stared one last time at the bulk of the old lion, now seemingly peaceful as it slept the big sleep of eternity, a swarm of flies rising as the human shaped hyenas gathered. Then he sighed and climbed to his feet and went back to the car.

An hour later Harry checked in at the Halali Game Lodge where he was met by the welcoming sight of his wife and the cold beer she seemed to conjure up from nowhere. How did she know he had arrived when only minutes earlier he had driven through the imposing gates to the place?

Female intuition, he decided, or perhaps just old fashioned magic. It didn't matter, holding her in his arms and smelling the honey in her hair it felt good and he told her so.

9

CHAPTER

Rising early the next morning Selena and Harry went for a leisurely stroll down by the river, sticking to the boardwalk that meandered for several hundred yards before petering out at a bend in the river. It was promising to be a beautiful day, no sign of the clouds that would gather out of nowhere in late afternoon, the opening act to the violent yet short lived thunderstorms that was the daily expectation that time of year.

The cicadas were out in strength, their synchronised singing all around and seemingly coming off the water as the reeds swayed gently in the breeze. In the distance, across the river and beyond the grass plains the early morning's rays of sunlight were tracing long fingers of old gold at it gently touched the folds and contours of the lush green hills.

It was indescribably beautiful and as her own hand nestled into the warmness of her husband's and she stole a glance at those familiar craggy features squinting as it took in nature's show, Selena could not help wondering why there was this deep sadness inside her. If made her think back of a time, long ago now, when she had been that young freshman student at Cape Town University, studying English literature as part of a Dramatic Arts degree. Robbie Burns her favourite poet, the words of the Scottish bard suddenly clear in her mind. *Ye flowery banks o' bonnie Doon. How can ye bloom sae fair. How can ye chant, ye little birds, And I sae fu' o' care!'*

She would have to tell him, sooner or later, about that phone call as she was about to board the plane to Halali. The impersonal voice of the surgeon telling her the lump in her breast had been what they feared, that further treatment would be needed. Further investigations too. Things they would face in future, once she was back in town.

That suddenly uncertain future...

But not now. Not with those little birds so full of life and singing their little hearts out as they went about the business of life... *Thou'll break my heart, thou bonie bird. That sings beside thy mate; for sae I sat and sae I sang. And wist na o' my fate...*

They were at a bend in the river now, the tent structures out of view and here the river was narrower and speeding up, the sounds of rapids disturbing the tranquillity of the slowly swirling waters. Selena watched as Harry knelt to examine a clump of fresh animal tracks in the mud at the river's bank. She could see it was a big animal and wondered if it could be the elephants. Harry nodded, it was possible but somehow he didn't think so.

'Rhinos, more likely,' he said as they paused to glance once more across the river to where they could make out the tiny in the distance speck that was the lodge, sunlight dancing on the roof tiles in hues of yellow and red. 'A bull and two cows. Didn't the ranger say there could be down here somewhere?'

Selena shuddered and pulled her light cardigan closer. At that early hour it was still nippy close to the water's edge. 'Well, let's hope they keep their distance,' she laughed, 'I have enough trouble keeping my own bull of a man under control!'

They had turned back, Harry's stomach telling him it was time for breakfast. A check at his watch confirmed that it was approaching the time they had arranged to be picked up for the trip to the lodge and minutes later they were at the landing site, Harry helping Selena onto the rocking platform before pulling them across with long steady hauls at the thick rope. Standing close to him and holding on to the small wooden railing raised on one side of the punt, Selena studied the observation deck rising above the reeds on the opposite bank.

Erected a short distance from the landing area it was set on stilts about twenty feet off the ground with a small thatched roof. Access was by a solid looking wooden ladder and Selena reckoned the bird watching platform – she thought that was what it was – would not be for the faint hearted. Certainly not for those afraid of heights.

Then they were alighting at the far side and bounding along the path leading to the lodge came the buggy sent to pick them up.

Colonel Ehlers stared at the photograph as a frown creased his deeply tanned brow. The image was grainy, a grab taken from an earlier CCTV recording at the check-in desk, but there was no mistaking Harry Dance and "Mr Harry Dean, husband of Mrs Selena Dean" as being one and the same person.

'So he's here,' he said to the man who had handed him the photo. 'Well, that means that idiot, Louw, told him about this place, just as we suspected.' Turning to face the bearded Hugo a sudden thought made him ask about the black man who had been brought in the night before.

'Vusi Luwago. We got that much from his driver's licence, which by the way was issued in Spain. Interestingly though are several credit cards in his wallet, all with different identities.'

'Hmm. Stolen cards perhaps?'

Hugo shook his head, 'Somehow I don't think so. There's something about him, well dressed and groomed, speaks in an educated way and has an air of confidence about him.' The last bit brought a wolfish smile to his lips and as always it was slightly lopsided, a legacy of where the plastic surgery had resulted in a partial facial palsy. 'Not that I expect the confidence to last much longer, not after I have another little session with him.'

It was the next bit of information that had the colonel rise from his seat behind the desk to cross to the window from where he had a view of the pool area. As usual at that midday hour the guests had returned from the morning game viewing drives and, having indulged in a satisfying lunch, were sunning themselves on the deck. Somewhere amongst them was Harry Dance but there was a glare and he couldn't spot the couple. 'The Elangeni Hotel, are you sure?'

'In Durban. Yes colonel, dead sure. He had a plastic room key card on him with the hotel's name and address.'

Ehlers nodded and resumed his pacing behind the desk. The Elangeni. The same hotel Selena Dance had been staying at when she made the booking for Halali. Could there be a connection between this mysterious captive and Harry Dance?

'How many five star hotels do you think there are in Durban, Hugo?'

Hugo shrugged, 'Dozens, colonel. Most on them on Marine Parade, a few at the new Waterfront.'

'And yet this man and the Dance couple are recently from that very same hotel.' Colonel Ehlers didn't believe in coincidence, in his mind it more often than not spelled enemy action. 'Contact the Elangeni and find out if this man is still booked in there, tell them you're a cop and there's been an accident. And Hugo, with this Harry Dance snooping around we'd better speed up things. We'll take the client up to the hut after dinner this evening and ship the cargo out shortly after. Meanwhile I want to meet this Vusi character.'

With the morning's game outings over and nothing scheduled for another two hours no guests would be outside of the Lodge area, a good time to visit the restricted compound. The colonel reached for his wide brimmed hat instructing Hugo to bring a car around to the front.

As the Land Rover climbed unsteadily over the loose rocks and deep ruts lining the track, the engine's throaty rumble at times rising to a protesting whine, the colonel braced himself against the unsteady ride, his thoughts once again on what to do with Harry Dance. That the man was there on a mission was in no doubt but just who was he working for – if anyone – and what was he after? And how much did he know about Halali?

Actually they knew the answer to the last bit. Mike Louw had finally, after some unpleasant persuasion from Hugo, divulged how he had been in contact with Smit, the police informant who had donated a pair of kidneys before falling prey to a bullet and a crocodile. Smit had already been through the process of Savannah, was about to leave the farm for the next phase of his journey and must somehow, against all orders and shortly before his agenda was uncovered, have communicated with Louw, told him about the process.

Louw in turn directing a snooping Harry Dance to their front door.

It was hot in the car, the smell of engine oil making for a heady mix with the pungent body odour of a cursing Hugo, the man having to stop to drag another fallen branch off the track. It was a chance for Ehlers to get out and stretch his legs. It had been raining the night before and the ever present humidity was bad, even at that altitude, the lodge way below them in the valley. Taking off his bush jacket he reached for the canvas water sac suspended from the vehicle's front fender and took a deep tug of the cool liquid before splashing some on his neck and back.

'When is the boss coming?' a profusely sweating Hugo asked as he took the offered water from Ehlers, taking a deep pull before hanging it over the fender once again. He was referring to the man both knew as "Mr Heidmann" and had both known in an earlier life under another moniker.

'Later to-day. He wants to meet with the client. Plans to leave to-morrow and Mike Louw is to go back with him, they lost two men in Baghdad and he needs to send the asshole in as a replacement. I hope you didn't rough him up too much yesterday, he was already a bit tender after travelling some distance in the boot of a car.' This elicited a soft chuckle from Hugo which quickly disappeared when he saw the other man's look of disapproval.

'Let me remind you, Hugo, that it costs Savannah a lot of money to recruit and prepare a suitable man for our line of business. You should know, you've been through it.'

Hugo suppressed a shudder. He knew only too well what the company's "other business" was and recognised the thinly veiled threat of watching his step so as not to be sent on another mission to whichever hellhole Savannah, operating as Phoenix Executive Solutions, was plying its security protection trade in. He was still getting those nightmares after his last stint and far preferred his current assignment.

Not that there were many options. Once you were onto the train that was Savannah the colonel, and Mr Heidmann, owned you for life. No way out, but it still beat a jail term in a South African prison. His eyes narrowed at the thought as a vague headache began clamouring for attention.

'I can't believe he still wants to hang on to that shit of a Louw. After the man placed out whole operation in jeopardy with his stupidity.'

The colonel was cleaning his sunglasses on a neatly folded handkerchief, holding them up for study before carefully putting them on. 'Mr Heidmann has plans for him. Business has been good and we need more men. Louw is an experienced soldier and the general – Mr Heidmann – is now also putting together a mercenary unit in Argentina for another venture.' He inwardly cursed himself for the slip, referring to the head of Savannah as "the general', something they had been careful to avoid ever since setting up the underground train. It was sheer bad luck that the big man was visiting just now when this damned Harry Dance was snooping and he knew instinctively that there would be hell to pay if he didn't sort the problem out before Heidmann even knew of its existence.

He knew all too well the wrath of his erstwhile commander and ruthless did not even come close to describing it.

10
CHAPTER

Detective Captain Piet Niemand stared gloomily at the report in front of him. The typing drifted in and out of focus as his thoughts – and mood – shifted between despair and frustration. The battered government issue desk was overflowing with paperwork testifying to a dozen open cases, none of which held much hope of being solved.

Then again, who the hell cared about illegal casino operators or brothels run out of the back of roaming minibuses. Or for that matter high level corruption amongst his colleagues and seniors. In the weary world of Piet Niemand just about the only thing he still gave a shit about was good old fashioned murder.

The sixth Commandment. Thou shalt not murder.

Mentally he ran through the list, memorised since the days of his confirmation in the Dutch Reformed Church of the small dusty town of Potgietersrust, deciding that over the years he'd pretty much broken every one of them. Blasphemy? Covet they neighbour's house or car? Screw his wife? (adultery he thought was the term the bible used) Been there, done that, got the T shirt.

But not murder. Every son of a bitch he'd ever shot or, in the good old days sent to the gallows, had deserved it. Justified and to hell with anyone who thought different.

Which was why this case was getting to him. With a sigh he picked up the folder running his eyes down the now familiar lines. Kidney transplants. More donor kidneys transplanted at Durban's St Theresa Private Hospital over the past two years than in the rest of the country's hospitals put together. One hundred and eighty three in total and all of them live donors.

That's where the rub came in; those "live" donors. Where were they? Who were they? So far twenty three had been traced, all of them indigent poor and functionally illiterate blacks unearthed from the local slums of Durban. And not a modicum of useful information from all those hours of interrogation. For the story was always the same. A man – a fellow black who spoke perfect Zulu but with an accent – would approach them with the offer of good money for an unspecified job. If they agreed a meeting would be set up where two white men would be present. It was at a secret venue and they would be blindfolded on the journey over. A local warehouse of sorts was the general impression.

One man was a doctor for he carried a stethoscope and asked a lot of doctor's questions. There was an X ray machine and chest films were taken. Also blood tests; lots of blood tests. They were given some money and a week later another meeting would be set up, again at the same venue. Not all would be called back and it did not take genius to figure one of the tests would have been for HIV, the omnipresent virus of doom amongst the population of Natal Province.

Jannie Smit. *His* undercover man, retrieved from a crocodile with a bullet in his brain and two missing kidneys. Where were those kidneys, better still, who was walking around with them and where was the transplant done?

Sighing deeply Niemand rummaged through the contents of an overfilled desk drawer, found a Cherry Ripe chocolate bar and set about the serious task of unwrapping the treat. As usual the air conditioning in the fifties era government building had given up the battle against the sweltering humidity that was Durban and the Cherry Ripe had melted into an amorphous blob of sugary components and wrapper. Lesser men would have been unequal to the task but Niemand was already scanning the next document as he chewed, spitting out the occasional shred of printed matter, washing the lot down with satisfying gulps from a can of Coke. Finally pushing away the pile of papers on the desk to create space for his size twelve Hush Puppies he leaned back in the swivel chair to ponder what he knew up to that point.

Medical tourism had come early to the New South Africa. First in the form of cosmetic plastic surgery offered at cut throat prices in the country's first class private clinics before long being followed by live donor organ transplants. It was all about money, thousands of wealthy people on seemingly endless waiting lists for that kidney and suddenly being offered the service at a fraction of the normal price and in a facility comparable to the best in first world countries.

It took off like wildfire. Initially donors were sourced locally but they had to be careful and within a matter of months demand far outstripped supply. Fortunately far flung corners of impoverished third world countries were fertile recruiting grounds for suitably young people only too willing to sell a kidney for often as little as a few thousand dollars. No problem, before long they were flown into Durban as "tourists", the kidney was removed and the donor sent back home. And everyone was happy, not least of all the team of Durban based surgeons of several specialties who saw their bank balances grow quite nicely thank you.

It could never last and it was the press that first uncovered the story. Public outrage and pressure led to clampdown by immigration authorities – from both sides of the ocean -- and the stream of donors dried up. By that stage the demand had become so great that another source of the prized organs had to be found and that was where Detective Captain Piet Niemand came into the picture.

The selling of human tissue for profit is illegal in South Africa and it didn't take long for the Vice Squad to cotton onto what was happening and things quickly started winding down. Arrests were made and the hospital in question named and shamed with a major investigation and court case still pending.

So far so good. But then things took a more sinister turn; people, young people, started disappearing. And turning up, dead, with body parts missing. Like his own man, Jannie Smit, by all appearances killed by a crocodile in a remote corner of the country. Except crocodiles weren't all that adept at neatly removing kidneys...

Which was when the first of the paperwork started piling up on his already overladen desk. Smit had been sent deep undercover to investigate a totally different matter, the underground "train" of wanted crimes against humanity fugitives out of the country, an investigation Niemand had been tasked with almost two years earlier and with little progress made. There was evidence of the dead man having undergone face altering plastic surgery, a new identity forged and in his last communication with his handler he had hinted at after the surgery being sent to a farm to recover before being whisked out of the country.

The feeling was that it was part of a "surgery plus safari" deal, a new innovation set up by enterprising plastic surgeons to lure the rich to sunny South Africa and her ever hungry private hospitals. Come for your face lift and then spend a few weeks on a luxury remote game farm being pampered while the wounds heal and upon returning home no-one would guess your refreshed new look had anything to do with the skilful application of a surgeon's scalpel.

Piet Niemand knew the identity of the surgeon who gave Smit a new face, as well as the location. At a guess there would have been other customers under similar circumstances. An easy trail to follow were it not for a small problem: Dr Basson, the plastic surgeon in question, was lying in a police morgue, an ID tag tied around a big toe, with his office firebombed and all records destroyed. His receptionist having come to a similar bloody end. And to add irony the search warrant he had been waiting for arrived later that same day. Apparently the minister responsible for the issue of the vital document had been indisposed, the matter being delayed for twenty four hours after the man had been presented with the documents containing the overwhelming evidence.

Two different crime scenarios, both involving the same prestigious private hospital. The harvesting and transplanting of kidneys and plastic surgery to give new faces to fugitives on the run. Both extremely lucrative business models, both now ostensibly curtailed. All evidence regarding the true identities of the fugitives up in smoke while, as far as the hospital was concerned, in his bitter experience it would be just another damp squib that would culminate in a slap on the wrist and the kind of fine the clinic would comfortably pay out of a well stuffed petty cash drawer.

Shifting his feet slightly so the chair would tilt enough to move his bulk out of the morning sun creeping across the desk, he called over his shoulder for someone to bring him a coffee. A weary reply from the corridor indicated that Santie, his long suffering secretary, would be onto it. And yes, she did remember to get more of those Romany Cream cookies he liked so much.

Rocking slowly against the padded back of the chair he turned his thoughts back to what the next step should be. As always he reckoned the best bet would be to follow the money. For there was simply too much money at stake for this all too cosy little venture to just fizzle out. So the live donor kidney transplants could no longer happen in South Africa but all those customers out there! Like the international narcotics trade there simply had to be another way and Piet Niemand thought he knew where that path led.

Wasn't there an old saying that if the mountain didn't want to come to Mohammed, Mohammed would have to go to the mountain? He tried to recall if that was something his bible punching daddy had vainly tried to beat into him, deciding it was all too long ago to matter. But like all sayings it carried more than a grain of truth. If the kidney's were no longer being harvested in his neck of the woods they were being harvested elsewhere. Early contacts with police authorities overseas, mainly in Asia, indicated that there was no evidence of the kidney for sale trafficking having increased, which suggested supplies were coming in from outside the country. There was however an interesting new development; where India had been a favoured site for the transplants there was growing evidence mainland China might just be the new playing field.

Could it be that kidneys were now shipped out from under his nose to be transported overseas, to be transplanted there? The case of Jannie Smit's missing kidneys would fit but the logistics of harvesting a live donor kidney locally then transporting it over thousands of miles and still having it arrive in a state suitable for transplant sounded a bit dicey.

It was a newspaper article the day before that had set him thinking. Due to unacceptably cruel practices in Middle Eastern abattoirs live cattle exports had been indefinitely banned by the Australian government.

Live cattle exports. Slaughter at the point of consumption. The missing children...

Cold blooded murder – his kind of business. The only thing in his miserable life that still got him out of bed in the mornings. Well, that and Romany Cream biscuits now plonked on his desk together with a steaming cup of tea by a glowering Santie who had waited silently for him to move his feet off the desk. A protest about having asked for coffee was met with a "we're out, I'll get some during the lunch break."

Which, he reckoned with weary resignation, meant you can't always get what you want. You get what you *need*. (He thought there was a song with those lines but couldn't quite place it.)

And he needed to solve this one. People were dying and if his hunch was right – he hoped to God it wasn't – then children were dying in far off hellholes for their kidneys. Dying even as he sat there munching his cookie.

The only shadow of a clue on his horizon a game farm in a far corner of Zululand where a man called Harry Dance was right now an agent provocateur and that might just mean another killing was about to happen.

Slurping the last of the sickly sweet tea, he climbed to his feet and stabbed the intercom button, calling for his sergeant. It seems he would have to make a trip of his own, take a closer look at a certain game farm. But first they would dig a little deeper into who could be the mysterious buyer and how these missing kids, if his hunch was right, were leaving the country.

There were only two realistic routes; overland across the porous border with Mozambique or by ship from Durban harbour. They would start with shipping records.

Durban harbour. The busiest port in Africa. Thirty one million tons of cargo and more than four thousand five hundred ships per year. Fifty eight berths with twenty terminal operators.

Where to start? With a grunt Niemand lowered the brochure the harbour master had given him to meet the man's slightly apprehensive look with his usual ill humoured scowl. 'Do you keep a register of all cargo plus destinations?'

'Of course. It's all stored on computers now, if only you could tell me exactly what you're looking for I could direct you to...'

'People. Passengers.' He wanted to add human cargo but that would probably spook the man who was casting fleeting glances at a hovering secretary trying to draw his attention to where a uniformed ship's captain was awaiting his attention.

'Passengers! Well why didn't you say so! Ingrid can get you a list of the passenger liners calling and from the companies you could get the lists.'

Recognising a dead end Niemand sighed. He had already ascertained the stunning number of vessels of all tonnage and sizes plying their trade between Durban and Asian ports, a good number from China and to double check the passengers or crew passing through customs would be the kind of exercise beyond his meagre manpower capabilities.

No, he decided, those kids wouldn't be going through customs; they'd be transferred in a soundproof container and that meant a cargo ship. Still, the list would be a daunting one.

Corrupt customs officers and dockworkers were a given. No percentage going there.

'What about CCTV?' he asked, absently unwrapping a stick of chewing gum.

The little harbour master was an old acquaintance – Niemand thought him about sixty odd and, judging by his pale grey complexion, in urgent need of stepping outside his bustling office for a bit of sunshine – glanced over his shoulder while handing back a clipboard to the secretary. 'CCTV? We have it all over the place. But it's monitored by the different operators and you'd have to go and ask them. The new car shipment dock has a lot of cameras, to cut down on the stealing of cars, you know.'

Piet Niemand indicated that he knew and was about to ask for a printout of Orient bound container ships when his phone rang. It was a colleague from vice, a black detective called Mandla he had worked with on a case eighteen months earlier. 'Howzat, boss?' Before Niemand could reply he went on, 'Remember that money launderer we caught, man had a false passport on him and he ended up hanging himself in the holding cell before we could question him?'

Niemand grunted. An image of the man in question, typical pimp with flashy clothes and a quick toothy smile, filled him with little pleasure.

'I'll take that as a yes,' Mandla said, 'Well, I think we've found the paper hanger whose doing those passports. I know you've been looking into people smugglers, getting fugitives out of the country ...'

'How do you know that?'

There was a muffled laugh at the far side of the line, 'C'mon, boss. This is the New South Africa! There's no secrets anymore!' His voice dropped off as he shouted something at a fellow policeman before coming back on the line. 'It's a routine raid, a tip-off and what should we find but one of the johns has no less than three false passports on him. Didn't take much persuasion to have him lead us to his little printing shop, a Berea flat.'

'I still don't see how this interests me.'

'At his place we found several completed passports; one belonged to a Thomas James, except the photograph looks a hell of a lot like your late friend, Jannie Smit...'

'I'm on my way,' Niemand said, hustling a startled harbour master out of his way as he headed for the exit while calling for his sergeant. He'd get the address while they drove.

The midday traffic was slow moving and it was thirty minutes later when he reached the top of the stairs leading to the third floor apartment. As usual there was a power outage and he paused for seconds to catch his breath while a bemused Detective Mandla, standing in the doorway, shook his head. 'You really have to start working out, captain. You look like a heart attack waiting for a place to happen!'

An expletive from the big man had him hastily lead the way inside the cramped quarters of the tiny one bedroom flat. A small dark complexioned man sat on a kitchen chair while holding a blood stained towel to his forehead. He glanced up as the newcomers came into the room and Niemand saw that he was Indian and middle aged. Dark eyes glittered behind gold rimmed pebble glasses. A clipped greying moustache was stained at one side where he had been bleeding from the mouth as well as the gash on his forehead.

'What happened to him?'

'Resisted arrest,' a smiling uniformed cop offered, 'Seems he bruises easily.'

Looking at the small frightened man surrounded by several burly policemen Niemand didn't put much stock in the resisting arrest story but, what the hell, maybe the little guy was just accident prone. He gestured towards the items arrayed on the small kitchen table. 'This the stuff?'

'Uh huh. There's more in that cupboard over there.'

A cursory perusal revealed the usual array of forger's tools. Blank RSA passport books, printer's paraphernalia and a bathroom with heavily shrouded window serving as a photographer's darkroom. The new passport issued to Thomas James had been found in a desk drawer and, despite the plastic surgery, Niemand easily recognised Jannie Smit's grinning features. The smile was a bit lopsided, probably a result of the surgery and the hair longer than the way he normally wore it. Enough to get him past a routine customs or police checkpoint but anyone who knew him would recognise the old Jannie Smit, the man's beak of a nose having proved too much for the plastic surgeon to tackle.

Jannie Smit who would not be needing that passport after all.

Two other passports where of men in their thirties or forties, both whites, one with a beard, that Niemand didn't recognise. The job on all three passports were professional enough for the little man in the corner to have done this before.

'Can I have copies of the face pages of these two?' he indicated the passports of the two unknown men and Mandla nodded. 'I'll have it on your desk by morning.' They both knew the originals would go into evidence only later, Niemand suspected, to surface elsewhere as a getaway pass for someone else. In the New South Africa nothing was ever wasted; especially not work of this quality.

Finally turning his attention to the man in the corner Niemand pulled up a chair to position himself face to face, close enough to see the fat drops of sweat form into tiny rivulets as they welled up from oversized pores, running into his eyes and steaming up the glasses. The bleeding had stopped and it looked like he might need stitches to the gash on his forehead.

'So,' Piet Niemand began conversationally, forcing his features into what he hoped was a friendly good cop look, 'want to tell me who these people are?' He indicated the passports on the table.

Faced with a combination of a throbbing head and a giant cop with hands the size of shovels looming in his personal space, it took no more than five minutes of gentle persuasion – no rough stuff needed – to get Mr Sunil Rajaruthnam to sing like the proverbial canary. It seemed the man they wanted was a certain Mr Naidoo, a fellow Indian, who as chance would have it he was due to meet at the usual place at three that afternoon.

The arrest took place at eight minutes past the hour and was witnessed by a fifteen year old pickpocket who was plying his trade near the entrance to the Gourmet India Deli in the sprawling Golden Dawn Shopping Mall. At that hour the place was busy and he had not noticed the Indian enter the small shop with its array of spices displayed in the large window and the merry tinkle of a suspended bell as customers drifted in and out. Business had been good and the rest of the team, unobtrusively mingling with the crowd, had been as expert as ever at "unloading" the pilfered products of his sleight of hand, so he never noticed the arrival of the big man whom he now recognised with dread certainty as being a cop.

As they exited the shop now, the Indian handcuffed and still protesting his innocence as the big cop ushered him towards the elevators and the car park, the boy noticed there was another, smaller, Indian who was also cuffed with two plainclothes cops bringing up the rear.

The shopkeeper, a man he knew simply as "Mr Gupta", was standing in the doorway, ashen faced and wringing his hands as the party disappeared down the hallway where shoppers, wearily used to the travails of the New South Africa, cleared ample space while studiously avoiding eye contact.

'That was Mr Naidoo,' the voice next to him said wonderingly, making him jump. It was Goodwill the biggest of them and the leader. The boy's frown was speculative, apart from the car heist business where the Indian had been of help they knew the arrested man as one of Mama Tembu's business contacts and the owner of the shop where they were standing. And Mama always paid well for any information where any of her known business contacts were involved.

'Should we go and tell her?'

'I'll go. You fetch the others and meet me at the usual spot.'

Hampered by the need for search warrants and the inevitable ordeal of having to listen to an increasingly desperate suspect whining about "rights" and "lawyers" (who inexplicably proved hard to contact) plus a growing awareness that he had missed lunch, it was two hours later that Detective captain Piet Niemand arrived at the address Mr Naidoo had finally coughed up after some gentle persuasion.

It was a dilapidated warehouse in an industrial area and set well back in a weed overgrown open lot. The ever vigilant ostrich posed no problem as they drove through the gates and up to the large loading doors. Someone had cut the heavy chain securing the gates and close inspection showed the cuts in the steel to be fresh. Heavy wire cutters Niemand reckoned as he realised with a heavy heart that someone had beaten them to the search.

But who?

Parked two hundred yards away, partially hidden by the rusting hulk of an abandoned trailer, Mama Tembu sighed and lowered the binoculars. Damn the fat detective who was now entering the place with what looked like two other cops in tow. Another fifteen minutes and she would have been able to conduct a better search of that dumb bastard, Naidoo's office. Especially the contents of the small safe bolted to the back of a heavy steel cabinet. As it was her scouts had spotted the cops four street blocks away giving her enough chance to get out and back to the car that was waiting, engine running.

Getting into the back of the gleaming black Mercedes she ordered the driver to head back to the shebeen while she leaned back to study the sheaf of documents she had snatched in her hasty scouting of the premises.

The driver cursed as he braked for a group of idle youngsters kicking a soccer ball and the Nigerian bodyguard riding up front laughed softly as he cocked an imaginary pistol at the smiling group who hastily made way for the big limousine.

Everybody knew Mama Tembu. Nobody wanted any trouble. Beside her Goodwill stirred as he tried to peer at the papers she was now dismissing one by one as she tossed them angrily in a corner. Junk! Receipts and bills, details of shipping cargoes. Nothing that would shed light on what the police were after.

Leaning back she lit a cigarette and thought of what she had witnessed; the cells and the small operating theatre. Didn't take genius to know what the man had been up to and to think all this time he kept it from her. Big money that would have been!

It was also the kind of operation that would need protection. High level protection. The kind that only someone in high office could provide. The thought brought a smile to her lips; this was her route back into the big time. It was time to make that phone call. With a curt command she instructed the driver to give the kid a hundred rand and drop him off. If the man thought it was a bit rough on the youngster, they were still miles away from his normal stomping grounds, a fleeting eye contact in his driver's mirror had him keep his concerns to himself. For Mama had her mobile phone out and the look on her face said business was in the air and that was no place for outside ears.

Seconds later, after a curt exchange with a private secretary who knew her all too well, she was put through to Uncle Cecil as she addressed him although in reality they were in-laws. She spoke in rapid Zulu and without interruption, the only sound at the other side that of a distant bustling office and after a few seconds a door was slammed and only the man's measured breathing remained.

'I see,' the voice said when she had finished. 'And you say the police have arrested him?'

'Yes.'

There was an audible sigh, the sound of a creaking chair. 'What do you want from me?'

'You owe me, you know that. I want to be in on whatever this deal is.'

The man's protests were cut short by the curt reminder that she was made the scapegoat when the lucrative public housing deal awarded to the extended family went sour, pointing out that it wasn't her fault that eighty percent of the structures deteriorated to the point of needing demolition within two years of construction. That it was the shady bunch of builders he, her brother-in-law, had hired that led to the mess for which she was kicked out of her job as public works overseer.

'But you were well compensated...'

Mama Tembu snorted, 'Peanuts compared to what you and my darling brothers have managed to skim off to overseas bank accounts!'

'And you think I can help in this matter?'

'We both know nothing moves in KwaZulu without the hand of the family at the wheel. If it's not you involved in protecting these people it's one of the cousins. I want you to get me into the deal.' With that she cut the connection, deciding there was no need to remind Uncle Cecil that she knew all too well where the bodies were buried.

At the far side of town the minister leaned back in his chair to contemplate his options, deciding his course of action was clear. Family obligations demanded that this troublesome in-law *sisi* be accommodated but first he had to stop the haemorrhage. A phone call established where

Naidoo was being held, as well as the name of the arresting officer, a certain Detective Captain Niemand.

A second call was answered by the receptionist at Halali Game Lodge who had him speaking to Colonel Ehlers within minutes. The usual fawning pleasantries brushed aside he came straight to the point. 'A small problem has arisen. I'll take care of it. What I need from you is the contact number for the man you use when problems need to be erased. I need you to phone him first and let him know Mr Tammany will be calling with a job offer.' The chosen moniker brought a wry smile to his lips. "Tammany", the slang the family used to denote big business of the kind to be kept from the public eye.

Ten minutes later Muller listened dispassionately as the contract was handed down.

11

CHAPTER

It was past four with the afternoon sun up high and baking and the birds just beginning to stir in the cooling shadows of the mopane trees when the small group of visitors gathered for the advertised walk with the lions. The meeting spot was in the parking lot of the lodge with two Land Cruisers ready to convey the excitedly chattering party to the enclosure where the big cats were kept. The guide explained that the large camp was fenced in with a sturdy ten foot steel mesh bordered by a conventional wire fence to keep outsiders away from the inside perimeter which was electrified, a sign every fifty yards proclaiming such.

Standing next to Harry and Selena Jamie Watson shouldered his heavy looking camera bag and remarked with a wry smile that no such precautions were needed on the inside with the big cats no doubt having learned the undesirability of contact with the wire early on in their stay. The young man had joined them for dinner the night before and Harry had enjoyed swapping stories of exotic parts of Africa with the well travelled photojournalist. They had agreed to cocktails on the lodge's veranda come happy hour later that day and Harry knew Selena too was looking forward to viewing more of the stunning photographs Jamie had taken.

The drive was a short one, no more than a few miles around the side of a steep hill bordering the valley overlooked by the main resort buildings, the enclosure out of sight of the compound but close enough for the roar of the lions to be a pleasant, if distant, reminder of the proximity of Wild Africa. Hemingway's Africa, the image Halali was striving for.

But without the smells. Or the flies.

Harry sat at back next to Selena who looked gorgeous in a brightly patterned summer dress with a wide brimmed straw hat and Garboesque sunglasses that looked at least two sizes too big for the little girl she had suddenly re-discovered. Her face was flushed with the sheer joy of being alive and Harry knew that behind the shades her eyes would be darting everywhere drinking in the splendour of an African afternoon in the veldt. They were sitting up high, higher than the others in the forward rows and as the vehicle rocked and skidded over the loose stones and deep ruts in the track Harry had to steady himself and it seemed the most natural thing in the world to have his arm around her slender shoulders.

The return hug and the hand on his thigh was a warm and wonderful thing and, as always, with it came that resolve to see this thing through, end it, and then finally start that new life he had promised her so long ago. And relaxing there, in the back seat of that rocking truck, feeling the pleasant heat on his neck and arms, drinking in the smells and sounds of Africa, *their* Africa, he knew this was where they belonged. This was where they would finally settle and find that inner peace that had been ever elusive on that distant horizon.

And as he gazed down and saw the look in his woman's eyes, he knew she felt it too.

The valley was falling away to their left now with the river a silvery band and dancing streaks of white water where it hurried over shallow rock piles in its long journey to the Indian Ocean.

The Umfolozi River.

Crocodiles down there. Not many and with the locations well known to local villagers in the remote areas. The occasional child taken when making the perilous crossing to a school on the far side of the river when the village punt was out of action and the river swollen from rain with the drifts no longer shallow and slow.

Somewhere in that river was where Jannie Smit was taken. Harry thought it was higher up, towards the distant Drakensberg mountains, yet not that far away from where they were now.

No more than an hour's drive from Halali Game Lodge.

They were approaching the gates to the lions' enclosure now, the engine high pitched in its struggle to overcome the last steep portion of the climb before easing into a gentle hum as they drew to a halt at the top of the hill. It was cold up there, a fresh breeze blowing down from the mountains as the passengers climbed stiffly from the truck, the driver ready to assist the women and elderly.

The last to alight, Harry stretched his legs and arched his back as he slowly turned to survey their surroundings. They were at the steep end of the largest of the hills, the track ahead winding down the gradually sloping escarpment in a series of lazy loops before disappearing in a section of thick bush a mile further on. Squinting against the brightness Harry thought he could make out the reflection off a windscreen of another sightseeing vehicle way down in the distance.

A great day for sightseeing, a good day to die as the saying went in Africa where death was always hovering in the shadows and not only for the wildlife. Returning his gaze to the gathered party he saw that they were parked just outside a twin set of electronically operated gates with just enough space in between those to accommodate a truck such as the one they came in. Smiling down at Selena who had come up beside him to nestle an arm through his he led the way to where the driver, the young ranger named Francois, was now explaining the next phase of the afternoon's outing.

'Alright everybody, gather around. We are about to enter the lions' enclosure.' He paused for a moment to let the weight of that statement sink in, a slight smile hovering as he scanned the eager faces now intensely focused as the thrill of anticipation set in. The young Afrikaner's accent was clipped, almost guttural, but the English was fluent. As he spoke he was setting up a series of coffee mugs on a tray top that opened up from the side of the vehicle, retrieving a flask of hot water and a large plastic container of biscuits.

'There are three lions inside at present, the male and two lionesses. All were reared in captivity but I must stress they are still wild animals and I want you all to sit quite still when we're inside there. Do not in any way try to provoke a reaction and at all times keep your limbs inside the vehicle.'

He paused for effect while deft fingers prepared the coffees from a tin of instant, an enquiring glance indicating the option of tea bags. Eager hands were reaching for the cookies, lunch a distant memory.

'How do you feed them?' one of the guests ventured, an elderly German tourist he was dressed in a khaki hunter's outfit, at least if one bought into

Cape Union Mart Outfitters' projection of what the well dressed safariteer was wearing that year. 'I mean, do you release some buck inside there for them to kill?'

Francois shook his head, 'No, their parents never taught them how to kill, so that would be cruel. We feed them twice a week with animals we slaughter.'

'Are there any other lions on the property?' asked another tourist, a young European backpacker.

'We have a breeding program on a neighbouring farm. A few miles that way.' He indicated the direction with an outstretched arm, necks craning to gaze back in the direction they had travelled. 'There is a daily tour, tickets available at the lodge and also the main gate reception area.'

'What about trophy hunting?' Harry asked, fixing the young guide with a quizzical look. 'Do you cater for that kind of business at all?'

He wanted to say "canned hunting," the kind he had witnessed the day before but decided to keep it polite, realising that his tone had already betrayed his views on the matter. It was no secret that the very lucrative practice of setting up the hunter's choice of prize animal in a simulated environment while babysitting the customer through the experience of stalking and killing it in a controlled environment was a fast growing business. A game for heroes where the only life in danger was usually that of the professional hunter poised to shoot the charging beast should the customer's nerve fail at the crucial moment. Harry knew this and he hated it.

'Many game farms in South Africa now offer this service to wealthy trophy hunters, mainly Americans, the prized trophy being any member of the big five,' Selena added while squeezing Harry's arm and giving him *the look*; the one that said "be nice."

'Yes,' offered the German, 'I read somewhere that this is the fate of old lions in Africa, they are bought up by the farmers and staked out to be killed by these hunters, no?' The small gathering had gone quiet now, the thought of an animal trapped and set up for the kill an uncomfortable one and not quite compatible with the pleasurable game sightseeing drive they were embarked on.

'We are purely a safari park and animal breeding facility,' Francois said hastily with a reassuring smile. 'We do not allow any hunting at Halali.'

After a moment's pause, as he retrieved empty mugs from his guests, he added. 'In fact, the name of our farm, Halali, is derived from the rising three notes of the huntsman's bugle announcing the end of the hunt.'

'Haa – laa – lii!!' the German sang to delighted applause from the others.

Harry had taken the binoculars from Selena's sling bag and was studying a series of low iron building at the distal end of the enclosed lion's camp. They were at least five hundred yards away and barely visible amongst a clump of acacia bush. A smaller hut set to one side had windows, by appearances an office of sorts with a tall radio antenna and satellite dish with a link chain enclosed tunnel connecting it with the largest of the sheds. A stovepipe chimney in the latter suggested a kitchen facility or possibly for heating in winter. Focusing the field glasses to maximum magnification Harry could just make out the perimeter fence at the rear of the buildings and there was no sign of a gate.

The only access to that distant clump of buildings was through the gate they were now about to enter.

It was also the only exit from the high voltage wire cage.

And the lions were the guards.

Interesting.

They were back on the vehicle now and waiting for the remote controlled gate to slide closed behind them before the inside gate would open. In the distance and leading off to the left hand corner of the camp Harry could make out another one of the farm's vehicles, a Range Rover with a man standing next to it and smiling a welcome as they bumped their way towards him across the uneven veldt.

It was Colonel Ehlers, dressed smartly in an olive green safari suit, the shirt sporting the Halali emblem, topped off with a blood red bandanna knotted at the neck cowboy style and the broad rimmed slouch hat had what looked like a leopard skin hatband.

All in all it vaguely reminded Harry of a character in a Hollywood version of Darkest Africa. John Wayne came to mind.

'Good afternoon! Great day for it, not so?!' came the hearty welcome, the man spreading his arms to indicate the fresh embrace of glorious nature all around. He was answered by a chorus of enthusiastic agreement from the excited newcomers who had spotted the lions, three of them, lying in the grass at the corner of the camp and no more than fifty yards away.

Their own vehicle had pulled up next to the Range Rover at an angle affording everyone the best possible view. Francois, the driver, had alighted and after exchanging a few muffled words with the Colonel, returned to the Land Cruiser mounting the running board to address his charges. 'We are very lucky to-day in that Colonel Ehlers is here on a regular inspection of the big cats and he has graciously offered to treat us to a display of extraordinary control and interaction with these kings of the jungle. The last phrase was expressed with some emphasis leaving Harry to conclude they had done this act before.

Still no sign of interest from the big cats, the only proof of life one of the lionesses lifting her head to gaze at the party for a few seconds before dropping back into what appeared to be a sound snooze. Francois was speaking again, cautioning everyone to stay inside the vehicle, explaining that the Colonel was one of only a handful of people in the world who had ever mastered the art of approaching a fully grown lion in the wild and with no weapon at hand should things go wrong.

'I want you all to sit quite still, no noise at all, as he approaches the lions. It's OK to take photos but, please, don't make a noise.'

The Colonel was already halfway across to where the lions were lying, moving slowly and crouched forward, his gaze fixed intently on the tan and grey shapes that now showed the first signs of stirring. The male – his name was Kibus the guide had informed them earlier – lifted his massive head to a sharp hiss from the spellbound group as the magnificent mane stirred in the breeze.

The Colonel paused and for the first time Harry noticed something in his right hand. Something white and at that distance indistinct and kept low at his side as if to shield it from the view of both lion and tourist.

'He's beyond the point of no return now,' whispered Jamie Watson who was peering through the viewer of a long lens camera, rapidly clicking away, the whirr of the autofocus suddenly loud in the breath holding silence. 'Should the lions charge now he will not be able to get back to the safety of his car before being caught...'

A low shudder of anticipation went through the gathering as they visualised such a dreadful event even before Francois reminded them that several people were still killed every year by lions in the wild.

Twenty yards. Advancing slowly now, crouching even lower.

The Colonel paused and his captive spectators held their collective breath.

For Kibus was moving. As he raised his massive torso a deep rolling roar, almost a moan, thundered across the veldt and Harry felt Selena's nails dig into his arm. 'Oh God!' she whispered and then the lion rose and turned towards the approaching man and moved towards him, slowly then picking up the pace and Harry aware of the ranger leaning across the Land Cruiser's roof turning rigid a hand hovering just inside the cabin as the tension gripped him. Rifle, Harry guessed but then a sigh from his fellow guest had him swivel back to where the Colonel, seemingly at the last second, had straightened up and raised his arm high, the sunlight catching the white object in his hand.

As if stopped by an invisible magic curtain, Kibus halted in his tracks. The lion stood there for what seemed an eternity, only a few yards separating it from the man. Then, slowly, it turned and headed back, flopping down next to the lionesses who had watched the whole spectacle without showing the slightest sign of wanting to join in. All watched as the Colonel took off the hat in mock salute to the lion who was watching him dispassionately, all the while emanating a guttural moan so low as to be almost inaudible.

Turning to the now chattering and visibly relieved audience, Ehlers accepted their applause with a flowering bow before striding purposefully back to the Range Rover. 'Please don't try this at home!' he offered with a smile to general laughter as it became clear to all that the mysterious white object in his hand was nothing other than a humble roll of white toilet paper.

But Harry was staring at a small object that lay on the ground near the vehicle's front, something that appeared to have been dropped earlier and not noticed by the man who was now, with a last smiling wave at his fans, climbing back behind the wheel.

Exchanging the binoculars for Selena's camera he brought the object, a small glass vial, into sharp focus and took a photo. "Ketamine" was the inscription, the rest of the writing too small to make out. Interesting, Harry mused as their own vehicle started up and prepared to follow the other car towards the gate. Harking back to his days living in Spain and being involved with raising fighting Miura bulls he was quite familiar with that drug. Ketamine, a veterinary sedative developed to tranquilize animals producing an effect known as neurolept analgesia – a state of deep sedation where the subject would not experience pain while all other physiological functions, such as breathing, went on normally. A drug, as far as Harry could recall, that was subsequently taken up by the medical profession for use in human anaesthetics.

Why had the Colonel found it necessary to put up that ridiculous show with three drugged lions? Ego? Or did it have something to do with what was at the far end of that camp? The collection of huts where the Range Rover was now headed, a short message on the two way radio that nestled on the passenger seat of the Land Cruiser informing their driver that the Colonel would catch up with them later.

'Phew!' exclaimed Selena as the outer gate slid closed behind them, 'I sure could do with a gin and tonic after all that!'

Harry smiled and returned her squeeze of his hand. 'Spectacular wasn't it?'

They were heading down the back of the hill now, towards where Francois moments earlier had mentioned a herd of African Buffalo had been spotted earlier that morning. Five hundred yards down the hill they stopped, the ranger alighting to point out a small bush next to the track. 'The *gonnabos*,' he explained, breaking off a section and passing it up to his charges to examine. 'When your vehicle is stuck and you need rope to pull it out but you don't have any, you can fashion a rope from this plant like this.' Stripping long sections of soft bark from one of the plant's many limpid sprouts he indicated how this could be woven together to form a surprisingly strong fabric.

Dutifully examining the piece of vegetation before passing it along Harry used the opportunity to question the young man regarding the section of outbuildings they had just passed on their descent down the winding track. Expecting a brush off stock reply of "storage" Harry was intrigued to hear the young man explain that it used to be a research facility, for animal breeding programs, but was now in disuse.

'So it's empty now?' Harry asked.

Francois shrugged and glanced at his watch. 'I suppose so, I've never been inside, I think the Colonel uses it as a kind of field office but we rangers never get to go there.' With a smile he indicated the fence just visible in the distance, 'As you can see, it's in the lion enclosure. Not the place to go wandering about is it?'

12

CHAPTER

B roadly speaking hitmen come in two groups. There's the traditional mow them down in the street with a tommy gun mobster much favoured by old time crime families and referred to as "torpedoes" or "mechanics." Nothing subtle there with collateral damage not given much thought and the more public the killing the better. Then there's the latter day faceless killer. The sophisticated professional who studies his target, often for weeks, before coming up with a customised and often novel method of getting the job done. Ideally disguised as a natural death or an act of God. The idea not to teach a lesson or publicly eliminate a competitor or threat but to smooth the path for a proposed venture by white collar businessmen who abhor violence and wish to be spared the details or draw attention to themselves. These killers are hard to find, work selectively and for exorbitant fees. They are seldom caught and often have a perfectly respectable "day job."

There is a third type. This man is usually from a military background, often special forces, and kills not because he likes it but because he's good at it. Skills honed during years of undercover "black ops" where the use of sophisticated state of the art killing tools are combined with meticulous planning and execution. Often such missions would come down at very short notice and require the mindset never to hesitate when faced with the target and the moment.

In practice this meant having at one's disposal not only the tools of the trade but a full set of ready made plans for different situations. All thought through and in many cases previously put to the test. A very special kind of man.

Muller was such a man.

The telephone conversation, taken in the privacy of his study so as not to disturb Ria and the kids, was of necessity a lengthy one. This was not to the liking of the man on the other side of the line, the man who liked to be called "Mr Tammany" but whose voice bore uncanny resemblance to a political figure in the Natal branch of the government Muller had seen often enough on national television. He wanted the job done quickly and with no comebacks, didn't seem to care about the details. Therein lay the problem: a twenty four hour deadline and the quarry under guard in a prison cell, didn't leave much scope for meticulous planning.

Or a delicate surgical job.

It would be messy and he would need outside help. Help? the man asked, what kind of help? So Muller told him. All in all it had taken him less than eight minutes to formulate the hit plus explain to the minister what he wanted. Lastly came the price and here there was no bickering. Half payable in advance, cash, at an agreed spot and at a time that gave Mr Tammany less than two hours to get the money.

After he hung up Muller sat behind his desk for a few minutes as he ran the plan through his mind, mentally checking off each required item. Satisfied that he could put things together with material stored in his backyard shed he smiled as his wife peered around the door to remind him that the lawn needing cutting.

It took the better part of an hour, working in the small workshop at the back of the garage, to prepare the device. Two pounds of C4 explosive attached to a magnetised base plate with a clip to hold the stolen mobile phone he would buy off a street urchin on the corner of Smith and Marine Parade. Carefully locking the workshop he went into the garage and kneeling next to the rear wheel bay of the wife's car checked that the package would attach easily and securely to the metal on the inside — excessive mud could be a problem. Satisfied, he placed the device in a small canvas shoulder bag and locked it in the trunk of his car.

A glance at his watch showed there was still an hour to go before meeting the client, time for a coffee and a slice of that apple crumble the wife made so well. He was feeling hungry.

Frustrated at her brother-in-law not getting back to her as promised, Mama Tembu decided to confront him in his office at Parliament House.

As an ANC "mother" from the days of protest marches she was well known in political circles and would have little trouble in getting past the security detail.

The Nigerian was driving, Mama Tembu in the back and thumbing through a glossy magazine when they were stopped by a black Mercedes exiting through the gates with little regard for the angry squeal of car tyres and the protesting blare of horns. It was the minister and more interesting, he was driving himself, alone in the car and that, Mama Tembu decided, meant business was afoot. Of the more private variety and on impulse she ordered her driver to follow.

Morning traffic was sparse, mostly pedestrians and light vehicles and the driver worked at keeping a few cars back, his mistresses limousine not the ideal vehicle when unobtrusiveness was the goal.

As arranged Muller and the minister met in a back booth of a Spur steakhouse twenty minutes later. Muller, who had arrived first, was halfway through his Hunga Busta burger when Mr Tammany slid into the seat facing him. No words were spoken as a briefcase was pushed across and its contents checked.

'What time?'

The minister blanched, although no newcomer to the art of the assassination he was taken aback by the cold callousness of the man calmly sipping his coffee across from him. 'Two thirty; the meeting in my office is at two thirty which means they will have to leave the prison at about two, maybe earlier.'

Muller nodded. 'No suspicion as to why the summons to your office?' The light grey eyes seemed to bore into his mind and the minister found himself glancing away, suddenly uncomfortable.

'It's not unusual for something like this, not when I inform the Chief of Police that the matter is a political one.' He could have added that it helped that the Police Chief was his brother but there seemed little point.

'You've arranged for an insider to signal me when they leave, identify the vehicle?'

Tammany nodded and pocketed the slip of paper with the mobile phone number Muller had scribbled down.

And then there was really nothing more to be said. He could have asked about what would happen to the cops accompanying the prisoner, to innocent bystanders but sometimes it was simply better not to know. A few final words regarding the next payment and then he was outside and feeling the midday sun warm on his back and shivering despite the heat.

In his haste to get out of that place of death he took no notice of the woman seated at one of the barstools facing the window counter, the woman in the hat and dark glasses that had been silently studying the transaction in the reflections of the large decorative mirror on an opposite wall. And Mama Tembu knew exactly what had gone down, she had been part of similar deals herself and now it was simply a matter of figuring out how she could play this to her own advantage.

Paying for her milkshake she went over to the car and spoke to the driver who nodded and held open the front passenger door for her to get in. They would follow when the man came out and might have to switch drivers quickly should the unforeseen arise.

At three minutes past two the white Toyota Camry swung through the gates, the uniformed driver gunning the engine as he jumped the amber traffic light narrowly missing a group of schoolgirls out on a supervised sightseeing trip. In the back sat a stony faced Naidoo, his handcuffs hidden under a folded coat. The front passenger seat was occupied by a plainclothes policeman with a uniformed cop sitting next to the prisoner and working the wrapper off a Mars Bar.

Inside the courtyard a police sergeant cradled his pocketed mobile phone, the device warm in his sweaty palm, as he grimly watched the car leave. As arranged he had made the call, the answer on the other side a grunt before the line went dead. He hated doing this but the minister was a powerful man and there were many mouths to feed. Something dies when the big dog feeds but there is always meat for those who follow him around.

An official police vehicle travelling fast with several cops inside was something to be kept away from and there was no need to run the flashers but what the hell. For good measure the driver, a rookie still into the job, flicked on the siren until the plainclothes cop, with a sidelong curse, told him to switch the damn thing off.

Traffic was light. The doors were locked.

Alerted by the expected call on his mobile seconds earlier, Muller had the engine of the Kawasaki running when the car came into view and swung into its slipstream, the powerful machine bucking slightly as the rear tyre struggled for grip on the melting in the heat tar. Settling twenty feet back, just enough space to prevent another vehicle from getting between him and his quarry, Muller waited for his chance. It would have to be at a traffic light stop, it was simply too risky to manoeuvre the bike while simultaneously trying to plant the bomb.

But, in a city – a country – where it was more dangerous to stop at a red traffic light than run through it, would the car stop? He shrugged off the thought, as always he would improvise if need be.

His chance came three minutes later as the driver, alerted to the fact they were running late, decided to take a short cut down a narrow side lane only to be held up by a double parked DHL delivery van, the man dropping off a package and seemingly oblivious to the angry blare of the police car's siren as he waited for the required signature on his e pad. With traffic coming the opposite way there was no chance of passing and nothing to do except sit there cursing as they watched the other driver make his way back to his cab, the man with all the time in the world.

A small compensation that they weren't the only traffic held up, a helmeted biker on a big Kawasaki revving the bike next to their blindside rear corner with another car, a black limousine, further back.

Working quickly Muller had the device out of the canvas bag slung around his chest and was clamping it to the underside of the wheel well, all the time keeping an eye on the mirrors of the Toyota for any signs of undue interest. The powerful magnets attached at once and that, Muller reflected, was pretty much that. All he had to do now was decide on the place of execution. For all his questionable attributes Muller was no callous mass murderer, simply a tradesman, one who took pride in his trade and limiting collateral damage was a matter of pride.

They had started moving again and coming into a busy street there were lots of pedestrians about. The mobile phone was resting on the machine's petrol tank, held securely by a clip, the number already dialled and all it needed was to hit the green dial button. Death at the fingertip of a patient man; was this what was in store for him one day? He shook off the thought, focused on the job at hand, the bike throbbing between his thighs, starting to sweat now under the leather gear, moisture running down on the inside of the all enclosing helmet.

And then the moment was there. Falling fifty feet back, a safe distance, he pushed the dial button.

As explosions go it wasn't much, not by modern movie standards anyway. Just a sudden fireball followed a microsecond later by a dull thunder that rocked the bike and had Muller instinctively raise a shielding arm to his face as shattered glass formed a brief halo of light around the car that was raised several feet off the road by the force of the blast.

Cruising slowly past the furiously burning wreck Muller thought he could vaguely make out several figures inside, they would all be dead now and part of him noted with clinical detachment that the burning effect must be due to the bomb having been in close proximity to the petrol tank – C4 doesn't normally produce a fireball such as he was witnessing now. Something to make a note of; next time he would use less of the stuff. At any rate, there was no need for the Colt Python tucked in his belt as a backup, the contract was completed.

Gunning the engine and working the traction control of the clutch as he wove patiently through the stalled traffic he pointed the big bike in the direction of home. Ria was preparing a *bobotie* for supper, her mother's recipe and one of his favourites. Life was good, he reflected but there was still unfinished business at hand.

A man called Harry Dance. The problem, the man was currently holed up at a place declared off limits by the contractor. He would have to wait and watch. Like all predators, he was good at waiting.

Out of her car—with chaos reigning all traffic had ground to a halt as the crowd gathered – Mama Tembu stood and watched the car burn. She knew Naidoo was inside, had seen his face when the Toyota had first come through the gates of the police station. Having followed the man on the motorbike and parked further down the street, Mama with binoculars trained on the scene, knowing something was happening.

Naidoo was dead now, of course. A professional hit, which cost money. Which meant even larger money was in play and Naidoo had been in the thick of it.

It was time to have that chat with dear brother-in-law.

13

CHAPTER

'Do you think we'll ever come back here, Harry? I mean back to Africa to stay for good?'

Harry looked at his wife. God she was beautiful! Dressed in a simple white cotton full length gown that even in the dim lighting of the pool deck contrasted vividly with her golden tan, she had a red hibiscus in her hair and a soft look in her eyes. Earlier, after a languid swim in the refreshingly cool water of the resort's infinity view pool, she had painted her nails a deep red and lying on the bed in their tent and studying her Harry had thought there was something on her mind. They had shared a life long enough for him to know this and also to know that she would tell him in her own good time. Now, relaxing in the comfort of soft cushioned cane chairs on the lodge's veranda and listening to the pleasant strains of a vaguely familiar song wafting through the open doors leading to the lounge and dining rooms, Harry thought, yeah, back in Africa – permanently this time – was something he too wanted.

He said so and was rewarded by a tight squeeze of his hand, nails drawing a pattern and holding promise of things to come.

Dinner long over most guests had retired to their cabins with only a group of teenagers still playing pool in the games room, the sharp clacking of the balls interspersed with sudden exclamations of excitement. Voices drifting in through the open windows were of couples taking a last stroll while soaking up the sheer beauty and tranquillity of the African night, the only sounds the excited twitter of birds settling into the trees and the distant hum of a generator.

A busy day sightseeing and being exposed to the heat and humidity meant everyone was pleasantly worn out and ready to turn in. Harry and Selena had joined the other guests for the cocktail hour followed by dinner which as the guests had come to expect by now meant a sumptuous three course meal served up in style by Norbert, the ever serious looking European chef. That was a few hours ago and, glancing at his watch Harry reckoned it was time to set in motion the second half of the evening. Minutes later they were being driven back to their quarters by a young female warden, Cassie.

The bumpy ride across the grass plain was an adventure in itself with the game ranging from springbok to kudu to wildebeest lazily making their way down to the river and its watering holes. The golf buggy had no lights and a nervous Selena was entrusted with the powerful torch used to light up the path as well as the brown and grey shapes suddenly looming up in the lights only to startle away with a thunder of hooves.

Suddenly chilly she wrapped the sweater tightly around her shoulders and asked the driver about the next day's activities.

'There's a walk with the lions at our breeding facility on a neighbouring farm, a minibus will leave from the lodge at ten, then there's the usual game drive at six in the morning and late afternoon as well as activities like horse riding or a ride on Hatari, our elephant.'

They were approaching the river now, the musical play of water over pebbles faintly audible, the reeds gently swaying in the evening breeze. Climbing our of the buggy Harry stretched his legs as he gazed across to the far side of the river. Something he saw there made him turn to the girl who was busy hauling the punt across to their side. 'I don't see any lights on in the tents over there, only ours.'

Cassie nodded as she concentrated on hauling the floating jetty onto the bank before offering Selena a steadying hand as she clambered aboard. 'I think you are the only ones staying on that side to-night, apart from Jamie, the young photographer in tent number four. (Did she blush just then? That hint of familiarity? It was too dark for Selena to be sure.) 'The other two families checked out to-day.'

'I didn't see Jamie at dinner,' Harry said to Selena, recalling the young man's promise to join them for a nightcap later.

'Jamie told me the best time for wildlife photography was dawn and dusk. He excused himself to try for a photo of the fish eagle he had spotted earlier.'

They were at the other side now and waving goodbye to Cassie who was taking the punt back, the outline of the khaki clad young woman quickly fading into the fast gathering gloom. A shout from the far side reassuring them she was OK they started up the boardwalk which was wet with dew, Harry remarking how the long grass was mowed down in an irregular fashion and Selena telling him that was the effect of the water buffalo coming down at night to graze between the tents and walkways. Nice then to know, Harry thought, that last he checked buffaloes didn't climb steps.

It was shortly after ten that evening when Madame Chen was helped out of the Land Cruiser and led into the well lit enclosure of the barn. The colonel led the way with Hugo and the young Chinese bringing up the rear. The lions were nowhere in sight and with Hugo sure they were at the far end of the enclosure there was no need for special precautions on the short trip from car to the safety of the building.

Once inside the motley collection of frightened young faces were quickly lined up and carefully scrutinized by an expressionless Madame Chen as she slowly passed down the row of shiny black faces, big eyes silently following her progress.

'They have all been checked?'

The colonel nodded. 'No diseases. Healthy specimens.' He might as well have been discussing cattle, a thought he kept to himself.

'Hmm. What about that big one in the cage over there?' All eyes turned to where Vusi was reclining on his cot, watching the proceedings with clinical interest as he weighed up any potential advantage to the appearance of the newcomers. And all the time his gaze would drift back to the bearded Hugo and once again the hatred would well up inside him bringing with it all the pent up rage of the caged predator.

'We think his son is with the previous batch. We caught him snooping around and brought him along.'

An arched brow had him quickly add, 'We believe he's been acting alone but so far he's been refusing to talk. There is no reason to believe our operation is compromised.' Seeing her frown he shrugged, 'If you want him we'll throw him in free of charge. It will save us having to dispose of him.'

Madame Chen nodded. 'Very well. As it is the previous shipment is still here in Durban. I decided it's less risky to do one big shipment after I'd inspected the facilities.' She glanced at her watch, a chunky gold Omega that looked too heavy for her slim wrist, 'What time is the truck due?'

'Any time now. But we'll only move the cargo at one in the morning. We'll have them at the harbour before dawn.'

In the corner Vusi felt his pulse quicken. Lukas was still in the country and most likely held with others in the hold of a ship in Durban harbour. And with luck that was where he was headed. And how many times had Harry reminded him that the best time for an ambush or escape is when the enemy is on the move. His chance would come.

Two hundred yards away, up close to the fence and hidden in the shadows of a small shrub, Jamie Watson adjusted the focus on his long lens and settled in for the wait. He had already captured the images of the newcomers – they had to be the buyers – and if he could get that photo of them in the same frame as the boys his mission would be complete. In any case he reckoned he had enough evidence now to blow this whole thing wide open. To-morrow he would return to Durban and a no doubt warm welcome from his colleagues at the paper. He knew the editor had been waiting for just this scoop and, boy, was this going to be the big one!

'Do you have to go? Remember what the game ranger said about the wildlife roaming outside after dark?'

Harry nodded, grimaced, as he laced up the soft leather hunting boots. 'I know, the rhinos haven't been seen for a few days now and sometimes the buffalo cross the river and graze on our side.' Sitting on the bed he glanced around for his bush jacket – it was bound to get cold towards dawn – and, after a moment's hesitation slipped the bulky Colt into his belt, resting against his back.

Selena watched him in silence as he collected the items laid out on the dressing table, placing them one by one into the small canvas sling bag.

Powerful flashlight, bulky night vision goggles, water bottle and finally a flat Perspex encased compass. She had watched in silence earlier when he strapped the matt black commando dagger to his calf where it nestled under cover of a trouser leg. Watching him now, turning the light from the lantern way down before stepping onto the porch, she tried one last time to change his mind. 'What exactly do you hope to find, Harry? These people know who you are and if you're right about this people smuggling thing they could be dangerous. Where will you even start?'

'The truth is out there somewhere. You know I have to go.'

Yes I do, Selena thought sadly. And fortune favours the brave but one day, perhaps a beautiful perfect day just like this one has been, your luck will finally run out. Suppressing a shudder she snuggled into his arm.

Standing on the wooden deck now and gazing out over the river below and the grass plain beyond Harry waited for his eyes to adjust. There was a sickle moon rising and it was after a minute, when his night sight came in that he started identifying the shapes of animals moving against the back drop of the horizon.

Buffalo, he thought. Most ill tempered of Africa's Big Five and a whole herd of them close by with only the river between us and them. There was a soft rustle and then Selena slid her arm through his and gave it a squeeze.

'Wouldn't it be nice,' she said softly, 'If for once we could enjoy all this like just another couple. Soaking it all in, letting it just wash around us, without there being some ugliness bearing down us?' She felt Harry stiffen, 'What is it?!'

'The lights, the lamps marking the wooden walkways between the huts, are out. Normally they burn all night. The lamp post at the river crossing has gone out as well.'

'Perhaps the generator...'

Harry shook his head, 'No. Our fridge is still working, I can hear it humming and,' taking her by the hand he led the way to the far end of the porch where they could just make out the lodge between the low hanging branches, 'The lights at the lodge are still burning.' Adding, after a second, 'I don't like it...'

'Shall I phone reception?'

Without waiting for an answer she went inside only to return seconds later. 'The line's dead.'

'What do you think, Harry?' There was a note of apprehension in her voice as she searched his face for a sign.

'I think they want to keep us confined to this side of the river, away from whatever's happening over at that lodge. At a guess I'd say the punt on the river would be rigged so we couldn't get across.'

A thought she had been harbouring for some time now, made her ask, 'Are we in danger?'

'I don't think so, not if we stay put. They cannot afford the publicity of a guest injured or dead while on the property. No, whatever is going down is happening to-night, by to-morrow there'll be nothing left to find.'

The guest arrived at ten that evening, while Colonel Ehlers was escorting the Chinese buyers to view the prisoners. Cassie, who had been alerted to his expected arrival, greeted him at the door to quickly escort him straight through to a small room upstairs where a meal had been laid out. The servants had been dismissed for the night and she was the one to serve, always careful to keep his wine glass well filled. She knew he would have flown in by small plane, the pilot dropping him off at the lodge before heading to the kitchen where his own meal would be waiting.

Heidmann chose to dine in silence and if he was aware of her presence hovering close by in the shadows he made no acknowledgement of it, the only sound in the room Bach playing softly on the CD player, the man occasionally drumming his fingers in rhythm with the more strident sections.

She knew it was the Brandenburg Concerto No 5 in D major because she had checked the label when putting it on. Also it was always that same piece of music when he dined during one of his infrequent and always secretive visits.

Her own taste in music being more in the line of Dire Straits not forgetting those good looking hunks from Boyzone.

He ate slowly, seemingly tasting every morsel of food before carefully chewing it and swallowing with a generous sip of wine. Like the music there was a rhythm to it as he methodically worked his way through the different courses, Cassie dutifully removing each plate and quickly substituting it with the next. For the hundredth time she wondered who this mysterious man was and how he fitted into the scheme of things at Halali. Living her dream of becoming a skilled game warden in a country where such jobs were rare, she had long suspected other business than game viewing might be happening at Halali but to date had managed to keep her suspicions to herself.

The meal finished the man had remained at the table, slowly twirling a glass of port. Saying nothing, just sitting there while Cassie, still on duty, hovered in the background.

Her relief was tangible when Colonel Ehlers arrived an hour later and she was allowed to retreat to her quarters.

Accepting a refill from the excellent bottle of Roodeberg 85 the guest leaned back and patted his pockets for a cigar which the colonel lit for him. After a few minutes of smoking in silence, seemingly lost in thought, the man known as Mr Heidmann swivelled his chair to face the colonel who had been scouring the sideboard for leftovers, finishing the last of the dessert, a truly excellent brandy pudding. 'So the Chinese contact is here and the plan is to shift to-night?'

'Yes. As instructed I have spoken to Tammany in Durban and there will be no problems with the customs or on the dockside. His own people will take care of that as always.'

'Hmm. I can't help wondering how long that idiot of a president intends keeping our man in his job as minister. As you know he keeps on shuffling the bloody cabinet to give everyone a chance to dip their snout into the trough. That's apparently how the buffoon stays in power. He sighed, tapped some ash on the carpet and held out his glass for a refill. 'Ah well, no doubt the next one will be as corrupt as the last and will be open for business. Now, tell me about the black you got holed up there with the others.'

'Vusi Luwago,' the colonel said, 'Known associate of Harry Dance. I'm not sure if Dance, whom you know is staying here, knows Luwago is held prisoner close by. I have already explained how this Luwago got to be here in the first place, most likely a co-incidence.'

'Has Dance been snooping around?'

'He's only been here twenty four hours and we have taken great care in keeping him away from the barn and also from the off limits quarters.'

'Unlike you, Jaap, I don't believe in co-incidences. Dance is here because that idiot Louw told him about this place. The man is here to snoop with God knows what agenda or who he's working for.'

The colonel had crossed over to a well stocked with liquors sideboard and was studying the label of a vintage port. His thoughts returned to the earlier meal, wondering whether there were any leftovers in the kitchen. The venison had been done just right, never an easy ask, and the wine excellent. Now it was time for something sweet and lingering. 'Port?'

'Make mine a cognac. Is Louw here?'"

'Yes. As instructed we have kept him confined to his quarters. Dance and his wife are on the other side of the river and I've given orders to make it difficult for them to get over here before dawn. A power failure.'

The other man had risen to pace the room now, puffs of cigar smoke highlighting his passage, a frown creasing his tanned brow. 'Something will have to be done about Dance. An accident. And not while he's on the farm.'

'But how can ...'

A raised hand stopped him midsentence. 'We will lure him off the property and the bait will be Mike Louw. Once outside an accident can easily be arranged...'

Sipping his port the colonel studied Heidmann over the rim of the glass, his gaze calculating. Should he tell the man about Muller, about the contract already out on Dance? No, he decided; in their game it was better to be that vital one step ahead. Who knows when *he* might become expedient, be the next blot on the man's landscape. When the services of the hitman might just stand between himself and a nasty end.

14

CHAPTER

Still dripping wet from his swim across the river Harry pressed deeper into the shadows of the portico carefully controlling his own breathing as he listened to the conversation taking place several feet above him. He couldn't see the faces, couldn't risk climbing onto the table located just below the window but there was no mistaking the voice of Colonel Ehlers. It was the other man who interested him, the one who was giving the orders. And as he listened Harry knew with growing certainty that he knew that voice. A different time, a different place. But when? Where!?

There was no doubt this was the big boss, the man in charge of Savannah but what was this other business, over in that mysterious shed? He had to know and that meant going up there, now. His ears pricked to the sound of a car drawing closer, the engine note rising and falling with the occasional gnashing of gears. At that hour of the night decidedly unusual but it could just be a game ranger on a mission.

A sudden movement had him freeze, pressing even deeper into the shadows of the overhanging window box. Was there someone moving at the far side of the large pool deck? He thought there was. But an earlier scout of the area had revealed no guards, the personnel all down at the small compound a few hundred yards away. He knew there was still a servant somewhere in the house, he had heard the dinner plates being cleared away minutes earlier and then of course, Mike Louw was in there somewhere.

He was about to move away when he saw it again, a man was coming up the path leading to the front of the lodge where the parking area was. He was half walking half running and clearly out of breath. Moving around the base of the pillar to remain unseen he watched as the man knocked on the patio door which was opened seconds later by one of the black servants. 'The colonel,' the man, Harry recognised him as one of the rangers, wheezed between snatches of breath, 'I must see him immediately. There's a man in the car outside who's been bitten by a snake. One of the guests. I need to get the snake bite kit in the colonel's office.'

He was trying to push the servant out of the way, the man hesitant as he had obviously had orders to let no-one in. It took Harry just seconds to decide this was his chance. As the newcomer was let in, Harry sprinted for the corner of the building and then he was running to where a Land Rover was parked, lights blazing and engine running.

A young man was slumped in the passenger seat and as Harry yanked open the door he saw it was Jamie Watson, the photographer dressed in camouflage with his face blackened. A long gash had been sliced down one trouser leg with a handkerchief tied tightly around the calf, a thin trickle of blood seeping from underneath. 'Hello, Harry... Cape Cobra,' the young man smiled weakly. 'Saw it too late and it got me. Didn't...didn't want to find... they mustn't find .... '

Harry could see him fading, the poison starting to paralyse the respiratory muscles. Instinctively he took the back pack Watson was indicating nestling at his feet while imploring the young man to lie still until help came.

But the eyes were fixed on him now, their message pleading and urgent. 'Mus...must not f.. find this... lives at s...stake. G...give paper, Natal Mercury...'

Lights were going on in the lodge behind him, shouts shattering the stillness of the night. Time to move but the young man's grip on his arm, even as its strength faded, had him hesitate. 'P...promise.'

'I promise.' With that he sprinted for the cover of the nearest bush from where he watched as the colonel came striding up rapidly with the warden in tow. Of the other man Harry had heard in the room upstairs there was no sign. The servant brought up the rear with a large first aid kit.

Harry watched as Jamie Watson was lifted from the car and laid down on the wet grass. He didn't seem to be moving and the colonel cursed as he tore the slitted trouser leg open to inspect the bite mark. 'Cobra?'

'That's what he said.'

'Where was this?' the colonel asked as he drew up the anti-venom while the ranger looked for a vein in the victim's limp arm. 'Over the back of the hill, near the barn camp. I was coming back from checking on the lions as you ordered when he suddenly stumbled into my headlights and waved me down.'

A vein had been found and the colonel injected the contents of the vial, adding a second injection before expertly connecting up a saline infusion, the plastic bottle handed to the servant to hold aloft. 'He's still breathing, but weakly. Help me move him to the house and call Miss Cassie to come up, she'll have to help.'

Still in the shadows Harry watched the limp form being carried inside and minutes later a golf buggy drew up in a cloud of dust and a young woman Harry recognised as the receptionist, jumped out and raced up the steps to the house where the servant was holding open the front door.

From experience Harry knew Jamie Watson was staring down the gaping chasm of death, he would have to be ventilated and then there was still the chance his heart might give out. Still, the people inside there looked like they knew what they were doing – snakebites an all too common occurrence in the wilds of Zululand and the journalist had youth on his side. So what was it he was risking his life for, up on that hill and the increasingly mysterious barn?

Settling down with his back to the wall of a small stoneworks at the edge of the car park, Harry went through the contents of the backpack. Setting aside the paraphernalia of a professional photographer, cameras, lenses and a small tripod, he found himself holding a bulky manila envelope. Inside was a thick sheaf of photographs, some of nature scenes and wildlife but it was the other photos that really interested him. For they were unmistakably of the barn and there was a vehicle parked with a stream of black children alighting and being hustled inside the building. He recognised one of the men as being present at the previous day's killing of the lion with Colonel Ehlers standing off to one side. Two other men were unknown to him. It was one of the last photos that had him go ice cold as that old familiar slow rage reared its head.

Framed against the light set high over the barn's open door stood his friend Vusi, handcuffed and with his ankles chained and standing unbowed while glaring with unmasked hatred at the bearded man who was smiling as he raised a club for the blow to follow.

There were more photos and Harry looked at them all as his mind raced and he forced the rage down and waited for his hands to become steady once more. The last photos were still stored in the digital camera, at a guess taken only hours earlier that night. They showed Madame Chen and Hilton, the young companion, being showed into the building, presumably to inspect the wares.

The second business venture of Colonel Ehlers and whoever his partners were.

The kidnapping and selling of children. And Vusi, in search of his son, had stumbled right into it. Shoving the items back into the pack his mind was made up. He would have to rescue Vusi immediately, then deal with the rest and for that it was time to send for the cavalry. A phone, he needed to call that number Detective Captain Niemand had given him but the only phone was inside that house and to get to it he would have to overcome a slight matter of odds.

He was about to move when the front door opened and the ranger came down the steps and over to the Land Rover. Harry watched as he opened the passenger side door to rummage about, finally searching the back of the vehicle as well. 'Looking for something?' Harry said as he swung the heavy piece of wood he had located nearby. It struck the startled man against the side of the head with sickening force and he slumped against the vehicle before collapsing soundlessly to the ground.

Harry reckoned him out for the count.

Moving quickly he dragged the limp body into the shades of some bushes and squatted next to the raggedly breathing form to wait.

He did not have to wait long, five minutes by his watch, before Colonel Ehlers stepped into the light of the porch. *'Piet! Waar de hel is jy!'*

No answer and seconds later, still swearing in Afrikaans under his breath, the colonel strode over to see for himself what the hold up was. Clearly it was the camera bag they were after. Harry waited until he was right up to the car before rising out of the shadows and showing Ehlers the Colt. 'Good evening, Colonel. Why don't the two of us go for a little drive. Let's say up to that cosy little barn of yours?'

Colonel Ehlers stood quite still. 'What do you want, Dance?'

Harry smiled. 'Ah yes, the masks are off, no more "Mr Dean."' I like that. He waved the pistol in the direction of the front door, indicating the man should follow but only after a brief but expert frisk had produced no weapon. 'But first things first. Let's go and make a phone call, Colonel. You lead the way, if you please.'

Minutes later they were in the office and Harry was making the call, the number memorised when he had got it from the detective. The sleepy voice on the far side was initially muffled and Harry had to ask why Niemand sounded different.

'Damned sleep apnoea mask,' came the spluttered reply, the voice now awake and familiar. 'Always a struggle to get the bloody thing off! What the fuck is it, Dance?! I've had a shit day and this had better be worth it!'

So Harry told him, in as few words as possible and as the cop, grunting between trying to retrieve various items of clothing and occasionally falling in the process, tried to persuade him to do nothing until he arrived with a team, Harry hung up.

He couldn't take that chance. For all he knew an alarm might have been sounded up at that hut, the life of his friend and all those young black faces on the line. He wanted to phone Selena, tried, but the line was down.

With a curse he yanked Ehlers to his feet, the man protesting as he crashed painfully against the desk, Harry having tied his hands behind his back with a length of rope found in the back of the Land Rover. A search of the desk had produced a Beretta automatic which Harry shoved down a jacket pocket. Jerking Ehler's head back, their faces inches apart Harry asked him about the other man. 'Who is he?!'

'A...a Mr Heidmann. A business associate. He...he's from S..South America.'

He didn't ask about the Chinese woman, her role was self explanatory. 'Where's this Heidmann now?'

He had Ehlers by his shirtfront and the spluttering noise from the other man had Harry realise he was strangling him. Easing up he repeated the question, softer but with no less venom. 'He's ... he went to his quarters at the other side of the house. He was t...tired after his l...long trip.'

Most likely a lie, Harry thought, but the clock was running, he'd deal with Mr Heidmann later. Now was the time to move.

As Harry bundled Ehlers into the passenger seat of the Land Rover, seconds later roaring off to follow the rocky track it had come down minutes earlier, the man at the window slowly released the curtain and stood there for a minute, enjoying the last of his Havana. Finally he turned to the man who had been silently watching him for what seemed like minutes. 'You know this Harry Dance, don't you?'

Mike Louw nodded. He said nothing.

'Of course you do. You were the one who told him about us. About Savannah.'

Shrugging Heidmann stubbed out the cigar. Like everything he did he did it patiently, with precision. Only then did he look at Louw. 'It doesn't matter anymore. Your friend died because he was a spy and I can understand that you were worried about his death.' Raised hands indicated that matter had been put to rest. 'Remind me, Louw, why you came to us, to Savannah?'

'Vlakplaas,' came the muted reply.

'Ah, yes. Vlakplaas and then that pesky Truth and Reconciliation Commission that seems to think everyone ever involved with that little police holiday farm were criminals that needed to be removed from society...'

'Including you, General.' Louw said softly.

'Don't call me that!' came the curt command, the sudden steel in the voice bringing the other man instinctively to a position of ramrod attention.

'Yes, Sergeant Louw; we are indeed in the same boat here and Savannah's promise to you still stands. Are you ready?'

Louw nodded. 'Yessir.'

'Good. Now we can't warn those up at the shed because Dance has cut the phone line,' he held up the frayed end of the main line at the switchboard where they were standing. 'Knowing Dance he's going to create all hell up there and it's time for us to leave but first there's the matter of a little bit of insurance.'

'Insurance?'

'Mrs Selena Dance. Hopefully awaiting her man's return and about to receive visitors.'

15
CHAPTER

As they rounded the last bend with the barn slowly rising into view Harry slowed to a crawl as he scanned the surroundings. Lights were on and a truck was parked at the entrance. The gates were closed but unlocked and it was a moment's work to swing them open and drive through. No sign of the lions but he took care to close the gates again.

The only sign of life was a figure leaning against the hood of the truck smoking a cigarette which he extinguished in a shower of sparks to stroll over as the Land Rover screeched to a halt. 'Colonel?'

Harry had his peaked cap pulled down to mask his features in the poor light and was taking care to keep the automatic out of sight. He had stopped twenty yards short of the barn cutting the engine but leaving the headlights on bright and shining straight at the doorway. It was a matter of seconds to cross to the passenger side and drag his prisoner into a standing position. With his hands tied behind his back and a gag stuffed in his mouth there was no protest forthcoming.

'What the...' the guard had moved out of the glare of the lights and recognising the situation was tugging at a gun in his belt and Harry shot him twice, the boom of the heavy calibre startling a crow nesting in a nearby tree which flew away in a flap of wings and loud protests. Four seconds went by, five and then a khaki clad man stepped into the light of the porch and seeing Harry's pointed gun slowly raised his hands.

Struggling in Harry's grip the colonel was trying to say something and Harry kneed him in the back as a reminder of his situation. His ears were still ringing from the shots and Harry's own voice sounded faraway as he shouted at the others inside to come out in single file, hands held high.

Moving quickly, pushing Ehlers ahead he was up against the wall, the man a shield between him and the light spraying through the open door. Harry reckoned there would only be one exit to the place and at least one more gun amongst whoever was inside.

As usual thirty years of experience served him well. The next man came through fast and shooting at whatever moved and Harry shot him in the back even as the man's own fire cut down his fellow still standing in the headlights of the Land Rover.

'I have the colonel as a hostage! The next bullet is for him! Last chance; come out with your hands held high. Now!'

Glancing down Harry confirmed that the Colt had jammed, a bullet stuck sideways in the breech and with a silent prayer he discarded it for the Beretta taken from the colonel's drawer earlier.

'*How do we know you're not going to shoot us all?!*'

The shout came from just inside the doorway and Harry thought it was a fair question and decided it was time the colonel had a say in matters. 'My name is Dance, Harry Dance. You have my word. I...' It was then, as he yanked the rolled up handkerchief from the colonel's mouth, that he heard it the first time.

The children screaming.

It had started as a low whine of fear, quickly building to a loud wail of sheer terror.

And somewhere inside there was Vusi. If he was still alive.

'How many of your men inside there, colonel?'

'Go to hell!' the colonel hissed, his voice hoarse from the effects of the gag, the man struggling to break free from Harry's grip.

Man has five senses. Hear, see, touch, taste, smell. Some men, a very small group of unusual men, have a sixth sense. Fewer still are fortunate enough to recognise the gift early enough to nurture that sense; and to rely on it.

Harry didn't hear the man, neither did he smell or see him. But he *knew* he was there, right behind him. Maybe it was the way the colonel kept pulling to one side, dragging Harry along with him, always facing the door. *There was a second exit and the man was right behind him and closing with the silent stalk of the cat!*

Pushing Ehlers violently face first into the wall, Harry spun to find himself six feet away from a snarling bearded giant who, crouched for the kill, held a gleaming hunting knife in the classic knife fighter's grip. Another second, Harry reckoned, and that sliver of shiny steel would have sent him permanently on his way.

Something the man saw had him hesitate and Harry realised it was the Beretta he had instinctively raised into a firing position. Only an idiot brings a knife to a gunfight and Jan Hugo was no idiot. Harry was about to order him to drop the knife when Colonel Ehlers, struggling to his feet, his face a mess of blood and gore, spoke. 'It's my gun he's holding, Jan. I never leave a bullet in the chamber and he hasn't cocked it! Kill him!!'

Out of the corner of his eye Harry saw the obscene grin on the colonel's face, teeth glinting white amongst streaks of blood, the man straining violently against the cord at his wrists.

With a fierce howl the bearded giant lunged forward and, twisting away in a fluid movement that had him lose his own balance, Harry shot him twice. There was a moment of baffled silence as the big man stared dumbly at the growing red stain on his belly, a second jagged line of blood off to one side. Slowly, lips silently mouthing a protest, he lifted his head to stare uncomprehendingly at Harry before slowly sinking to his knees and toppling over with his face in the dust.

Back on his feet Harry was still looking down at the fallen man as he spoke. 'I'm a professional, Ehlers, I *always* have one in the chamber. You just didn't see me do it.'

'You bastard!!' Ehlers snarled as, enraged beyond reason, he lunged towards Harry charging head down like an enraged buffalo. Stepping back to parry the sudden attack, Harry stumbled over the fallen man, losing his grip on the gun in the process even as the colonel twisted his body to get his tied hands onto the knife.

His progress was brought to a sudden halt as a tall black shadow stepped into the light and with lightning speed draped manacled hands and chain over the colonel's neck jerking back with a snarl of rage. Such was the strength of that grip that the colonel's feet were dangling in the air, kicking and jerking as he desperately struggled for air.

'Vusi! Noooo!!'

On his feet now Harry pleaded with his friend to let the man live, pointing out they needed information only he could provide.

They stood like that for what seemed a long time then, with an audible sigh of frustration, Vusi released his prey which dropped to the ground like a sack of potatoes, purple faced and gasping for breath in jagged hoarse gulps that reminded Harry of another death. Another place; another time.

'We really have to stop meeting like this, people will talk,' Harry said with a smile. A thought made him frown, 'Lukas…?'

Vusi shook his head. 'No, but he was taken as part of an earlier group. With a bit of luck we'll find him soon.'

'Any more of them inside?!' Harry nodded in the direction of the light streaming through the open door.

'Two Chinese, one an old woman. They made for the back door seconds ago…'

At that moment the Land Rover's engine sprang into life, the car kicking up dust as spinning wheels sought and found grip slewing the vehicle sideways before roaring away into the night as the headlights jumped and weaved across the rugged landscape.

'And there they go…' Vusi added somewhat needlessly.

'The kids OK?'

Vusi nodded and Harry stiffened as he saw his friend stride purposefully across to where the bearded Hugo was struggling to a sitting position using the back drop of the wall as support. His gritted teeth glinted in the pale light and when he looked down at his hand clutched to his chest he seemed surprised to see it come away glistening with blood. Then Vusi was squatting next to him and saying something so softly Harry couldn't hear and the bearded man responding with a curse and Vusi crushing his larynx with a stiff fingered blade jab so fast that neither Harry not its victim ever saw anything more than a blur.

It took maybe ten seconds for Jan Hugo to die. Ten seconds of staring his hatred at the strangely calm features of his executioner as lips moved soundlessly over bared teeth, ten seconds of Harry wordlessly watching the unfolding tableau, oblivious to the protesting form of a Colonel Ehlers struggling to free himself from the rope that had chafed his wrists to raw meat.

'Vusi…?'

Harry watched as his friend – a man he thought he knew, until now – slowly straightened up to walk past him and back into the barn. Inside Harry could hear the sudden burst of excitement amongst a chorus of child voices, suddenly growing louder as the first faces began to peer around the open doorway. With a grunt Harry yanked the colonel to his feet, ushering him into the brightly lit room where he pushed him into a chair facing a metal office desk near the entrance.

A quick glance revealed a large steel wired cage occupying most of the central part of the spacious room with dozens of mattresses strewn about the cement floor, basic ablutions at back and a single steel mesh cell door that stood wide open. A lit corridor led off to one side and a room beyond and Harry presumed that was where the back door exited from.

A dozen faces stared back at him. Young faces with big white eyes and teeth to match and a shared look of apprehension as to what new horrors fate could have planned for them. It was Vusi's voice, once again normal and composed, that spoke to them in soft Zulu, explaining that they were safe and this man was their friend. All at once an excited chatter broke out to be quickly silenced by Vusi who asked who knew where the keys to their shackles were. It proved to be in the pocket of the bearded Hugo lying dead outside and while Vusi went to retrieve it Harry turned his attention to Ehlers who was now eyeing him coldly.

'What is the name of the ship lying in Durban Harbour, the one these boys were meant to be on?'

His reward was an expletive, the colonel's voice rolling thick over a swollen tongue and lips. Harry smiled grimly as he pulled up another chair to face the man who glared at him with unmasked hatred, 'Perhaps we can work a deal? You give me the name and you might get to live, I'll hand you over to a policeman who's on his way here right now instead of taking things into my own hands.'

'Fuck you, Dance!'

'Want me to work him over?' It was Vusi, he had discarded his own manacles and was in the process of removing the shackles from the ankles of the others. Harry shook his head, his memory still fresh from what he had witnessed his friend do minutes earlier. 'He won't talk. I've known his type all my life. We'll get the information some other way, the important thing now is to get to Durban Harbour quickly before that Chinese couple and the ship escape.'

'What do we do with him?'

Harry smiled grimly, 'Oh I have just the plan for him. You could almost call it poetic justice. Get the kids into the truck parked outside while I scout around for anything that could provide a clue to our quarry.

While Vusi shepherded the chattering bunch of erstwhile prisoners into the back of the truck Harry ran a quick search of the desk drawers. He dragged Ehlers along as he scanned the back rooms of the building finding little more than a sparsely furnished living quarters for the jail keeper and a small kitchen. On the way out he collected the airgun he had spotted the previous day, together with several of the ketamine loaded cartridges, shoving the latter into a jacket pocket.

Silent now the colonel allowed himself to be manhandled along until they reached the front door, Harry switching off the lights. 'What are you going to do?' he asked suspiciously.

'Oh, you'll find out soon enough,' Harry said as he proceeded to shackle the colonel to the steel front door of the barn which he carefully locked. The man was now attached to the solid door handle by the twenty foot heavy chain that had earlier tethered the prisoners. 'Tell me, colonel, just between us, why *these* kids?'

There was a long pause as Harry, satisfied that Ehlers was securely shackled, collected the Colt and knife where it had fetched up near the dead Hugo before fixing the other man with a stare as cold as an Arctic night. 'Is it because nobody was bound to come looking for them? Is it because their lives are worthless anyway, trapped in poverty and corruption and a government only interested in lining its own filthy pockets?' The last few words almost a whisper as Harry fought to control the growing rage once again welling inside him.

Flinching from the menacing face, suddenly very white and much too close for comfort and gradually becoming aware of what Harry planned for him, Ehlers backed away until the taut chain brought him up sharply. 'W...what are you doing?!'

'Tell me, you soulless bastard or, God help me, I'll kill you right here, right now!!'

'I... You see... you say they're endangered and that's what Heidmann always says, the best way to preserve an endangered species is to farm it. That's how we can save the elephants, the whales, the...'

But Harry had heard enough. Sickened to his stomach he turned away, started walking towards the waiting truck. He could have asked about the general but he knew anyway and it was time to go.

'Dance! Damn you, you can't leave me here!! The lions!!'

As Harry climbed into the passenger side of the truck, Vusi with the engine running, he could make out the reflections of three sets of bright green eyes motionless just yards outside the pool of light from the headlights.

Kibus and the two lionesses. Recovered from the tranquilisers and drawn to the commotion inside their compound. He knew the colonel would have seen it too, would have worked out why Harry had doused the building's lights – lions are wary of fires and lights.

'Harry!! For God's sake, leave me a gun!'

As Vusi meshed the gears, Harry laid a restraining hand on his arm. 'Just give me a minute.' He reached for an object he had spotted wedged behind the driver's seat and climbed down from the cab to stride over to where the colonel, now a jabbering wreck, was crouching next to the wall. Stopping a few yards away Harry flung the object which fetched up at the other man's feet. 'Try this. It seemed to work well enough the other day.'

And as the colonel stared uncomprehendingly at the toilet roll, very white in the moonlight, lying at his feet, Harry climbed back into the truck and seconds later they were at the gates, Harry dismounting once again to carefully secure them before driving off into the night.

And as he listened to the fading sound of the engine, strove vainly to catch a last glimpse of a taillight, Colonel Ehlers could see the ashen grey shape of Kibus as the lion slowly came closer, very green eyes never wavering from his own.

The night quite still now, the only sound the low growl of a big cat as all animal life held its breath, watched and waited, for nature to reassert herself and a rightful king to approach his throne.

The truck was halfway down the rocky track, lurching and protesting as Vusi fought the bucking wheel, when Harry spoke. 'Want to tell me what that was all about. You and that bearded one?' He was staring straight ahead, not looking at his friend whose features were inscrutable in the eerie glow from the dashboard lights.

It was a while before Vusi spoke. 'Vlakplaas. A long time ago.' He spoke softly and Harry had to strain to pick up the words. 'A comrade – a friend – was being held there by the police torturers, by that bastard, De Kock, who is now serving a life sentence in Pretoria. Remember him?'

Harry nodded. All South Africans of a certain generation knew about the head of the Police Counter Insurgency Unit, C10, the man who became known to his victims as Prime Evil, a man thought to have been responsible for the deaths of well over one hundred opponents of the apartheid state at the isolated prison farm ten miles west of Pretoria.

'At that stage three of my unit had already died as a direct result of this man's actions. I was on the run at the time, in hiding in Soweto but when I heard my friend had been caught, was at that place of torture, I simply had to get him out. His name was Headman Bazi – funny how you never forget the names of the ones you failed, isn't it?'

'The names,' Harry said, 'And the faces...'

'I went in alone, at the dead of night, cut the fence and avoided the dog patrols long enough to reach the main bungalow where there were lights and the sound of voices. There were no blinds at the windows which were open, it was a hot February night, and I could see clearly from my hiding spot in the shadows...' Vusi cursed as he braked suddenly to avoid a small herd of buffalo blocking the road, the engine settling to a low gurgle as they waited for the animals to slowly, reluctantly, move off into the surrounding bush. Sitting there in the dark, watching the dust swirl lazily in the headlight beams, Harry found his mind drifting back to those times, so long ago now, when he had been in that same situation. So many faces, most of them dead now...

'... Headman was tied to a chair that was fixed to the floor. His face was a mess of blood and I could see long knife wounds criss-crossing his naked breast. He was barely conscious and moaning softly. That man back there,' he tossed his head in the direction they had come, 'was standing over him, holding the knife. Another man in the room but out of my line of sight. I had a gun and was still thinking what to do when I heard the barking of the dogs coming closer, shouts in the darkness. They had found the gap in the fence and time was up. At that moment Headman saw me and so did the torturer. He shouted for the other cop to hit the light switch and in that brief second Headman reached out to me. Too weak to speak, the words soundlessly trembling over his swollen lips, his eyes said it all...'

'He wanted you to shoot him...' Harry said softly. They were moving again, the track ahead clear.

'I shot him,' Vusi said, 'but it was that man back there who killed him.'

'And you recognised him, after all these years?'

'He didn't have a beard then and I think his face has had work done. No, it was the voice that gave him away. The voice and the sadism – that never changes.'

'You were lucky to get away,' Harry said.

'Very lucky,' his friend agreed, 'A long story; for another day.'

16
CHAPTER

Selena stood quite still. Aware of her heart beating a tattoo, palms suddenly sweaty she forced herself to ease the tightness of her grip on the backpack. All the while striving desperately to peer through the darkness at whatever was lurking, no *moving* not fifty yards away. Now oblivious to the coldness of the night that had her minutes earlier rug up in a felt lined bush jacket, she strained her ears for the slightest sound that could offer a clue to what was down there beside the river.

Three bulky grey shapes. Moving slowly. Coming nearer?

The problem was too many sounds, coming from all around. The lowing of the buffalo somewhere in the distance to the sudden clatter of a startled white breasted crow, its squawks of protest fast fading in the distance. Wild geese splashing by the river.

The routine sounds of night on the African veldt. And good to hear; she recalled Harry saying that in Africa silence was everything but golden. Silence was what you feared. Silence meant a predator close by. There was nothing as comforting as the symphony of nature at peace with herself.

A three sixty survey of the surroundings showed no other signs of nightlife. In the absence of light there were no reflecting sets of eyes, no glinting teeth. Just those three slow moving grey shapes. Go back to the tent like she had promised Harry she would do? Measuring the distance it was clear she was closer now to the punt mooring than the tent. But was the punt there? Harry had promised to send it over to that side of the river but still...

Another thought crossed her mind, brought on a further rush of adrenalin, she could always run for the safety of the river if confronted but what if those grey shapes were hippopotamuses? She knew all too well that the hippo was in terms of humans killed Africa's most dangerous animal. Huge and fast and above all aggressive they were fiercely territorial and diving into a river was going to offer no escape.

Were there even any hippos at Halali? The game rangers had never mentioned that. Which left, *Rhinos!!*

Of course! Francois had mentioned it the day before when they were taken on that safari drive and someone asked. Halali had three rhinos which had not been seen for the past four or five days. The area was huge, much of it covered in dense bush and the plan was to go look for them later that day. The warden had mentioned that sooner or later they would make their way down to the river in search of water.

Rhinos. And didn't they have bad eyesight? She seemed to think they had.

Feeling slightly more comfortable but still wary she decided to press on to the water. Moving slowly, carefully placing every footstep to avoid the snap of dry twigs, she finally reached the punt. Heaving a small sigh of relief to find it there she quickly got on board and minutes later reached the other side.

What now? Where was Harry? Setting down the rucksack she considered her options. Go up to the house? But that could be dangerous if Harry was right and he usually was. They had earlier considered the option of her accompanying Harry but on balance he thought her lack of experience in the kind of bush skills he thought might be needed would prove a handicap. What about my safety here? She had asked. Why are we the only guests left down here and suddenly there's no power and no phone. Isn't that suspicious?

Harry had smiled his old devil may care smile, the one that always melted any resistance she could muster, and told her that being a female she was deadlier than the male and then, on a more serious note, suggested she moved to one of the empty cabins closer to the river and wait there for him. Anyone up to mischief would go looking for her in their designated lodgings and she would have ample warning and could take the necessary action.

What action, she had asked. Hit him with my handbag?

Harry's remark that it always worked for Margaret Thatcher earned him a playful punch to the arm.

Seconds later he had disappeared into the night, Selena watching her man go and wryly thinking of his favourite saying at times like these. "If I go into the Valley of Death I shall fear no evil. For I am the meanest son of a bitch in the Valley of Death."

Oh Harry...

Then, as the minutes ticked away, turned into an hour then beyond she started having second thoughts. Suddenly it didn't seem safe to be here, away from the rest of the people. Surely all couldn't be part of whatever evil was being practised here? After all there were still a few fellow guests over at the main lodge and at least some of the game rangers had to be just that, game rangers?

Jamie was out there too. She would be safer there. Harry would understand.

But now, suddenly, she wasn't so sure anymore. Still hesitant she became aware of a rustling sound and before she knew it was halfway up the ladder to the observation deck. It was a water buffalo, drinking and seemingly oblivious of her presence. Sitting down on the wooden boards to catch her breath she realised that between her and the nearest of the lodge buildings, the quarters of the game rangers, was a vast open field with scores of buck and buffalo roaming. Perhaps not the safest place for a bush novice to venture alone.

The decision was made. She would stay on that platform knowing that Harry would pass that way on his return.

Barely had she settled down, her back to the wooden balustrade, when she saw the lights of the approaching vehicle, seconds later hearing the growl of the engine as it bucked and weaved its way towards the river and the punt crossing. Instinctively hunkering down into the shadows she saw the Land Rover pull up, the lights switched off and two men getting out. For a moment when the doors were open she saw their faces in the courtesy light and neither man was familiar.

With the engine switched off silence returned and perched twenty feet above and within easy earshot she could hear every word of the conversation.

'The punt is supposed to be tied up on this side of the river,' the older man of the two snapped. 'That bloody Dance must have swum across and sent the thing back.'

'I'll haul it back,' the other man, an Afrikaner by the broad accent, offered as he set about rhythmically pulling on the thick rope. The older man went back to the car and rummaged in the back, returning with a coil of rope and a torch which he flashed onto the approaching hulk of the punt.

'Think the woman will be expecting us?' the young man asked, adding, 'Knowing Harry he would have warned her about this possibility.'

The other man grunted, waited for the punt to ground, before clambering aboard, 'Doesn't matter. There's two of us, she won't get away. Now pull us across.'

Selena felt an icy claw tighten around her heart. Was Harry OK? Clearly these men were out to kidnap her but why? Whatever the answer, she had to elude them, then get up to that house and find her man. Rummaging in her bag she found the binoculars they had used the day before for the game viewing and seconds later the three grey shapes jumped into sharp focus. She had been right, it was the rhinos and they were now only thirty yards away from the punt landing site. Huge heads lowered they were peacefully grazing, all three facing her way and quite close to the water.

Perfect.

She wasn't Harry's girl for nothing. Moving quickly she scrambled down the ladder and a quick search of the Land Rover – she wriggled through the open passenger side window to avoid opening the door and activating the roof light – produced what she had been hoping for.

A weapon. More precisely, something she could use to startle the rhinos, force them into a stampede.

It was a flare, nestling in the glove box, a parachute magnesium flare and no doubt there to light up an area during a night search or a hunt. Another bonus: the keys to the vehicle were in the ignition.

Climbing back onto the wooden platform she waited for the two men to alight, the young man moving ahead at a muted instruction for the other who appeared to be in charge. She could see it was to be a sweeping manoeuvre, one going around the back of her and Harry's tent, the older man blocking the exit from the front.

The rhinos were no more than thirty yards away and neither man had spotted them.

Taking careful aim, Selena angled the flare and pulled the ring cord.

She had done this before -- during their adventures as arms dealers Harry had insisted she learn to operate every bit of military kit passing through their hands – but, despite her bracing stance, the kick of the rocketing flare took her breath away. Whoosh! And a microsecond later, a huge unbearably bright white balloon high above and behind the grey forms of the rhinos and lighting up the night sky for what seemed like miles around.

For a second, a moment in eternity, she was staring at a snapshot tableau. Two men, frozen in position, necks craned to the sky. Three African rhinos, lifting their heads from what had been a peaceful evening's grazing. And seeing, dead ahead, two alien animals that could only represent a threat.

Then all hell broke loose.

With a low deep throated bellow the rhinos charged. Furthest away from the relative safety of the river the young man had no chance. A fully grown rhinoceros can reach a speed of 35 miles per hour over a short distance. Maybe an Olympic standard sprinter could have made it but Mike Louw was no athlete. The lead animal caught him in mid-stride, the huge leading horn scooping him up like a sack of potatoes, tossing him eight, ten, feet into the air, the last of the trio trampling him into the dust the moment he hit the ground.

Selena reckoned him dead on impact.

The older man had been luckier. Seeing what was coming he jumped back on board the punt and was hauling as if his life depended on it. Which, of course, it did. He was perhaps fifteen feet away from the river's edge when the rhinos reached the spot and his fear crazed scream penetrated the night like a spear. Against all the odds, it proved to be his lucky night. For at that point the river bank dived steeply under the water and the first rhino took seconds to resurface, its horn like a periscope on a surfacing submarine. In close pursuit the other two managed to halt when still only belly deep in the water.

The night was deathly quiet now, all animal life awake and watching and waiting for whatever had caused this night time drama to go away and let peace reign once more. Selena watched as the rhinos regained the river bank to pause there for a minute, slowly milling about, before resuming their rudely interrupted grazing. The dead man lay a few yards away and seemed of little interest to the animals who simply strolled past the limp form as if it had never been a factor.

Which, Selena decided, left the matter of how to handle the man now halfway back towards her side, hauling on the rope like his life depended on it.

Was he armed? No way of knowing. Did he know she was up in that observation spot? Probably. Didn't really matter, she needed that Land Rover and with that she reached the water's edge and it took her no more than seconds of furious sawing, using the razor sharp hunting knife Harry had insisted she have, to cut through both the ropes attached to the punt.

There's a thing known as a Missouri River Ride and standing on that punt, a fast flowing river beneath and the rope suddenly gone slack, Heidmann knew he was in for that ride. Not that he knew it by that name of course, but Selena did. Her memory stretched back to a trip she and Harry had once done going down that 2,540 mile long American river, Harry remarking how he'd once seen a western where the ropes were cut, the raft being swept away with horses falling off, panicky men jumping into the water. A ride of a lifetime, he had remarked, wishing he could have been there.

Well, she thought wryly, it's every bit as much fun to watch as you suspected, Harry. Gazing through the binoculars she could see the punt spin slowly around and around as it gathered speed, heading for the rapids she knew was downstream. The solitary figure was standing quite still, staring back at her, the face quite expressionless, eyes too small and distant to make out but somehow she knew they were boring into her, seeing and hating.

Shivering she went back up the ladder to collect the rucksack and minutes later she was in the Land Rover and bumping along the rough track heading for the lights that had now gone on in the building housing the game wardens.

'How many more of these children do you think there are?'

Piet Niemand shrugged, 'We didn't get much from Naidoo but the impression was these ones were part of a larger shipment and that they're being smuggled out on a cargo ship; from Durban.' Bleary eyed and unshaven his general appearance was more dishevelled than the usual and, like Harry and the rest of them, he could do with a hot drink and perhaps some breakfast.

They were seated in the dining room of the Halali Lodge and from the direction of the kitchen came the enticing aroma of frying bacon. Seated at several tables were the children, largely quiet as they tucked into a hastily prepared meal of eggs, sausages and copious amounts of buttered bread and jam. Harry had insisted they be fed first and as he ran an appraising eye over the bedraggled looking little group he felt something almost akin to tenderness.

In a long life journey of seemingly endless encounters with the evil men do it had never been about the children. Until now. The unspeakable horror of what had been in store for these truly helpless youths was completely alien to him and he realised that from now on life would be viewed through a different spectrum.

What had he been up to until now? An endless chase after what? Vengeance? Righting old wrongs while increasingly realising that like that elusive rainbow he would never find that pot of gold, the dream always just that one step ahead. What was that old African saying? He who sees the shadow of the rainbow walks a lonely path...

Increasingly that path, that mission, was becoming an odyssey into isolation and loneliness. He did not have to glance at Selena, sitting across from him at the other side of the table and next to Vusi, to know she felt it too.

He wasn't that way any more. None of them were. Changes would have to be made.

He was brought back from his reverie by the big policeman nudging him to pass the butter. 'Did we get the name of the ship?'

Niemand shook his head, 'No. He refused to talk without his lawyer present and before that could happen he was killed.'

'Unusual, don't you think? This business of a prisoner being taken away to the offices of the Minister of Customs and Immigration?'

'It's never happened before,' Niemand agreed between large bites at a jam laden slice of toast, 'but this is the New South Africa, my friend. Anything is possible.'

'So you think the minister is part of this whole business?'

The big man snorted, 'Gee, you reckon?'

It was a sign of the times that neither man sought to explore.

They were interrupted by a young police lieutenant in a pilot's jumpsuit who informed Niemand that the hastily set up roadblock outside Empangeni had not encountered the Chinese couple and neither had the patrols on the peripheral roads.

'Tell them to maintain the operation until further notice. Is the chopper ready to go?'

'Yes sir. How many are we taking?' He nodded in the direction of the gathering, all eyes fixed on Niemand who was in turn eyeing the remainder of the sausages on offer.

'Apart from the sergeant and myself, three adults. That OK?'

The pilot nodded and collected a sandwich from a plate held out by a smiling waiter before returning to his machine.

'It looks like the fugitives have escaped,' Harry said, they should be quite close to Durban by now, no doubt heading for that waiting ship.' A thought made him frown, 'A plane! Of course! They didn't drive up here but flew in a small plane. That's why we haven't stopped them.'

Beckoning over Francois who had been seated at a distant table with the other game rangers, the group being interviewed by a grim faced Sergeant Gericke, Harry asked the apprehensive young man about airstrips in the vicinity. It turned out there were several, many of the local farmers having their own aircraft. And, yes, guests did occasionally fly in on commercial chartered flights, mainly using the airstrip at a nearby flying club.

Which, Harry thought, pretty much answered his question. A nod from Niemand had the sergeant get onto the phone to the nearest police station, the duty constable promising to drive out to check the airstrip, usually unmanned, and detain anyone that might be waiting there for a flight out.

Both men reckoned it would prove a fruitless exercise.

The gloomy silence was broken by Niemand who pushed back his chair and announced it was time to return to Durban, see what could be salvaged. The children would for the moment remain at the lodge and all staff, as well as the few remaining guests, were not to leave the premises. A police team was on its way by road and would take care of the situation. The whole area to be considered a crime scene.

As for the young snake bite victim, he was conscious and stable with the district general practitioner in attendance and confident the patient could be safely managed locally. For now the plan was to get back to Durban as soon as possible and organise a search of the ships in port.

A grim thought Harry kept to himself was the possibility of the captive children being hastily disposed of, murdered, with the weighted bodies dumped overboard under the cover of darkness. In a long journey through life's shadows nothing surprised him any more.

'I think I know how we can perhaps find out the name of the ship.' It was Vusi, the first time he had spoken, until then having being huddled in deep conversation with Tsotsi at the other table. All eyes turned to him.

'It's a long shot, but worth a try. Naidoo was a close associate with a shebeen boss called Mama Tembu. That's where I first saw him. According to my young friend here,' he indicated a smiling Tstotsi, 'they were involved in several criminal enterprises together. She might just have that name for us.'

'Do you know where to find her?' Niemand asked, raising a bushy eyebrow.

'No but he does,' Vusi replied nodding towards the boy.

The duiker stiffened, lifting its head, oversized ears twisting and turning like the nature's antennas they were as they searched for the source of the sound. Finally pinpointing it as coming from the mud encased log lying half submerged on the river bank twenty yards away, the little deer whirled and, amongst the sudden chatter of startled weaver birds, darted into the dense shelter of the reeds close by.

The log stirred, a man's head slowly, painfully, lifting from the mud as bleary eyes scanned the surroundings. Finally, at the third attempt, he managed to drag himself into a sitting position. Heidmann sat like that for a while, vaguely aware of the river bubbling and swirling around him, the distant sound of the rapids, as he methodically checked for any lasting damage, broken bones, the such. Deciding that, apart from a splitting headache and a killer thirst, he was intact, Heidmann pondered his next step.

He was above all a businessman. Anger, revenge, all that was for lesser men; he lived in the here and now. So Dance had won, after all. There was little doubt their lucrative little venture with the Chinese had come to a close but that still left Phoenix Outcome Solutions with big money to be made out there.

Glancing up at the sun – his fine gold Cartier hadn't survived the trip over the rapids -- he judged it to be after eight and no doubt a police search party would be coming that way soon once the woman had told her story.

The woman! With a smile he shook his head. She sure was something else. Wasn't it typical of Dance to always pick the winning hand?

With a grunt he climbed to his feet and set of downstream to where he knew there was a ford with a road leading to a farmhouse a few miles away. From there he could place a call for someone to retrieve him. It was a pity he had sent the charter flight back to Durban but then he had been expecting to spend a few days at Halali, didn't he? Enjoy some of its facilities for a change. On balance the safest option would be to persuade the farmer to drive him to one of the more remote airstrips arranging for the pilot to pick him up there. He would offer the man money, of course, spin him some story about a boating accident on the river, whatever. Comforting in an outside pocket of his mud caked jacket was the weight of his .38 Special. He was banking on the farmer being a man of reason, hopefully there would be no unpleasantness.

With the temperature climbing and the mosquitoes buzzing around his ears he slung the jacket over his shoulder and focused on wearily exchanging one mud sucking footstep for the next. It was going to be a long day.

17
CHAPTER

Mama Tembu was at her desk, going over the previous night's takings, when there was a knock at the door. 'Come,' she said, absently, wondering where she had left the keys to the office safe.

It was Lovelace, the Nigerian's frame filling the doorway. As always he was smartly dressed in a pair of slim fit jeans, a neatly pressed light yellow Lacrosse tee shirt and the latest model Nike trainers. Mama Tembu smiled appreciatively, she liked her men well groomed even if she did treat them like dirt.

'What is it? If you want time off to go to the gym, go now. Before it gets busy.'

'It's not that. There's people out here who want to see you. One is that tall Zulu who came looking for his son. The other man looks like a cop.'

Without saying a word Mama Tembu motioned him to come in, close the door. He watched her cross the room to pause in front of a small monitor screen, adjusting the controls until the roving camera eye brought the two newcomers into sharp focus.

'Did they say what they want?'

'Uh uh. Just that it's a business matter.' Anticipating her question he added, 'No search warrant.'

Mama Tembu grunted, 'That means nothing. I recognise the fat one as a police captain from the vice squad.' A frown furrowed her brow as she hurriedly scooped up the ledgers on the desk, locking them in the safe. What was this about? The fact that the black man was there suggested it had something to do with Naidoo. And that was not good. Her eye fell on the papers she had removed from the Indian's premises the day before, papers she had not had the time to properly go over as yet. Could this be what they were after? Moving quickly she shoved them into a shopping bag.

'I'm heading out the back. Tell them I must have gone out earlier but that you expect me back here this evening. If they insist on searching the place, call my lawyer at this number.' She handed him a card from a desk calendar then turned on her heels to head for the door at the other end of the room. It led to a small washroom but, more importantly, a hidden exit from behind a closet gave access to a short alleyway guarded by a sturdy iron gate secured by a chain and padlock.

Weaving her way between stacked crates of empty beer bottles and dustbins overflowing with foul smelling trash, she reached the gate, a cautious scan through the bars showing the side street to be devoid of traffic. During business hours the gate was left unlocked and seconds later she was standing on the pavement, dialling on her mobile phone.

'Looks like you were right,' Vusi said to a smiling Tsotsi who held out an open palm, fingers motioning where cash was due.

Vusi sighed, 'Put it on my tab.' Then he stepped out from the dark recess of an adjacent alley and strolled over to where the woman had not yet spotted him. She was talking rapidly into the phone and Vusi guessed it was a taxi service.

'Hello, Mama,' he said conversationally. 'Remember me? The missing kids? I feel you might be able to help me after all.'

Only to find himself staring down the barrel of a small automatic that had appeared in her hand seemingly from nowhere. Slowly raising his hands, the boy doing the same, he wondered whether he'd mentioned friends of his, policemen, were just around the corner, said as much.

'Shut up or I'll shoot the boy first.' Eyeing the deep shadows the pair had emerged from and deciding there was a risk of passers by spotting them at any moment, she motioned her captives towards the alleyway, following closely behind. Five minutes, she reckoned, the taxi would be there in less than five minutes and, it being one of her brother's operation, there would be a guard riding shotgun.

She was four feet from the alley, pausing for a second to allow her eyes to adjust to the gloom when she became aware of another person, a spectre stepping out of the darkness.

The Taser S26 delivers 50,000 volts to its target, instantly rendering that person a helpless convulsing bundle of violently contracting muscles and nerves. In that split second before discharge Mama Tembu saw Selena step forward, the weapon held at arm's length. At that close quarters she had removed the projectile cap with its darts, simply pressing the two naked electrodes to the other woman's exposed neck.

For perhaps five seconds they stood there waiting for Mama Tembu to stop jerking, the first sign of slow recovery a string of expletives.

'I think those things are illegal in South Africa,' Vusi said off-handedly as he cuffed a chortling Tsotsi over the back of the head, admonishing him to respect his elders.

'That's what Harry said, that's why no-one sees it coming. Help me get her up, I'll get Sergeant Gericke to bring the car over.'

'Tsotsi, run around to the front and tell the captain that we've caught her.'

Still grinning broadly the boy raced off and seconds later was standing in front of Niemand who was growing increasingly frustrated with a chocolate bar vending machine refusing to co-operate. Bracing himself for a strategically placed kick to the machine's nether regions the big man turned to listen to the breathless messenger blurting out the news.

Standing a few paces away Harry saw the Nigerian stiffen then rush forward with a snarl only to be tripped by Niemand and crashing into a table sending chairs flying. As the boy backed away in alarm Harry grabbed hold of the back of a chair, ready to use it as a weapon against the now clearly furious bodyguard,

'See this?' Piet Niemand said, holding up the five rand coin he had been trying to pay the machine with. Scrambling to his feet, a hand slowly stretching towards a nearby broken off chair leg, the Nigerian hesitated. Stunned all watched as the cop placed the edge of the coin between his molars before, with almost no effort, bending it to a ninety degree angle between thumb and forefinger. It was as an astonishing show of strength as Harry had ever witnessed.

'If you can do that,' NIemand said pleasantly to the now hesitant Nigerian, 'You and I can step outside, have a little chat. If not you'd just be wasting my time.'

Common sense prevailed. Still scowling the bodyguard tossed away the stool leg and did as he was told, went and sat at a table and kept his hands where Niemand could see them.

A shout from the doorway had them turn to see Selena standing there, holding up a Pick and Pay shopping bag and telling them she thought that might be what they were looking for. As for the woman, the sergeant was putting her into the back of the car as they were speaking.

'Time for a little chat in my office,' Niemand said, 'But first things first. This machine took my money.'

He turned his attention back to the vending machine followed by a flurry of backhand punches delivered so fast the human eye couldn't follow. There was a sudden groan from the machine, a deep whirr from somewhere inside its workings, followed by a shower of Snicker Bars onto the floor. They watched as Niemand bent to retrieve the prize, all except Tsotsi politely refusing a share of the booty. In the big man's defence, Harry thought the machine looked pretty dodgy to start off, various dents and scratches suggesting a survivor of many an encounter with a dissatisfied customer.

Minutes later they drove off in NIemand's Camry, a handcuffed Mama Tembu in the back next to Selena, the rest of the team following in a second vehicle. Harry studied Niemand who was driving. 'That coin thing back there , it *was* a party trick, right?'

Niemand grunted as he leaned on the horn, clearing a way through the midday traffic, 'I don't do party tricks.'

Which made Harry look at the big man in a new light.

Shrugging he turned his attention to the sheaf of papers they had retrieved from the shopping bag.

'Do you have any idea how many ships sail from Durban Harbour every day?'

Harry shook his head glumly, 'The busiest harbour in Africa. I reckon more than we could search...'

'Not that we'd ever get the necessary search warrants.'

The big cop scratched his head, flicked over the scattered pile of papers on his overcrowded desk before pushing them away with a sigh and leaning back in a battered swivel chair that protested under the burden. 'And nothing here to give us a clue.'

'Well,' Harry corrected him, 'We *do* know it's a ship that's being used to transport the captives; that much is clear from Naidoo's papers.'

They were sitting in Niemand's office at the Point Road police station, the little room crowded to capacity with a scowling Mama Tembu seated in a corner under the watchful eye of the sergeant. Selena and Vusi had gone on to the harbour to see what they could discover.

The mood in the room had distinctly soured after twenty minutes of close scrutiny had failed to produce any tangible clue as to their quarry.

All attempts at getting their captive to talk had proven fruitless and Harry was beginning to think she did not know anything beyond what they had gleaned from the documents. For the umpteenth time she repeated her demand to see a lawyer, her face taut with suppressed rage. Twice she had tried to rise from the chair only to be restrained by an admonishing finger from Sergeant Gericke and a glimpse of the Taser in his other hand. The one Selena had reluctantly agreed to relinquish after a curt command from Niemand accompanied by a resigned shrug from Harry.

A look in his eyes saying I can get you another one any time, sweetie.

True they had gotten some information from the lady, carefully lifted from the steady stream of expletives and threats, and it would seem she was little more than an opportunist who had stumbled onto a nice little racket and wanted in. Of more concern was her family connections, something she saw fit to mention more than once.

More specifically, the Minister of Customs and Immigration.

'Any news of the Chinese pair?' Harry asked.

'We found the truck abandoned at a rural airfield. There's little doubt they flew into Durban and by now would be on board that ship and preparing to sail.' Seeing Harry's quizzical look, Niemand added, 'No point in trying to determine who went into the harbour area, there's very little control regarding that. Customs are more interested in what comes into the country. Besides, plenty of Chinese about the city.'

'What do we do with her?'

'Yeah,' snarled Mama Tembu, 'Either book me or release me!'

Niemand looked at her with eyes that had seen all there was to see and was tired of it all. 'Oh geez, oh geez' he said, 'Are those my choices?' He scratched his head while patting his pockets for presumably something to chew on. 'I choose to *book* you.'

'On what?' Harry asked. 'Jaywalking? Possession of an unregistered firearm? You'd have to arrest half the country.'

'Serving liquor to underage kids.'

Harry shook his head in bemusement, glanced at his watch. 'We're wasting time. What about that call you made earlier to the Harbour Police? Any word?'

'It turns out they're on a go slow strike. Something about danger pay. Most of them would be taking kickbacks anyway, don't expect much help there.' He reached for his hat, instructed the sergeant to escort Tembu to the front desk, book her, then meet them at the car parked at back.

'You're kidding!' Gericke pleaded; 'On what charge?'

Piet Niemand sighed, placed a paternalistic hand the size of a shovel on the sergeant's shoulder and said in a voice worn thin of patience: 'It doesn't matter, sergeant. Spitting on sidewalks will do. All I want is for you to take her out of circulation for a while, keep her away from phoning people.'

'You think she knows more than she's letting on?'

'Hold that thought,' Niemand said, 'And one day you might make lieutenant.'

It was time to head for where the ships were waiting. Nothing else seemed to make sense.

In the event Mama Tembu never needed to make that call. The desk sergeant, a grey "ringhead" Zulu approaching retirement, instantly recognised her, knew only too well the family connections.

Knew where his bread was buttered.

Waiting for Gericke to depart, the prisoner having been taken down to the holding cells by a hefty policewoman whose disapproving glare suggested she still believed in the justice system, he took a tea break and, when alone, dialled the number he had stored in his mobile for just such an occasion.

The big break.

Five minutes later, after negotiating a series of minions of rising rank, he was put through to the Minister of Custom and Immigration's private secretary. Mention of a family member in serious trouble with the police, an increasingly sensitive matter of late when a series of embarrassing incidents had led to charges of nepotism and rampant corruption in the press, secured him access to the man himself.

Sitting in his swivel desk chair, a half eaten upsized Big Mac Meal temporarily forgotten, Mr Tammany listened in silence, only interrupting once to ask for a description of the two men that had been with the captain. Finally ascertained of the facts he thanked the desk sergeant and asked the man to leave his details with the secretary. His service to the state would not be forgotten.

Then he asked to be put through to the Durban Homicide headquarters and minutes later he was speaking to a Colonel Robbs who confirmed he was, indeed, the boss of "that renegade Captain Niemand who was causing major embarrassment to our vital Chinese business partners, the whole thing threatening to become an international diplomatic incident."

John Robbs came from an old sugar cane farming family that could trace their roots in Natal back to the time of the nineteenth century Zulu wars. One of the last remaining whites in high office he was only too aware of his dinosaur status. And of the reason he hadn't been retired yet, being that he was seen to be "reasonable" and "understanding" of the realities of the New South Africa.

That, and the fact that his younger brother, the black sheep of the family, was deeply involved in the shadier dealings of the New South Africa and threatening to break their old mother's heart when her darling little Richie's luck finally runs out and big brother is no longer there to tidy up the mess.

A caretaker, he thought bitterly, that's what I've become. And once again I'm being asked to take care of business.

After leaving no less than five messages on the errant captain's phone to urgently contact him, Colonel Robbs decided that once again the fat man was up to his old tricks of ignoring authority, knowing all too well he was about to be reined in. With a sigh he asked for his car to be brought round.

Lunch hour traffic and wearily negotiating the interminable potholes and half hearted road works meant the inevitable holdups but with generous use of the car's police siren as well as a motorcycle traffic cop clearing the way, he entered the harbour gates forty minutes later.

Stationed at the gates, a sentry for exactly this event, Sergeant Gericke was speaking to his captain seconds later. 'It's as you said, Captain. The big boss has just rolled up, no prize for guessing who he's looking for.'

Suppressing a curse Niemand asked whether Gericke had been spotted. 'I don't think so. He's chatting to the guards at the moment. Looks like they're pointing him in the direction of the harbourmaster's office.'

'OK,' Niemand said, 'Now listen, go up to him and identify yourself. Tell him I'm somewhere over at the Safmarine container yard, the one at the far side away from the offices. Tell him I posted you at the gate to block any escape attempt from the gang I'm after.'

'What gang?'

'Bonnie and Clyde; whoever. For fuck's sake make something up! Just buy me ten minutes!'

The sergeant's protest was cut short as Niemand pocketed the phone, turning his attention back to the harbourmaster who had just been handed a phone by a red faced flustered looking female employee who glared at the intruders with unmasked indignation. Any attempt at drawing the man into conversation again was stalled by a halting gesture and a vigorous shake of the head as he listened to the voice on the other side. Finally mumbling an affirmative he handed the phone back to the woman, turning back to Niemand and the others.

'That was a Colonel Robbs, your boss, I believe. He says he knows you're here and under no circumstances are you allowed to board any vessel or prevent any vessel about to depart, from leaving. You are to await further instructions. He's on his way.'

'Gerickeee!!!' Niemand cursed, 'Can't the damn man carry out the simplest bloody mission?!'

Glancing wildly about he motioned the others to head for the door, hesitating to ask what the harbourmaster held in his hand, was paging through.

'The list of ships due to sail on the evening tide,' the other man's expression one of sweet innocence. And if there was a protest forming on his tongue it died a natural death as Niemand snatched the list before following the others clattering down the metal staircase and heading for the shelter, and hiding places, of a busy dockyard.

Temporarily out of sight of the harbourmaster's office Vusi, Selena and Harry gathered around Piet Niemand who was studying the sheaf of papers he had just snatched from the official's hands. It was a list of departing vessels scheduled for later that day, about twenty in all. Listed next to the vessel's name and port of registration was the next port of call followed by details regarding cargo, passengers if any and if a pilot was needed. Something that applied only to the larger ships.

Twenty ships. Amongst them one carrying several dozen young black faces, brutalized and frightened and headed for the slaughterhouse of a far flung country.

Twenty names, different listed cargoes and types of vessels, from bulk carriers to container ships to coastal traders. Half a dozen countries of registration, almost all known tax havens.

An impossible task in the time left to them which could be minutes only. An unvoiced but shared thought that the ship could have sailed that morning, the Chinese couple planning a rendezvous later. It didn't bear thinking; the ship *had* to be here still, the boys still in South African waters and nominally at least able to be rescued.

Collective eyes scanned the rest of the page, the final listing the next destination. It was Selena who spotted it. 'Look!' she shouted, pointing at a name three up from the bottom, her voice rising with excitement. 'The Mako Venturer. Registered in Monrovia, a thirteen thousand tonne bulk carrier, no cargo listed. Point of call Dar es Salaam to pick up a load of bananas. But look at this bit here...' They watched as a finely manicured nail stripped away the remainder of an almost unobtrusive stick-on tag, the obliterated word underneath there for all to see. 'Shanghai!!' she shouted triumphantly, wildly glancing around to see if all shared her revelation. 'They changed the destination at the last minute to throw us off the scent!'

'Departure time 15h00,' Vusi said, 'Which is now. She's about to sail!'

There was a moment's silence as the realisation sank in that this was their only chance. To be wrong would be to lose.

'It *must* be the one,' Harry said, his voice betraying his inner desperation. 'We have to get on board!'

'But how?!' Selena asked as she glanced urgently about, searching for something, anything, that could offer a solution. She was about to suggest taking a leaf out of the Somali ship hijackers' book, intercepting the ship offshore with a fast motorboat and boarding using a long hook fitted ladder, when Niemand spoke.

'The pilot vessel,' he offered, nodding in the direction of the Harbour Captain's office where several small cabin cruisers were berthed, all bearing the markings: Pilot. One was being readied for departure, a uniformed official stepping aboard while a figure in the wheelhouse had the engine going, another moving forward to cast off. 'It will be heading over to escort them out of the estuary, compulsory in a busy harbour like this.'

But Harry was already racing for the boat, a cursing Vusi in hot pursuit.

'Aren't you going to follow?' Selena asked raising an eyebrow. Harry had motioned for her and Tsotsi to stay behind.

'No need,' the big man said, 'I have this.' With that he produced his mobile and seconds later was speaking to the harbourmaster. 'NIemand. Yeah, me again. Two of my men are at present on board your pilot boat. I want them taken to the Mako Venturer and on board. What?' There was a crackle over the line, the connection dodgy between the stacked metal containers and Niemand had to turn one eighty degrees before contact was restored. 'No pilot, you say?'

'...slow traffic day, not needed.' They were on speakerphone now, the other man's voice crisp and edgy. 'That pilot boat your two assholes have just hijacked is heading out to check on a tanker with engine trouble two miles offshore.'

'Well, I want you to change that. Get the Mako Venturer on the radio and tell them there's a problem at the estuary heads, that you're sending a pilot out.'

'Fuck you, Niemand. I'm tired of our bullsh...'

'Listen here, you two cent little piece of shit! This is a matter of national importance. Unless I get those men on board right now I'm going to come over there and kick your skinny little arse all the way to Cape Town and back. You get me?!!'

A barrage of expletives were cut off as Niemand pocketed the phone, turned his scowl back to where the pilot boat was now on its way, both

Harry and Vusi out of sight in the cabin. 'Dumb bastard!' he growled before stuffing half the contents of a Tic Tacs mints packet down his throat while simultaneously trying to set light to a crumpled cigarette that had appeared from seemingly nowhere.

'Aren't you courting disaster here?' Selena ventured, 'Talking to the harbourmaster like that?'

'You mean old Smokie back there? Naah...,' he laughed, almost choking on a mint in the process, 'We go back a long way. Poker on Friday nights. Poor bastard's wife left him for the postman. Wasn't even their postman, just one she met in the checkout queue at Pick and Pay.' He chuckled at the thought, shook his head at the mystery of it all. 'Don't be fooled by the language; we're good.' Seeing her expression of incredulity he smiled, 'You didn't think our friend just happened to have that list of departing ships in his hand, now did you?'

Which made Selena, once again, puzzle over the weird world of men without women

18
CHAPTER

On the pilot boat Nina Harry shivered and pulled tight the lightweight jacket he was wearing. Out on the open water there was a cool breeze off the ocean and as the boat picked up speed and encountered the first of the choppy estuary waters, the wind chill factor added to his discomfort. Sitting on a passenger bench further aft Vusi looked as impervious to the chill as always. The helmsman, a broadly grinning black by the name of Fourteen – Harry didn't ask – spun the wheel to bring them into the lee side of the ship which had slowed down as instructed and was now barely making way, her bulk serving to calm the water the pilot vessel was now motoring across.

'Good day for fishing, cap'n' came the cheery observation as the helmsman ducked his head to scan the looming deck rail of the ship that was now dead ahead.

Harry got the impression he called everyone "cap'n" and didn't debate the issue. He pointed to where a side loading door had been opened on the side of the Mako Venturer, a lone sailor balanced in its darkened portal and waving them on. 'Hold us steady for a few seconds after the pilot goes on board, give Vusi and I a chance to sneak aboard, before standing off.' Harry knew the practice would be to come briefly alongside, let the pilot jump across, then move fifty or more feet away to avoid collision.

'Will do, cap'n.' They were slowing now, a deckhand in the bows ready with a boat hook. Next to Harry the pilot, a weather beaten craggy eyed man of indeterminate age, adjusted his white rimmed cap. 'I hope you know what you're doing,' he mumbled without seeming to move his lips. 'Don't think we're coming back for you.'

'Wouldn't dream of asking,' Harry said as the man slid open the cabin door to step outside and move to the front. Seconds later, timing the ride of the swells with ease, they watched him jump the narrow gap between the two vessels, grabbing the arm of the waiting sailor, the two of them disappearing inside the darkness.

'No-one on the deck,' Vusi shouted from where he was peering up at the guardrail, 'Let's go!'

Moving unsteadily over the slippery prow of the Nina, Fourteen fighting the wheel to keep her steady, Harry waited until they were in a trough, the boat seemingly motionless for a second, then jumped for the open hatchway. A serrated rubber mat inside the doorway steadied his landing, the small space beyond wet from sea spray and slippery with moss. Vusi was less lucky, mistiming his lunge, the Nina moving away at the very moment he jumped, he slammed into the side of the bigger vessel, managing to grab onto the lowermost edge of the hatch where he clung, desperately striving for a grip on the slimy surface.

With the pilot boat standing off the Mako Venturer swung her bows facing the open sea once more, the swells instantly picking up. For Harry to move to the edge to try and help Vusi would risk both ending up in the water. A quick search produced a coil of rope he quickly tied around his waist in a bowline, setting the length just long enough for him to reach the other man while preventing him losing his footing. Vusi was shouting now, a desperate call for help, hanging by one hand now as the other flailed numbed fingers failing to find traction.

Then Harry was bending down and reaching for him.

Seconds later they were lying side by side on the stinking rubber mat, Harry's breath coming in rasps, the younger man rubbing a shin that was badly grazed from the desperate clamber aboard.

'You OK?'

Vusi nodded, then indicated they should find a hiding spot before the pilot and the sailor, returned. 'A minor problem,' Vusi said which had Harry pause. He hated minor problems.

'What?'

'I seem to have lost my gun, must have dropped into the sea just then.'

Harry sighed, took comfort at the press of his own Beretta against the hollow of his back. 'At least you've still got your sense of humour. Try holding on to that.'

At just over thirteen thousand tonnes the Mako Adventurer started life in the early sixties as a coastal trader working the East African coast all the way to Aden and as far north as Jeddah on the Red Sea. Carrying a mix of dry goods and assorted electrical appliances as well as furniture and household white ware items, the odd motor vehicle, in the period before container ships took over. Twenty five years later she was sold to a grain trader and converted to a bulk carrier transporting wheat from South Africa to Indian Ocean destinations. Contrary to shipping regulations her Arab owners sealed off access between the two main holds, stripping them of all trappings to carry a greater load.

This meant the loss of many air vents as well as interconnecting passages to other areas of the ship.

It made her the ideal prison ship where one was not burdened by the close eye of officialdom such as customs as well as law enforcement. At least not if one plied one's trade between understanding like minded souls in, say Southern Africa and Shanghai.

When the market for illegal organ trade opened up she was exactly what the Triad was looking for. Bought for a song, the ageing vessel was given a complete refit, new engines and a few innovations such as toilets and shower facilities installed in the rearmost hold which also had thirty bunk beds and a small sickbay off to one side. A bulkhead door had been re-established between number one and two holds and this was a sturdy steel affair and kept locked at all times. There were no portholes and for good measure the whole of the hold had been soundproofed. When in harbour the ventilator shafts were shut to prevent noise from the hold penetrating to the outside, a large air conditioner providing relief for the prisoners trapped inside.

A large and modern kitchen manned by a cook and assistant provided meals for the prisoners as well as the crew of ten which included three guards.

Moving stealthily, Harry leading the way, they found themselves minutes later in a passageway leading to cabins on each side, six in total and all silent behind those closed doors. Their way lit by dim overhead lighting they reached a T section, a short passage leading to a steep stairwell with daylight coming through an open hatchway, at a guess the way the pilot and escort had gone on their way to the bridge. The second option was a short corridor ending at a sturdy steel door, shut by two heavy folding bars and, unusual for a ship's crew quarters, a large keyhole.

Of more immediate interest was the man seated on a chair guarding the door and absently leafing through a girlie magazine, a cigarette dangling from his lips. A short and stocky Chinese he wore faded dungarees and a badly crumpled T shirt with a New York logo on the front. Well worn boat shoes made for a good grip while the dragon's head tattoo on an arm spelt trouble.

Big trouble, especially seeing that arm now reached for the AK 47 balanced against a bulkhead.

It took Harry all of a microsecond to take all that in and then he was showing the man the Beretta accompanied by a disapproving shake of the head at the other's disappointing intentions. It took another second to realise this was Triad, the penalty for failure death, as a hand grasped the assault rifle, the short ugly snout rearing its head. But Harry had crossed the divide in a running tackle that came so fast that in that cramped space the Chinese could not get out of the way, his head crashing against the steel wall with sickening force. Two sharp elbow jabs to the slumping man's temple had him slowly sink into a heap in the corner, a trickle of blood seeping from the side of his mouth.

It took Vusi just seconds to locate the keys to the door from the man's trouser pocket and then they were inside, Harry dragging the unconscious man through the door which he pulled closed behind them.

They found themselves in a large hold devoid of any viewing portals to the outside and no sign of another exit, the whole lit by several steel mesh encased wall mounted lights. A series of bunk beds against a far wall next to two toilet stalls and a shower, none with doors.

Scattered blankets on the floor and the fetid smell of too many bodies cramped together in a space where fresh air came at a premium and only at intervals.

Thirty shiny black faces staring back at them, large white eyes apprehensive at what new horror life was about to visit upon them. Thirty kids, the oldest maybe eighteen, the youngest probably only thirteen.

Dressed in a variety of filthy rags, most likely the clothing they had on the day they were taken. At least two in what looked like school uniform.

'Sweet Jesus Christ!' Vusi said softly.

Too numbed to speak Harry could only nod.

They had found the Holy Grail of Africa. The riches other nations would kill for. Her children.

The moment's stunned silence was broken by a sudden stirring in the rearmost ranks of the boys, a slow murmur building as the group opened its ranks to let through one of their number, the young man – he was older than the rest – pausing as he stepped into the open, eyes fixed on Vusi who had suddenly gone quite still.

'*Tata?* ...Dad?'

'Lukas...'

There is something deeply emotional about a father embracing a long lost son and Harry looked away so he wouldn't have to see the tears running down the cheeks of his old friend.

By now there was a building hubbub of excited chatter amongst the kids and Harry had to raise his voice in order to quieten them down. He had guessed the room would be soundproofed but there was always the risk of a microphone linked to the bridge. Leaving Vusi and son to their own muted chatter Harry led the others to the far side of the room and quickly ascertained that since being brought to the ship they had never left that prison cell. All meals –twice a day – being wheeled in by a cook who would dole the slop, mainly stews and bread out in metal food trays under the watchful eye of two guards. Enigmatically it would always be followed by chewy sweet vitamin tablets they had to swallow under the watchful eye of the cook. The only way out of the room was if anyone got sick, one boy fell ill with severe stomach pain a week earlier and was taken away, never to return.

A grim Harry could only guess at the likely fate of that unfortunate individual.

A sickly specimen was of no value to the trade.

How often did the guards check on them? Only at feeding times, it appeared.

How many guards, did they know? An agitated discussion amongst the huddled batch came up with the consensus of three, armed with machine guns. All Chinese and none ever said a word, just glared at them in a menacing way.

Harry pointed to a door he had now spotted in a corner, until then hidden from view by the stacked bunk beds. 'Where does that go?'

'It is kept locked,' one of the older boys ventured, 'Only once did it open when someone came in to fix the air conditioner. We could hear the sounds of a big engine from somewhere deep inside then.'

Engine room, Harry guessed. He looked them over; dirty and bedraggled but fit enough at a glance, no obvious signs of physical abuse but then there wouldn't be, would there? Not with prize human cattle on the way to the marketplace.

Shaking off the negative thoughts he turned his attention to the immediate. How long did they have before someone came looking, how long before the unconscious guard was due to be relieved?

He asked, no-one seemed to know. Motioning the kids to stay he moved to the door they had come through and gun in hand, opened it to confirm that the passageway was still empty. A slight stirring behind him confirmed that Vusi had now joined him, an animated Lukas hovering in the background.

'How long have the kids been held prisoner down here?' Harry asked.

'Lukas has been here almost three weeks, others came more recently,' Vusi replied. There was the hint of a tremor in his voice and Harry had it down for pent up rage. It was something he would have to watch; emotion was a handicap when it came to the kind of split second life or death decisions that was the pointy end of their game.

'Hmm...' Harry had settled with his back to a bulkhead, a frown creasing his forehead. Years of experience told Vusi the man was not pondering the health status of their charges, nutrition, that kind of thing. Or was he? Casting an eye over the sea of faces staring up at them with a mix of fear and hope, he had to admit that on the whole they looked in reasonable shape. His son had confirmed that there had been no instances of abuse and the food, although basic and often tasteless, had been adequate and regular.

Which, he reflected, made sense. These boys were valuable commodities. Pound for pound more valuable than gold. But only if in premium shape, no diseased kidneys wanted.

Disease! It struck him like a sledgehammer and as he glanced up it was to see his friend grinning back at him. 'I suspect,' Harry said softly, 'That you've come to the same conclusion as me?'

'They cannot afford any damage to the shipment.' Vusi said flatly.

Harry nodded. 'Would you say the sailors we've seen have been mainly Chinese?'

It was Vusi's turn to nod.

'And they're a superstitious bunch, wouldn't you say. Especially sailors?'

'Well known,' Vusi agreed.

'Do you remember the strange case of the Marie Celeste?'

Vusi shook his head.

'A merchant ship, not unlike this one, found adrift in the middle of the Atlantic with all lights on, the dinner table set, no sign of anything wrong and yet not a soul on board. The crew had taken to the ship's lifeboat in a panic, and none were ever seen again. Theories range from abduction by aliens to ghosts to you name it. And then, of course, the fear of the kind of disease that would spread through a ship like wildfire. A disease for which, at the time, there was no cure...'

'Cholera?' Vusi ventured.

'Yellow fever,' Harry replied. 'The scourge of ships and ports and the sailor's worst nightmare.'

There was a long pause as they mulled it over. 'It's a long shot,' Harry said at length, 'And it will take some co-operation from the prisoners.'

'What are the signs of this Yellow Fever?'

Harry shrugged, his mind going back to an earlier life as a mercenary in the Congo when there had been an outbreak, 'As far as I recall, there's a short incubation period followed by headaches, cramps and the vomiting of blood. Also jaundice, hence the name. The death rate, often within days, is particularly high amongst non-Africans and thousands of sailors died during outbreaks in the past.'

A thought had him pause before adding, 'And then, of course, there's also Ebola... Kills even faster, sufferers simply bleed from every orifice. Very few survive.'

'Ebola,' Vusi said softly. 'Why not? This is after all Africa.' For the first time a smile hovered on his lips as he conjured up the scene. 'Will these Chinese sailors fall for it?'

'They just might.'

Which left them with the challenge of setting the scene and for that a few basic materials would be needed. There would be nothing of use in that prison of a hold but then he had the guard's keys now, didn't he? With a bit of luck...

Seconds later he had unlocked the door and located a storage locker at the end of a walkway which seemed to grant access to both galley and engine room somewhere below his feet. A quick search produced a large tin of dark red antifouling mix, a bag of bright yellow turmeric from the galley stores would have to suffice for the rest of the visual effects. While Harry was hunting down the props Vusi huddled with the wide eyed and now excited youngsters to explain the scenario and illustrate the required role play.

How long before someone came looking for the guard they had overpowered? By Harry's watch it had been almost twenty minutes since they had dragged the unconscious man into the holding cell. Time would be running out, sooner or later someone would come down to the hold and finding him missing, raise the alarm. Better, Harry decided, to make the man part of the plan, dress him up as another victim of the feared disease.

While Vusi, with the enthusiastic help from a few of the older boys, was applying the make-up and distributing the "bodies" in the required positions, Harry retrieved the Chinese, dragging him to the door leading to the passageway and placing him half through the open doorway. A quick application of the red antifouling around the mouth and lips, a puddle on the floor, created the effect of having vomited blood and a few strategic dabs of turmeric provided for the jaundice. Harry decided that the man's moaning and stirring – he was coming around – added to the desired effect but it wouldn't do for him to wake up completely. With this in mind another hopefully well judged karate chop to the neck was delivered which, by Harry's calculation, should buy them another ten minutes or so.

Realistically the man's AK 47 would have to be left next to him – a pity but necessary to avoid raising the wrong alarm – and Harry emptied the magazine into a coat pocket before replacing the rifle near the unconscious man's body.

A glance into the hold was met by the thumbs up sign from Vusi indicating the scene was set, the boys in position and ready for the performance of their lives. And a convincing sight it was too. Strewn about in haphazard fashion was an array of prostate bodies, some apparently unconscious with others curled up and softly moaning as they clutched their stomachs.

All showed signs of vomiting blood and even in the pale light Harry could make out the carefully rehearsed grimaces of agony on the young faces.

They were ready.

At his signal Vusi joined him in the corridor, slipping into a nearby cabin where he would be joined by Harry seconds later. The final step was to raise the alarm on the two way radio taken off the Chinese guard. As neither of them spoke any Chinese or being likely to imitate the man's voice and tone, the only answer was a soft moaning over the air followed by a falling sound and sudden silence.

Harry reckoned they had fifteen seconds. His hand was clenched around the grip of the Beretta, sweat running down the nape of his neck and back as he fought his breathing down and willed the tension from his coiled like a spring body. This was going to be close! In the old days it would have been just Vusi and him and against a bunch of sailors, even pirates, he would have favoured their chances.

This was different. Other lives, innocent lives, were at stake. There was no room for error...

They came fast and they came hard; several of them judging by the rapid exchange of words audible through the thin partitioning of the cabin wall. There was a sudden cry of alarm as the prostate form of the guard was spotted followed by rapid conversation over what Harry guessed was a walkie talkie. He reckoned they would have entered the hold by now, been confronted by the scenario hopefully being played out right now.

God he wished he could see! Should he have left Vusi with the others? How would that have helped?

A sudden howl, quickly climbing to a crescendo to be followed almost instantly by the clatter of heavy boots on steel as the first of the men made for the safety of the gangway, the sound of a painful grunt as someone tried to slam shut the heavy steel door to the hold only to have it crush onto the prone body of Harry's still unconscious victim. Listening hard while raising a finger to his lips to caution a ready to prance Vusi, Harry thought he heard other footsteps follow but was it all of them? It was a safe bet they were armed and he couldn't afford even a single shot being fired, it would sink the whole plan.

For maybe four or five seconds now, silence had reigned. Apart from the increasing groaning from the man collapsed across the bulkhead door, that was. Harry would have to chance it. He would also have to move fast in case a third crew member was still in that corridor.

The door slammed open into the passageway and Harry came through it with all the force he could muster, twisting as his lead shoulder crashed into the far wall and facing the man who had been kneeling next to the body of his knocked out fellow sailor. The expression on the man's startled face turned from puzzlement to "what the –" in a microsecond and that was all the time Harry needed to kick him full in the face, his head snapping back with a sound like an errant baseball striking a wet sheet on a clothesline.

It took Vusi only seconds to slop antifouling around the man's face and on the floor while Harry slipped inside the hold to take up position flattened against the wall just inside the darkened room. Vusi resumed his position inside the cabin, this time leaving the door open just a crack.

From their hiding places both men could hear the rapid and heated conversation now taking place on the deck above. One voice appeared to be that of a woman, the tone higher and also angry. The voice of someone in command and climbing to overcome the protesting chorus of others trying to drown her out.

Clearly all hell had broken loose and the only question now was would the plan work?

Harry didn't think they had long to wait before finding out.

Seconds later he heard it, audible above a hubbub of frantic shouts and excited chatter, the unmistakeable whine of heavy winches. Someone was lowering the lifeboat he had noticed earlier swinging from its mountings immediately above their heads.

Another sound had him stiffen. Someone was coming down the gangway. Moving slowly and stealthily. Someone careful and not wearing the heavy sailor's boots the earlier visitors had in common. In the cabin Vusi waited and listened, knowing Harry would be listening too. Slowly, a carefully placed footstep following the next the person moved towards the open hold hatchway, stepping soundlessly over the collapsed forms of the two fallen sailors.

Peering around the cabin door, now open at just more than a crack, Vusi found himself staring at the back of a woman. A tiny creature, to be more precise. And old, judging by the tufts of grey hair poking out beneath a knitted cap of sorts.

The woman he knew to be Madame Chen.

Intrigued he watched as she stepped over the fallen bodies in the passageway to step into the hold, a torch in her hand casting a sweeping yellow beam across the scenario spread across the floor.

She stood there for what seemed like minutes before saying something softly in Chinese and stepping back into the corridor. Hanging well back in the shadows of the darkened cabin Vusi watched her glide past, noting the heavily wrinkled features in the parched yellow expressionless face. Eyes like tiny black berries flitted from side to side and if she thought the open at a crack cabin door was suspicious she made no sign of showing it.

Cradled under an arm she had the two AK 47s the guards had dropped.

Watching from deep inside the shadows of the darkened hold Harry wondered why she bothered? Was it a woman's inherent taste for tidiness or was it because some of the victims down there were still alive, could pose a problem hefting a rifle?

Or was it because she suspected all was not as it seemed and an uninvited party was lurking aboard her ship?

Only one way to find out. After a muted discussion with Vusi who had now joined him they decided to wait a further five minutes to give the lifeboat and escaping crew time to get a distance away before the next step.

With Harry, pistol at the ready, keeping watch at the bottom of the gangway leading to the deck, Vusi herded the boys together, struggling to quell their excited chatter, as they helped him drag the two guards to a spot where they could be tied to a convenient pipe structure using a coil of rope he had found earlier stashed under a tarpaulin in the storage locker. Both were fully awake now and glaring silently at their assailants with hatred filled eyes. Neither said a word but for good measure Vusi tore strips off one of the men's shirts and gagged them with it. Then he set off on a quick reconnaissance mission, Harry giving him five minutes to get the layout of the vessel, find their route out.

Minutes later he was back. 'I checked the passage leading to the galley and beyond that another corridor with cabins leading off it. All deserted; I reckon your plan has worked, the crew have taken off.'

Harry listened while Vusi drew a verbal picture of the layout of the upper deck forward of their current position, nodding as different avenues to the outside deck was outlined. Their problem was at least two people up there, suspicious and armed with serious firepower. When Harry weighed up their solitary handgun against the firepower of an AK 47 he concluded sadly that only an idiot brings a handgun to a machine gun duel and not for the first time cursed himself for not retaining one of the weapons.

Again they listened; all quiet outside that open hatchway, the only sound the fleeting cry of an errant seagull against the backdrop of the steady deep throated vibration from the Mako Venturer's diesels. To go through that hatchway was to invite death and Harry decided they would both go back, through the galley and then take different routes to the outside deck, approaching the area from opposite sides, hoping for the element of surprise.

What to do with the boys? Leave them down there with the chance their adversaries would decide to come down that gangway, find them there, alive and well and take them hostage, strike a new deal? Or, worse, solve the problem with a few bursts from an AK 47? Harry couldn't take that chance, their precious cargo would have to come with, stay close.

Minutes later they were on their way, Harry leading with Vusi bringing up the rear. Passing through the deserted galley, a pot of rice cooking dry on the stove top smoking the place up, Harry collected a paring knife, carefully shoving it down the outside of a sock where it was hidden under his trouser leg. Without looking he knew Vusi would follow suit. Against an automatic rifle it wasn't much but it made for a small measure of comfort.

On impulse Harry decided to take a detour through the engine room and look for another exit further aft. Once down the steep and slippery steel steps he paused for a moment to gain his bearings, the others bunched behind him. The noise was deafening, a rhythmic clanging and hissing as rows of exposed valves bobbed and dipped, the long crankshaft in its oil bathed bed groaning in its endless revolutions. To his left was a bank of switches with an array of indicator lights and gauges. On the far side, wedged between several thick pipes, a ventilator shaft Harry guessed would lead up to the outside deck.

Peering into the dark space immediately beyond Harry saw it first; the movement. A sudden furtive ducking of a head when his own was turned in that direction. He raised a warning hand to caution the others and, gun at the ready, moved quickly while keeping a lookout for myriad cables and tubing criss-crossing his path.

The Chinaman, Harry guessed him at least sixty, was cowering amongst a pile of dirty oil rags and cans and held up a defensive hand when Harry towered over him. Judging by his dirty overalls he was in his workplace and somehow, in the panic to abandon ship, the message had not reached him. And Harry was glad to see him, for later, when he had taken over the ship he would need to keep those engines going for the next phase of the plan that had been forming at the back of his mind.

'Let's chase him out ahead of us at the hatchway, see if they're watching that spot and whether they're ready to shoot.' Vusi's voice was urgent, Harry guessed the tension was getting to them all now.

'No. We'll need him for later. Tie him up.'

Then there was nothing more for it but to lead the procession to where a bulkhead door at the top of a steel walkway promised access to the deck if the blue sky showing through a porthole to the side was to be believed. Seconds later Harry was crouched at the door, a hand on the heavy steel handle with the other sweating palm clutched tightly around the butt of the Beretta. He would have liked to place that last phone call to Selena – didn't a condemned man get a call? – but there was no reception and it was now or never and holding the gun at the ready he released the door handle and tensed his shoulder for the rush through.

Only to be momentarily stunned by the sharp typewriter clatter of an AK 47 being fired from the direction of the far side whence they had come earlier. Moving fast Harry was through the hatchway and in the leeway of a deck structure, Vusi bumping into him and spinning to cover the other side.

Thirty yards away one of the guards they had overpowered and tied up earlier lay sprawled at the top of the gangway, a pool of crimson spreading around his head. Standing over him was the lanky Chinese Harry recognised from the day a lion died from a crossbow arrow. The assault rifle was still pointed at the space the fallen man had emerged from, the man with the gun staring intently down the steeply descending passageway, trying to see through the darkness beyond and thinking about going down there. There was a wailing sound now and it took Harry a moment to decide it was their other prisoner, also now free, imploring the gunman not to shoot as he came up.

There was no time to lose. Until now the bodyguard and the old lady had had no certain way of knowing intruders were aboard but that was about to change within seconds.

Thirty yards. Too far for any accuracy with a handgun on a rolling deck of a ship. He would have to get close. Fast.

And then Harry was up and sprinting, side stepping like a star quarterback as he danced and wove, all considerations for cover now a side issue, the only blessing that his rope soled shoes were noiseless on the steel deck and the gunman still deafened from the burst of gunfire.

Things slowing down now, like it always seemed to for Harry. The slow motion thing, senses heightened to screaming point, the mind processing so fast everything became a blur yet part of the acute awareness that divided the thin line between living and dying.

Twenty yards. And starting to raise the Beretta as he ran.

Fifteen yards. The gunman turning and starting to raise the snout of the AK 47, the barrel still smoking, a snarl curling the man's lip, baring his teeth.

Harry fired as he ran. Two, three shots, the Beretta at arm's length but without the steadying of a two handed grip. The second or third bullet, Harry couldn't be sure, sprouted a pink mist as it thudded into the man's side, spinning him sideways, the rifle clattering onto the deck. So intense was Harry's concentration on those shots that he failed to see the coiled rope and as he went down it saved his life.

Crouching in the shadow of a deck structure Madame Chen brought the fire axe down with all the force that wiry frame, consumed by rage, could muster. It missed where Harry's head had been a microsecond earlier, the heavy wooden handle crashing down on his shoulder, rendering his arm instantly numb, the handgun spinning from his grasp. As he crashed onto the cold steel deck, his arm a sea of pain, Harry could make out the wizened features of the woman through a red mist that threatened to engulf his consciousness.

Was that Vusi grappling with her? The woman slashing at him with what looked like a wicked stiletto, Vusi twisting out of the way and almost tripping over Harry in the process.

Focus now! Must get to the gun!

Raising himself on his good arm he saw that the gunman had regained his feet and was clutching his side with a blood smeared hand as he moved towards the dropped AK 47, hatred filled jet black eyes squinting as he saw Harry stagger erect.

Both men paused, the situation frozen for a split second. No more than fifteen feet separated them. For either, in their wounded state, to bend down, go for their respective weapon, was not on. It would offer the easy target for a well aimed game ending kick to the head. Harry's Beretta was the nearer, maybe five feet away, but his right hand was still numb and functionally useless and it just wasn't on.

Warily they circled, eyes flicking alternately from an opponent's narrowed gaze to the dropped guns. So near, so far...

From the corner of his eye Harry could see that the macabre dance between the knife wielding woman and his partner was still in progress but moving away as Vusi held her sudden thrusting movements at bay with what looked like a fire blanket yanked from the same wall mounted closet the axe had come from.

The woman shouted something at the young man in clipped rapid Chinese and whatever it was, it had him visibly stiffen. Harry didn't speak Chinese, didn't have to. The change in the man's body language was enough to tell him the man had been told to do his job, defend her.

Martial arts had never been a passion with Harry. He thought them overrated, opera for weirdoes who foolishly believed they really had a chance in unarmed confrontation with a six foot four two hundred and forty pound hard man who had fought his way up from the gutter and knew every dirty trick in the book. A man who did this kind of thing for a living. Sure, he had been subjected to the usual unarmed combat training that formed part of the Special Forces training, but somehow always reverted to the kind of tactics that had him survive many a scrap growing up on the wrong side of the tracks in old Bulawayo. It got to a point where

Jock Barr, tough old Selous Scouts drill sergeant and martial arts instructor that he was, had wearily signed Harry off as "untrained but competent."

And Harry found a great calmness settle over him, finding its way down to evenly planted feet and a still lame arm that was showing signs of life in the stinging fingertips. For the stance his opponent had taken up was the classic kick boxer position with both feet close together, arms held close to the chest with fists at port, torso leaning forwards. Except, with blood pouring out his side and that arm restrained by the pain of any movement, not quite so classic.

It was going to be a kick, Harry wagered, delivered from an upright position and aimed at his midriff. A snap kick that, if well connected, would have him stagger back, give the other man chance to get to that rifle. That was the problem with classical martial arts training, Harry thought as he waited for, invited, the kick. It comes with rules. That and the expectancy the other man knows those rules and respects them.

When the kick came, a lightning fast straight forward delivered from hip height, the man putting his weight into it, Harry was ready. He had correctly guessed it would be the left leg, the man's wound on the right trunk limiting movement on that side and it was with relative ease that he could twist his body away at the same time grabbing hold of the leg. Then it was simply a matter of swinging his own leg over that of the other man and throwing his own weight behind it as he went down onto the deck. The violent twisting movement snapping every ligament in the would-be kick boxer's knee with a sound like a branch breaking off from a weather beaten dry as dust tree.

He went down like a dropped sack of potatoes and even before he hit the wail of pain was ear splitting and he probably never heard Harry's hiss, between clenched teeth. 'Sorry, old sport, I guess it's against the rules to hold onto that leg.'

Turning away Harry recovered both weapons and went over to where Vusi had tossed the fire blanket over the still struggling Chinese woman, grimacing at a torrent of rapid abuse flowing from beneath its folds. 'Really, Vusi,' he said, smiling, 'Is that the way to treat a lady?'

Vusi was scowling, 'That's easy for you to say, you always pick the easy ones. This one's as lethal as a spitting cobra!' He indicated the knife that had dropped to the floor.

'Let her go,' Harry said. 'Let's hear what she has to say.'

They watched with interest as she shook herself free from the folds of the blanket to draw herself up to all of her five foot nothing, clenched fists by the side as she glared at them with all the venom of a coiled snake. The children had come onto the deck now and were clustered around, shiny black faces upturned and apprehensively smiling as they stared at the woman they recognised from the shed at Halali.

She didn't say anything and Harry knew it would be a waste of time trying to interrogate her. For he had spotted the tattoo on her forearm, a snarling dragon with five red balls circling it. She was Triad, mainland China and sent to oversee this mission. Her masters did not tolerate failure. Failure meant losing face and that was not allowed.

Madame Chen knew this. The lined features were calm now, entirely devoid of any expression. Slowly she retreated away from them and as Vusi moved to stop her Harry laid a restraining hand on his arm. They watched in silence as she climbed onto the rail to sit there for a moment, inscrutable as ever. Then she tilted her head to seek out the sun one last time and then she toppled backwards.

The splash was barely audible and Harry did not have to move to the rail to see if she came up. He knew she was dead; probably couldn't swim in the first place. Slowly he raised his eyes to gaze out towards the horizon to where a tiny lifeboat was still visible. Just a speck in a vast wilderness with the dark continent somewhere beyond.

Turning to Vusi he asked him to round up the other guard they had seen peeking around the gangway a minute earlier. 'Shoot him if you must,' then untie the engineer and let's get some steam up. I'm going up to the bridge, try and find out where we are.

'Where are we going?' Vusi asked as he beckoned the last of the guards to come forward from his hiding place at the top of the gangway, the man suddenly eager to co-operate, maybe stay alive.

'Mozambique,' Harry said, 'Maputo Harbour to be precise. Shouldn't be more than a few hours steaming away.'

On the bridge Harry surveyed the battery of controls, dials and LED screens confronting him. All were brightly lit, the rhythmic sweep of the radar showing a solitary and fast receding blip – presumably the last sight of the Mako Venturer's errant crew. Central was the wheel, swinging gently in a narrow arc as the swells rolled under the hull. The compass, set directly in front of the helmsman pointed thirty degrees north northeast, the needle steady and putting his hand to the wheel Harry decided it was locked in position. A check of the control lever signalling the engineer confirmed that the ship was in a stationary position with the propeller disengaged. Which, he reflected, made sense: when deciding to abandon ship you don't want the thing moving at speed.

Now where was the radio? For a ship this size there often would not be a separate radio room, simply a small station set up to one side of the bridge. His search took in the chart table set in a small recess to the rear of the bridge and the alcove beside the galley way where the radio was located. No expert at the operation of ship's radios Harry had nevertheless had a fair bit of experience with military field radios going back to his mercenary years and it took him less than ten minutes to raise the Durban port authorities and have a call put through to Selena's mobile.

A soldier's woman, Selena knew better than to gush about how worried she was and whether he was OK. Instead the conversation went straight to business. 'Do you remember Gomez, the Mozambican customs inspector?'

'You mean that sleazy man who wanted to bust you that time in Beira when you brought those guns in for the deal with...?'

'Yeah, yeah. *Him,*' Harry interrupted hastily, mindful of who might be listening in. 'I want you to get hold of him. Tell him I'm bringing the Mako Venturer in to Maputo Harbour, I reckon about dawn to-morrow. I'll need a port pilot and will make radio contact when approaching. Tell him it's an abandoned ship, a salvage situation, and that there's a deal in it for him. He's a businessman, he'll understand.'

'What about me? You want me to fly up there?' There was a fair degree of static now, her voice drifting in and out and Harry thought the squall fast approaching through a portside window view might be the explanation. Waiting for the ship to ride the crest of a swell he had to steady himself against the increasing roll as he clasped the headset closer. 'Yes. You should be there before us, see if you can meet up with Gomez and put him in the picture.' A sudden thought made him add, 'Where's Piet Niemand? I need to talk to him.'

'As a matter of fact,' Selena said sweetly, 'He's right here with me as we enjoy a rather delicious meal of Tiger prawns washed down with a delicate little white...'

'Shut up,' Harry said, aware of his own gnawing hunger pains, 'And put the man on.'

There was the sounds of laughter followed by the gruff voice of the detective. 'What's up, Dance?'

Harry sighed, 'Enough of the pleasantries. I have control of the ship and the cargo is what we expected and safe and intact. Heading for Maputo Harbour.' There was no need to explain why that was the preferred option to Durban. Both men knew of the potential complications of bringing the ship back to South African waters. 'What's the situation back there?'

There was a pause followed by an audible swallow and a noisy gulp of liquid before the big man came back on the ether. 'Fluid, I'd have to say. Yeah, *fluid* is a good word here. Oil on troubled waters. Could go either way but I can handle it.'

'Good,' Harry said. 'Now, listen carefully.'

19
CHAPTER

Captain Fernando Gomez of the Mozambican Customs Services was a man who liked to smile and at times it even reached his eyes. He was smiling now and the beneficiary of that dazzling display of gleaming white teeth was a weary and somewhat shop worn looking Harry Dance.

'Haree!' he exclaimed with a broad sweeping gesture, 'How wonderful to see you again, amigo!' The voice was melodious with just a hint of an accent, the way Harry remembered it the latter would become more pronounced after about the fourth bourbon. A lanky six feet in his Italian loafers the businessman – Gomez preferred to think of himself as a businessman rather than public official – was immaculately clad in an off white tropical suit with an open necked floral shirt displaying a broad golden chain against a deeply tanned chest. A finely chiselled nose dominated a pencil thin black moustache, the whole topped off by a wide brimmed Panama hat.

Gold rimmed shades hid the eyes which Harry seemed to recall as resembling those of a pit viper, dark and fathomless and totally devoid of any humour.

The slender fingers of one hand caressed a slim panatela. The other arm was curled around the waist of a relaxed looking Selena.

'Hello, darling,' She said, disengaging herself from Gomez to come over and on tiptoe kiss Harry before turning to Vusi who also received a hug and a kiss. It was good to have her boys back safely but she knew Harry hated sentimentality and smiling sweetly she explained that Captain Gomez had been the perfect gentleman, as always, and was indeed very interested in the little proposition she had put forward on behalf of Harry.

'From what I understand,' Gomez said between lazy clouds of cigar smoke, 'this rustbucket, ' a sweeping gesture indicated the Mako Venturer where she was rubbing against the fenders quayside, 'is an abandoned ship, the crew having taken off in a lifeboat leaving you in charge?'

'Something like that,' Harry said. 'I'm sure we can work out the details later. Suffice it to say you will find her owners extremely hard to trace; in fact, I'll wager no-one will lay claim to this magnificent, and may I add very seaworthy, vessel you see before you.' And, he mused, seeing as to the nature of the cargo, it was unlikely any insurance claim would be forthcoming either.

Gomez nodded, drifting an appraising eye over the lines of the ship, sharp reflections off the water having Harry squint as he turned to study the sea of shiny black faces that had now appeared at the ship's railings. 'This being the cargo?' Gomez said with an inclination of his head.

Harry nodded.

'Hmm...I suppose we could come to some sort of arrangement. Safe passage you say, back to South Africa?'

'Through the border post at Komatipoort, not running for their lives from lions in the Kruger Park.'

This elicited a silent laugh from the Portuguese who, like Harry, knew all too well of the plight of the thousands of Mozambican illegal jobseekers who cross the border through the size of England national park many to be taken by the lions and crocodiles that serve as a very efficient deterrent.

'Quite. Passports should not be a problem between friendly countries. My men at the border will be very understanding.'

'Uh huh.' Indicating the ship Harry remarked that someone suitable would, of course, have to be found who would offer to take care of the ship, the vessel being an orphan so to speak. After all, she would need new papers, a coat of paint, perhaps even a new name...?

'I think I could take care of that,' Gomez said as he returned Selena's smile.

Harry said, 'Yes.'

'There is still the matter of that small debt between us,' Gomez said, studying the cigar absently, 'Going back to that time that you imported a shipment of AK 47 rifles through one of our sovereign ports without the necessary, ah shall we say, importation documents?'

Which, Harry mused, meant the bribe having been misappropriated at the time by colleagues of the customs man even more crooked than he was.

'A small oversight,' Harry said, 'and something I sincerely apologize for. Hopefully the gift of a ship as valuable as the one behind us will suffice...'

Studiously avoiding the gaze of Vusi whom he knew was in his mind reliving their experiences at the time they had to make a hasty exit from Beira, Harry added, 'Then, of course there's the other matter.'

Harry couldn't be sure but he thought there was an arched eyebrow behind those mirror shades. 'The other matter?'

Harry said, 'Uh huh. The way I see it the cargo this ship was carrying was undeniably illegal. To the point that if its very nature was ever to become public to the world out there heads would roll.'

'Some very *big* heads,' Vusi affirmed. It was the first time he had spoken which had both parties glance at him.

Harry said, 'Uh huh. Now, as it turns out, the shipping documents and cargo clearance in Durban was signed off by no less a person than the Minister of Customs and Immigration. A man closely connected to the President and many other members of the South African Government. A very important man, you might say.'

Gomez nodded thoughtfully. 'You can prove that?'

'Harry said, 'Uh huh. An associate of mine have those very papers in his possession as we speak.' A glance at Selena confirmed that Big Piet Niemand had been in contact earlier, confirming that aspect.

They were strolling in the direction of a nearby cafe now, the late afternoon sun baking and it being happy hour and all that. Harry did not have to spell out the significance of possession of those documents to a "businessman" such as the captain of customs. Leverage over a man as powerful as the minister was something to be dreamed about. The lucrative illegal trade of cigarettes and alcohol between the two countries would be so much easier once a certain understanding was reached between men of reason.

'I can perhaps keep those documents in a safe place where they could, shall we say accumulate interest?'

'An excellent idea,' Harry said. 'Now, how about that drink you were talking about?'

A taxi had pulled up next to the gangway and Harry watched as the Chinese hitman was helped into a back seat by the engineer and the remaining guard, the men studiously avoiding glances in their direction. At Harry's questioning glance Vusi confirmed that he had given instructions for the trio to be driven to the Chinese Embassy. If Gomez took any interest he didn't let on, simply held out an angled arm for Selena to hook an arm through and led the way to where welcome shadows and cool drinks were beckoning.

Myriad colourful birds were creating a cacophony of sound in the overhead palms and far out on the breakwater Harry could see the backs of semi-naked boys as they cast their fishing lines and drank their beers and watched the first of the fishing boats come in.

Africa! Harry thought and suddenly, from nowhere at all, a deeply buried nostalgia welled up inside him and for once he was glad his wife wasn't looking at him just then, for as well as she knew him he would never be able to hide that show of vulnerability from her.

Harry Dance, he said to himself, you're getting a bit old for this game now. It's time, boyo. Time to go home. And without having to look at Vusi and without having to look at Selena, he knew they felt it too. What was it Tsotsi had said when Vusi had asked the boy what he wanted most in life? *To learn to read...*

He, and Selena and Vusi, could make that happen.

He knew what he had to do.

And as Selena leaned back against the plush cushions of the latticed recliner she studied her man and she knew him well enough to know that, in his own enigmatic way, Harry Dance was happy. She knew without asking that he was pondering a new future for all of them. A future that was far away from this world of violence and ugliness and the evil men do.

They would talk about it later, in bed and in that tranquil period when the day's tensions ebb away to be replaced by a pleasant weariness, the mind winding down as it reviewed the day gone by. She would feel secure in the embrace of her man and Harry would tell her about things and, as always he would leave out the mean and the ugly and focus on the positive.

Harry the optimist is how she would always think of him. And now, now she would have to tell him about the news she had received earlier.

The phone call from an impersonal voice informing her of the results of that breast biopsy. Of the cancer that would need treatment and soon.

Of the uncertain future.

But that would be later. For now the sun's dying rays was turning her skin a golden colour and Harry was laughing at something Gomez said and Vusi was in earnest conversation with a son he thought he had lost and all around them was the sound of lively chatter and bustle and...

Life... Oh Harry, she mused, we're all on borrowed time here, all just waiting for the next act and that final curtain. But right now life was good, with an olive in her martini and the little umbrella so very bright and the calypso music from the three piece band over the road just starting to lazily waft through the sounds of a tropical evening coming down.

Piet Niemand's dad had always held a man shouldn't eat breakfast on an empty stomach. It just wasn't natural. Of course that had all been a long time ago, the old man gone now. At the time Piet, he was a boy then, had put it down to the old man's habit of helping himself to a little nip from the dregs of last night's brandy bottle – "hair of the dog" he called it – before rolling out of bed to face the day. Over time he had begun to realise there had been a grain of truth in all that. As much as he loved his food he simply couldn't stomach the idea of a big breakfast at bloody six in the morning. At that ungodly hour the night's heartburn had hardly settled not to mention the slight lingering nausea from that nightcap he shouldn't have had.

No, far better to swallow the paracetamol down with a strong coffee then stumble off to work and round about ten, the time a decent man started waking up properly, his stomach would tell him now's the time.

Only one snag. That was back when he was working with the aroma of bacon and eggs wafting through his office windows from the Wimpy down the street, his secretary ready to send the cleaner down to fetch his regular order.

Sometimes donuts too, the lady behind the counter at the deli letting him know when a fresh batch comes through...

Now, being suspended, he wasn't at the office and it seemed an effort to drive downtown at an hour when most of the shops weren't even open yet. With a sigh he dug the blender out of a kitchen cabinet, started searching for something to feed it with. The fridge did not hold much promise once he had hauled out the mouldy cheese, a few slices of meat he vaguely connected with a takeaway chicken, some coleslaw and a soggy rotting mess in the vegetable drawer that might have been a cucumber once. Or possibly a lettuce.

The pleasures of a single man's life he mused wearily, where every meal is a takeaway and, if you're a cop, washed down with bad coffee while hunched behind the wheel of a stakeout car. Time he got himself a woman again, he reckoned, idly wondering if the police psychologist would be open to an invitation. Somehow he didn't think so, not after what she had called him when last they parted.

Most unprofessional he had thought at the time.

With a sigh he fed the items he thought salvageable into the blender, adding some milk as an afterthought. Moving to plug it in his foot bumped against something on the floor. A slice of pizza, supreme by the look of it, with anchovies. He couldn't quite remember when he'd had that but it could have been the previous night. It looked OK and he added it to the mix, switching on the machine.

Breakfast, he thought, the most important meal of the day. Sitting down in front of the television with a bowl of the blender mix he let his mind drift over the previous day's events.

The Police Chief had been quite civil about the whole thing, come to think of it. Taking him by the arm to lead him away from Selena and the kid while apologising for the abrupt interruption. Then keeping his voice down as he laid down the new rules. Except he called it "clarifying matters." Used terms like we all have to work together while building a new nation. Not rocking the boat. And, speaking of boats, what the hell had he been thinking when he set about searching foreign flagged vessels without so much as checking with his superiors?

Was he even aware of the ructions this would cause in the delicate relations we have with important trade partners like, for instance, China? It went on like that, the man waffling on about police procedurals and correct channels, all the while leading the detective in a slow walk down the quay, away from where the others were standing. At the man's instructions

Detective Sergeant Gericke had remained with Selena and Tsotsi, ensure they wouldn't get lost or in harm's way, the harbour being a busy place.

Piet Niemand knew better. It was to get out of earshot of the sergeant. In the dog eat dog world the department had become no-one was to be entrusted, spies were everywhere.

'For God's sake, Piet, what's going on?' Robbs finally asked as they shared a light for a cigarette. 'All hell is breaking loose. The bloody Minister of Customs and Immigration wants you fired, something about harassing the Chinese.'

'Mr Tammany? That clown? What's he got to do with police business?'

Dismissing the question with a sad shake of the head at such naivety while conducting a slow sweep of the harbour traffic, Robbs resumed the stroll. 'It seems you have a spy in your ranks,' he said reflectively, 'someone who knows all your moves and reports back to most likely the Minister of Police.'

Niemand shrugged, 'So what? I still don't see...'

'He's the brother of Tamm... the Customs and Immigration Minister...'

'Business as usual,' Niemand said bitterly, 'South Africa Incorporated. Except here it's all government business. So you reckon our friend Tammany is up to his fat greasy neck in this people smuggling business?'

'What people smuggling business?' the Chief asked sweetly, flicking his cigarette into the water.

'Oh come on!'

'Just kidding! I've read your reports and there lies half the problem; so have others.'

Taking Niemand by the arm he led him into the leeway of a large container. 'How long have we known each other, Piet? Twenty years? '

'More like thirty,' the big man growled.

'Right. And all that time I've been straight with you, right?' Taking the other man's silence as assent he went on, keeping his voice down. 'Changes are coming. Big changes. Word is that the cabinet is due for a shake up, certain individuals having made too much of a spectacle of themselves at the feeding trough, enough to embarrass the president. The idea for the likes of you and I is to survive the trashing of the mortally wounded beast, you get my meaning?'

'You want me to lay off for a few weeks,' Niemand said.

'A paid vacation. You're due for leave anyway.'

Both men knew the official entry on the records would be that of suspension pending an enquiry.

NIemand's phone rang. It was Harry Dance, the reception poor. 'Bingo!' he said simply. Without replying Niemand cut the call.

There was a pause as the Chief studied the detective with interest. 'That was Dance, wasn't it?'

Ignoring the question Piet Niemand said, 'It seems we have a shipload of stolen children, our children, aboard a foreign ship about to leave South African waters. All that stands between them and likely death are a few good men. On the other side a sea of corruption and unspeakable callousness. I think, Commissioner, that I might just need your help on this one.'

They were sitting on stone bollards now, gazing out over the oily slick that was Durban harbour, the Chief lighting another cigarette while his big companion was searching his pockets for a stick of gum. 'What do you need?' Robbs said at length.

'All the information you can give me. Access to the usual police channels...'

'We can't stop that ship, not against the express orders of the minister.'

'No. But Harry Dance can.'

Robbs nodded. 'I've seen his dossier. That of Vusi Luwago as well. God help us if they don't make it.'

After a moment he seemed to reach a decision. 'There *is* something else I can do for you.' Not looking at Niemand he went on, 'It's all about survival, isn't it? For all of us. As part of my own survival kit I have over the past few months collected information on the activities of certain high ranking officials, people like the minister in question. The kind of things that would be too damaging to survive should they come to light.' Fixing the detective with a wry smile he rose to head back to where the others were waiting.

'I'm going to give that information to you, Piet. I trust you'll know what to do with it. I want you to save the children.'

Five paces away, he paused, turned to point an admonishing finger at Niemand. 'And you're still suspended!'

He got the call at eight that evening, the number unlisted on his phone, the clicking of engaging coins suggesting public phone. Must be one of the few phones still in working order he reckoned. The voice muffled, disguised, the message short and to the point. Twenty minutes later he picked up the package where the voice had told him it would be waiting, bulky in a manila envelope and sealed with generous amounts of clear tape. It was at his usual hamburger joint on the beach, the long suffering owner handing over the package with a smile, adding for good measure a donut and a coffee to go.

No, he didn't know who was behind it, the drop off had been one of the street urchins who had been paid handsomely by a white man of nondescript features. A printed note bore Niemand's name and it was marked private.

His regular morning breakfast stop. Christ, was he that predictable?!

It was all there, enough to bury Tammany as well as the police minister. Why hadn't Robbs used it by now? But, of course, he knew the answer to that one. The man would just be replaced by another stooge even more corrupt. Better the devil you know, at least until your hand was forced.

Like now.

Of even more interest was the information about Savannah, that nefarious underground human chain he had been hunting for so long now. Most of it he knew anyhow, in fact had been the source in the first place. However, there was the interesting bit about a certain Mr Heidmann and a company called Phoenix Enterprise Solutions. Even a photo of the mysterious Mr Heidmann, one he would pass on to Harry Dance who might just be able to place him.

How long was the Commissioner going to sit on this keg of dynamite? He could only speculate that there was a connection between Heidmann and Tammany and that the man had been waiting for the right moment.

Pushing away the dregs of his breakfast Piet Niemand leaned back in the armchair and thought back to the conversation he had with Harry Dance earlier that morning, the ship now docked in Maputo and Selena already there to help with the return of the children. It had been good to hear they were all OK and that a plan was already forming at the back of that computer Dance called a brain. A plan to terminate Savannah once and for all.

20
CHAPTER

The beauty of an airgun is its silence. Little more than a hiss of escaping compressed air. Audible perhaps for up to eight feet.

And no recoil to speak of.

Also, when mounted with a hunting telescope, quite accurate up to thirty yards.

The only noise the sharp yelp of the big Alsatian as the dart went home. The guard dog whirling sharply around in an attempt to get at the sharp sting in its hindquarters where the tranquilizer dart had struck. A further series of howls as it turned in rapidly slowing circles, the ketamine quickly taking effect in the animal's fast flowing circulatory system.

From where he had been crouching in the shadows Harry straightened up as he worked the lever to recharge the gun's compressed air cylinder, the next ketamine dart already loaded.

'Shaka! Shaka! Wat de fok maak jy?!' Came the perplexed shout from the large man who loomed in the lit doorway of the small granny flat set just inside the gates of the walled garden. But Shaka was already down, the whimpering now soft and replaced by the regular breathing of an animal in deep sleep. After a moment's hesitation the man retreated inside the flat to return seconds later clutching a handgun. As he moved into the open it triggered a spotlight mounted at the corner of the building bathing the driveway in brilliant light.

'Shaka, oubaas, is jy OK?' There was genuine concern in the big man's voice as he carefully circled the prone animal while warily scanning the darkness beyond the focused circle of the light. Standing in the shadows of a large Pittosporum bush Harry waited until his target – the man was

now kneeling next to the sleeping dog a look of puzzlement on his face as he extracted the dart – was square on before firing again the dart striking home in the right upper chest as intended. With a curse the guard dropped the gun, the arm instantly lame and staggered to his feet a shout dying on his lips as Harry stepped into the light and showed him the automatic now lined up on his midriff.

The guard was slowly backing off while eyeing the dropped pistol. 'Don't even think about it.' Harry said softly, 'It's ketamine, a major tranquilizer that will knock both you and the dog out for about half an hour or so. Go gently to sleep and you'll live. Cry out and I'll kill you.'

But the man's options were already running out, with limbs growing heavy and a building buzz in his ears he found himself sitting flat on the ground before slowly keeling over, a final protest dying on his lips.

No surprise there really, Harry thought, seeing he'd given him the pre-loaded dosage clearly marked on the cartridge as for Kibus, the lion. Apparently the stuff had a wide safety margin, what with not impairing spontaneous breathing and other vital reflexes. Not that Harry cared that much about possible collateral damage. For he was about to enter the den of a creature far more lethal than any lion he had ever encountered and by Harry's reckoning those that sought to seek darkness should expect darkness to seek them out in turn.

Minutes later he had scaled the gates and was heading for the large double storey house set at the far end of a sweeping lawn, having first dragged both unconscious beings into the shadows and out of sight of the street.

Heidmann came into the room slowly, cautiously, the first sign of his presence the creeping shadow cast by the hallway light framing his silhouette in the doorway. He was wrapped in a dressing gown and his footsteps were almost inaudible in soft leather slippers. White ankles protruding from too short pyjama pants were marked by bulging blue varicosities.

In one hand was a *knobkerrie,* a formidable looking cudgel, the other reached for the light switch. Eyes glinting behind steel rimmed glasses peering through the darkness at the flickering images on the plasma TV screen. *'Bastian? Wat de donder maak jy?!'* came the angry growl as he called out to the minder in Afrikaans.

The light switch activated two table lamps at the far end of the room leaving Harry's armchair in the opposite corner in semi-darkness, something he had checked earlier. He waited until the now visibly angry man was several steps into the room before speaking. 'Hello, general, or should I say Mr Heidmann?' he said pleasantly, 'Isn't this a bit late for you to be up?'

The other man whirled round the cudgel raised instinctively only to slowly drop to his side as Harry lifted the Beretta, the ugly snout of the automatic catching the light. 'Careful, wouldn't do to have an accident now, would it?'

Noting the man's searching glance in the direction of the door, Harry shook his head, 'If it's Mr Olympia you're looking for, I'm afraid he's dropped off to sleep. I've given him the evening off.'

On his feet now Harry motioned the general towards the desk, deftly relieving him of the *knobkerrie* and patting the pockets of the dressing gown to satisfy himself no nasty surprises were hidden amongst its folds. A quick shove had Heidmann slumped in the swivel chair behind the desk with a heavy grunt.

Picking up the TV remote control from the desk Harry killed the game, a pity because his old team, the Cape Town Stormers were doing surprisingly well for a change. The sudden silence in the room was broken only by the seated man's heavy breathing. Harry stared down at the old man for what seemed ages, taking in the altered features and yet, now that the mask of a new identity was finally removed to be replaced by one of naked fear, able to clearly make out the vestiges of an old hated nemesis. For a moment, a split second of insanity, there was an almost overwhelming impulse to pull the trigger, blow away the death's head that was now grinning up at him uncertainly.

'What do you want?' the general asked at length, a note of the old assertiveness creeping back into a still unsteady voice. The eyes, now hooded behind the lenses, were fixed on the gun.

'Put both hands on the desk where I can see them,' Harry commanded. He was still standing and had moved to place the light streaming in from the open doorway at his back. 'It took me a while to figure you out, general, too long to prevent more killings, but your time is over now. Ever heard of Blue Ice? It's when on a beautiful sunny day you're strolling on that boulevard, heading for your favourite restaurant, enjoying the crisp morning air and smiling at the pretty girls passing by, the pleasant memory of that last business killing easy on your mind. And then, thirty three thousand feet overhead a chunk of ice the size of a beer barrel detaches from the outside of a jetliner's toilet door and hurtles down gaining terminal velocity. And at exactly the moment you are at your most content, the whole world at your feet, it crushes you like a bug on a sidewalk.'

Harry was seated now, the gun resting on his lap, his eyes fixed on those of his quarry. Was that a flicker or fear? Of looming horror? He hoped so. 'Blue Ice, general. Totally random, seems so unfair. You never see it coming.' He leaned forward to better stare into those two dead pools of nothingness. And when he spoke again his voice had hardened. 'I'm your Blue Ice, general. I wish I had the time to chat with you about old times, all those missions, all the dead and the maimed and God knows what else hatched in that evil thing you call a mind. But truth be told, I find it all a bit sickening now, I'm not like that any more.'

'But you're still going to kill me?'

Harry's smile was a whimsical one, almost sad. How many good men, all dead now, had never seen it coming, never got to meet Death face to face before crossing over and all because of this monster? 'Oh yes, general. I'm going to kill you.'

And, Harry mused, that was pretty much that. How many times had he planned this moment, revelled in the sweetness of the long delayed revenge? And now? Now it all seemed so empty, so pointless. This pathetic creature cowering in front of him was hardly worth a bullet. Inside that horrible shell of a man the creature was dead. He was staring at an empty suit of armour, the knight inside long gone.

Images floating through his mind now, threatening to cloud his vision; that night so long ago, in old Tangier, when Ramon the matador had him at his mercy, Harry wounded and bleeding and barely able to stand, Ramon staring down at him and tossing the stiletto aside and walking away because he couldn't, wouldn't, do the killing thing any longer. *No mas, no mas...*'

'Please...' The thundering in his ears slowly subsiding Harry found himself staring down at the man who now had both shaking hands raised above his head, glasses fogged from the sweat breaking out on his forehead in large drops while wide open eyes were fixed on the gun now pointed unwaveringly at a spot between his eyes. 'I...Wait! Why? Is it because of people that accidentally died? It was a *war*, for heaven's sake! The communists would have destroyed our way of life...'

'His name was Quinn,' Harry said softly, 'We called him Koos, he was the biggest of the litter and reminded me of a big bumbling kid I went to school with... I loved him and you killed him as sure as if you were there that day.'

Sensing Harry was referring to the attack that destroyed his home in Marbella the day his wife was kidnapped, the general worked at a placatory tone. Perhaps, if he played his cards right, this sentimental idiot could be manipulated, hell knows he'd done it before. 'Was it the gardener at the villa that died, you know collateral damage sometimes...'

'He was my dog,' Harry said softly. There was a new edge to his voice, a slight hardening and the general didn't like that at all. 'My beautiful red setter. We loved him like a child, Selena and I. And your men killed him and a man is supposed to do something about that.' And with that Harry lifted the heavy automatic, 'Goodbye, general.'

'WAIT!!' Something in the ashen faced man's voice had Harry hesitate, his expression saying, what?

'Diamonds,' came the stuttered response, 'Twenty one briefcases full of diamonds. I... well, we used some of it over the years but most are still left, millions of dollars. We can strike a deal...'

With a sigh Harry lowered the gun once more. He was feeling really tired now and a dull headache was starting up behind his left eye. The only thing that made him pause was the thought of all those young black faces and, if the bastard wasn't lying yet again, what that kind of money could accomplish. 'Go on,' he sighed. 'Keep it short, tell me why you should live.'

It took five minutes for the general to tell his story, the first sixty seconds haltingly as the now profusely sweating man repeatedly mopped his brow and battled with a dry throat. It was an old and familiar story, going back all the way to 1975, the Angolan civil war and Harry had heard parts of it before. The fall of the Portuguese government leading to the overnight withdrawal of the Portuguese army, the new government abandoning its African colonies. The Anglo American diamond mine abandoned by its personnel when about to be overrun by advancing communist rebels, the

Johannesburg based company asking the South African government for help. A special forces team accompanied by two senior SAP diamond squad officers hastily flown in to retrieve a king's ransom of uncut diamonds from a locked bunker they had to blow open to get access to.

Diamonds that subsequently disappeared.

When the general's story trailed off into an expectant silence it left Harry wondering how much he could trust the man, was it yet another ruse to stay alive, hope to reverse the tables when the chance came?

Perhaps some good could still come from all this? A lot could be financed should those diamonds come into the hands of a man who knew how to convert them to cold cash.

A man like Harry Dance.

But he had made up his mind. In a way he had been kidding himself, nurturing a dream of instant, gratifying, revenge, when the big picture was much more important. 'I'm not going to kill you, general. Instead I'm handing you over to people who have been dying to speak to you for a long time now.'

The general snorted, 'The Truth and Reconciliation Commission is dead and gone. We're in the New South Africa now where it's every man for himself.'

'I seem to recall your disappearance while appearing in front of that body and there are people who see that as unfinished business.' Harry paused as his ears pricked to a new noise, dismissing it after a few seconds as passing traffic in the street outside. Feeling tired now and with a growing desire to be spared the old yet still vivid memories that were threatening to swamp his senses, he went on. 'I'm going to hand you into the custody of a certain policeman who has been looking for you for a long time. Some time later, perhaps months later, there will be a short piece in the national newspapers about your conviction and long term imprisonment. I will read it with some interest and think about you for a few minutes. Then I'll turn to the sports pages and never think of you again.'

Hesitant he thought of tying the man up, getting Piet Niemand on the phone then going off to the kitchen to get a coffee, give himself time to think things over when the voice behind him told him softly to stand quite still.

Harry stood quite still.

'Raise the gun above your head pointing it to the ceiling,' Muller instructed, 'Then bring up the other arm. Slowly, that's right. Take the gun by the barrel then hold it out at arm's length and drop it.'

Harry knew it was Muller, he recognised the crisp clear tone. Acting slow and deliberately he did as told.

'Move three paces to the right while keeping your hands where I can see them.' Harry could hear the man coming closer, moving off to his side to approach the general who was, visibly relaxed, leaning back in his chair with a smile.

'Turn around,' came the order, the voice flat and soft. Harry watched as Muller stooped to retrieve the gun on the carpet. Moving slowly the hitman paused next to the seated form of the general who was restrained from rising by the man looming over him.

'The *volk* will thank you for this, my friend,' the general said hesitatingly as he glanced up uncertainly at Muller, Harry realising the man was as surprised at the presence of the gunman as he was.

The move, when it came, was so unexpected, so smooth, that not Harry nor the man in the chair saw it coming. Lifting Harry's gun in his left hand Muller placed it against the general's temple and fired.

In a lifetime of violence Harry Dance had witnessed a thousand gunshots, seen a hundred men die violently, been a party to a good few himself, but never had he witnessed death appear that suddenly, that unannounced. That callously.

The awesome voice of the big nine millimetre rang in his ears as eyes and mind struggled to process the image of what had been a man's head microseconds earlier exploding in a pulped mess of pink mist and grey gore and fragments of seared bone.

Harry winced.

Then he braced himself for the inevitable next phase.

'Did you touch anything in the room?' came the matter-of-fact question as a stunned Harry watched Muller rub the gun free of fingerprints before carefully placing it in the dead man's right hand. The assassin's own gun now tucked into his belt and nestling against his lower spine. Still too numb to move Harry shook his head as he watched the other man deftly wipe the desk, covering the areas Harry had searched earlier as he went through the dead man's papers.

'You're not after me, are you?'

Sparing Harry only a cursory glance as he scanned the rest of the room, Muller offered a wolfish smile. 'I would have liked that,' he said wryly, 'but it's a new contract. You're no longer it.'

Harry nodded, suddenly aware that the cold sweat of moments earlier was pooling at the nape of his neck, running down the small of his back in sudden rushes. Thank God for professionals, he thought grimly. An amateur would have killed him simply in revenge, the professional took emotion out of the equation.

'May I ask who ordered the hit?' Harry heard himself ask from somewhere far away. Fixed to the same spot – no call to alarm the man with the gun – Harry's eyes followed him around the room as the killer wiped the armrests of the chair Harry had sat in minutes earlier. He felt strangely neglected, a mere spectator, as quick keen eyes flitted across his person with no more interest than it spared for the furnishings.

The eyes of a professional killer who knew with deadly certainty he could deal with any foolishness the other party might inadvisably come up with.

'You'd never believe me if I told you.'

Which, Harry mused, summed up the "New South Africa" in a way only men like them could ever fathom. Nowhere was the past more difficult to predict.

'Forensics will fail to find gunpowder residue on the hand holding the gun,' Harry offered as he, acting on the polite gesture of Muller, headed for the door, the man switching off lights in their wake, leaving only a corner side lamp on. A last scan of the room leading to a satisfactory nod before the two of them headed down the hallway to the front door.

'A small technical detail that will not come up in the police investigation. In fact, I strongly doubt whether this will even get into the national newspapers.'

They had reached the end of the driveway now, the night air suddenly cool in the light sea breeze that had sprung up. Pausing at the driver's door of the now familiar American muscle car , Muller glanced across at Harry, 'Can I drop you off somewhere?'

'No, thanks. My car's parked nearby.' He hesitated before adding, 'You wore a bullet proof vest, I should have thought of that,'

The other man smiled broadly, 'Never leave home without it.'
'Must have hurt like hell.'
'Still does. But only when I laugh.'
The door unlocked he was about to get in when an afterthought had him pause, straighten up to face Harry across the roof of the car. 'I guess you wonder why I'm letting you go?'
'The thought has crossed my mind.'
'Do you remember Leon Joubert, a young medic at the time?'
A name from a distant past. Yet Harry conjured up the image of a young face as if it was yesterday. A terribly young face, hardly a shaver, pain wracked and dirt smeared with eyes wide in fear and the horror of war. 'Rhodesia, April seventy eight. The retreat from Mtoko. He was wounded, captured. We managed to get him out.'
Muller smiled, 'More correctly, you went back for him when the Dakota was already pointed for take-off, engines running. The way I heard it you had your sergeant hold a gun to the pilot's head with orders to shoot if he didn't wait for your return. Which you did, with Leon. All the while fighting off an enemy in close pursuit.'
With a deep sigh Harry shook off the memory of that distant night. 'How is he?' he asked softly.
'My cousin? He's just fine. Runs a used car lot in Germiston now.'
'Tell him I said hey.'
Muller nodded, reached for his keys. 'Let's not meet again,' he said as the engine sprung into life. With the car in gear Muller paused then leaned out the window smiling, 'Having said all that sentimental stuff, if the contract hadn't changed, I would still have killed you. Just thought I'd let you know.' And then he was off, Harry watching until the taillights disappeared around a corner, the sounds of a big car blending with the background hum of a big city.

21
CHAPTER

It was past three and Harry was glad to get out of the sweltering humidity as they stepped into the cool embrace of a downtown bar. At that hour the large room with its wheezing air conditioners and tired looking furnishings was empty of customers, the lunch time crowd having moved on to better pastures. The lone barman, a reedy middle aged battler with pock marked sallow skin lowered his newspaper as Piet Niemand dragged over a barstool. 'What'll be it bud?' he rasped wearily in a voice that suggested a thousand summers, all of them hard and sad.

Then he lifted his gaze to settle on the frowning features of the cop and underwent an instant miraculous change. 'Sorry, captain, I didn't recognise you there for a moment. It's the bad light in here.'

Niemand grunted and motioned Harry and Vusi to pull up stools and join him at the counter. 'Three beers,' he growled, 'Cold Castles. And a double Johnnie Walker, hold the ice.'

For the uninitiated it would have been easy to assume the detective was ordering for all of them but Harry knew better. He ordered a beer for himself and Vusi settled for a Coke.

'Now,' Niemand said as he downed the first of his beers with what seemed like a single gulp, 'Let's talk turkey. There was something important you wanted to discuss?' He was about to add the bit about being a busy man but both men knew that wasn't true. Not any longer, anyway. Being suspended, waiting for that loaded gun of an enquiry, does that to a man.

'A little business deal,' Harry said conversationally, 'something that might give the old pension a nice little boost. But first, let's talk about that night at the house, the night the general died.'

'Suicide, I believe the coroner called it,' Niemand corrected him, as he waved a waiter over for a refill.

'Of course it was,' Harry agreed deciding to have another himself, the temperature outside now in the high thirties range where a man could die of thirst. He leaned closer. 'The bodyguard at the general's house was alive when I left him,' he said softly. 'Sleeping off a dose of ketamine. Yet his body was found, where I had left him, with several bullet holes, all from a nine mill, much like the one on your belt there...'

The big man sighed, reached for his second beer. 'He resisted arrest.'

'He was unconscious.'

'He had Jannie Smit's watch on his wrist. I recognised it from the old 32 Battalion inscription on the back. He was there when Jannie was killed, fed to that crocodile.'

Harry nodded. It all made sense.

'You were close, weren't you?' he asked softly. His beer still untouched he picked it up and took a sip, the icy liquid momentarily catching at the back of his throat.

'He was my nephew,' Niemand said, 'My late sister's only child. I was responsible for him.' After a while he added. 'They offered me counselling but after I'd screwed her twice there seemed little point in carrying on.'

There seemed little to add and they sat like that in silence for a while, the only sounds the clash of pool balls somewhere at back and the sudden rush of traffic noise as a customer came in from the street.

They were in a working man's bar just off the harbour side of the Esplanade and the steady whirr of the ceiling fans mingled with the hum of traffic outside, the afternoon's racing results silently rolling off the corner TV screen, the barman polishing glasses while studiously avoiding glancing their way, being accused of snooping. Behind the bar came the clink of bottles as a young man in a sweat stained singlet stacked beers into the fridges, surfacing at intervals to wipe his brow and take a pull from a can of Coke on the counter.

From further back came the sounds of activity in the kitchen, a hint of fries wafting lazily across.

Bruce Springsteen on the radio, Streets of Philadelphia; taking it slow.

Harry reckoned he'd been in a thousand bars just like this one, different parts of the world, different drinking companions but somehow the same.

Music on the radio, foam on his beer. He liked it.

The big man clearing his throat, irate fingers tapping on the beer stained table had him sigh, bring him back to the present and business at hand.

'What would you say if I told you I knew where a fortune in uncut diamonds were waiting to be collected by an enterprising team including yourself.'

'As a police officer sworn to uphold the law I'd have to read you your rights before taking you in.'

'What if I added these are diamonds stolen back in 1975 by right wing factions who have been using it to finance a mercenary enterprise run – until his untimely demise – by the late general. Money used to run the Savannah operation that led to the death of your nephew and several other innocent lives. A ruthless band of right wing renegades out there and for hire, all financed by the general and used to provide protection for ventures such as the kidnapping of those kids?'

'And you know this...?'

'The general told me, just before he died.' Before the policeman could interrupt, Harry hastened to add. 'He gave me the details, all of it. Hoping it would save his life.'

There was a moment's silence as the big man sipped his beer, the level in the glass dropping dramatically with what seemed like a long single gulp. They waited for the burp that usually followed this display before Harry went on. 'It will need detailed planning and a team of close knit and dedicated professionals to liberate these diamonds, set them to good use.'

'Good use?'

'The lost children. Vusi and I are planning to buy Halali, set the place up as a refuge for those kids we rescued. A sort of retirement venture that will also provide us with that South African home we have come to miss.'

'Why me?'

'Two reasons: I feel I can trust you, God knows enough has happened between us to build that. Secondly, you are a man of many contacts, right here in Natal. We will need that if this enterprise is to have any chance of success. Just imagine yourself, a few weeks from now, sitting by the pool at Halali, watching the sun set over the river, listening to the fish eagles screeching as they swoop over the cool still water...'

'Fishing. I like fishing...'

'Plenty of fish in that river,' Harry said, 'Isn't that so, Vusi?'

'How the hell should I know?' Vusi said, 'I was shut away in a barn, remember?'

'Still, you grew up around here didn't you?' Harry countered, a motion of the hands saying *give me a little backup here, for chrissake!*

'...and hunting, how about hunting?' Piet Niemand said thoughtfully.

'Of course,' Harry agreed, 'We'd have to be selective though, perhaps limit it to the old bucks on their way out, manage our stock so to speak. It *is* after all a game farm.'

'And parties,' Niemand wondered aloud, the big man immersed in the picture, 'with lots of pretty girls and good food, booze...'

'Quite,' Harry hastened to add, 'Once we open to the public again. We'll certainly have a Christmas party for the kids.' *You would be a perfect Santa* he mused, keeping the thought to himself.

'And fireworks?'

Harry nodded. 'There will be fireworks!'

'I love fireworks,' the big man said whimsically, draining the last of his beer without seeming to notice. 'I'm in. Let's hear the details.'

'There's a slight problem,' Harry said softly, glancing at Vusi who smiled wolfishly.

'Oh?'

'Guards. Mercenaries, who may by now know what happened to their boss, maybe figuring to keep the goods for themselves.'

Niemand nodded, 'I should have known it sounds too easy.' He shrugged, took another gulp of beer, mulled it over for a minute. 'I take it the diamonds are here, in Durban?'

Harry nodded. 'In a safe house in Berea, the headquarters for their mercenary operations.'

'How many?'

'The general said four. Of course, he could have been lying...'

'I hate that, people lying,' Piet Niemand sighed and downed the last of his beer.

Five days later.

In its heyday Ridge Road in the Durban suburb of Berea was where many of the city's wealthy white businessmen and professionals had their homes. On the crest of the low hills that surround the city it offered sweeping views of downtown with the bay further out. On the other side rose the lush green folds of the Valley of a Thousand Hills with Pinetown and beyond it Pietermaritzburg lost in the hazy distance. A cool sea breeze would blow in the late afternoons offering welcome respite from the sweltering heat of the smog bound urban maze sprawling way below.

These days the old colonial homes had been largely replaced by high rise blocks of flats as well as upmarket business addresses but the languid atmosphere of the place still prevailed, in a way trapped by the wealth of tropical growth that was everywhere. But there were still signs of the Durban of long ago, set in lush gardens and surrounded by high walls and locked steel gates, some of those stately homes survived.

Hlangana was such a home. Built of blue granite blocks mined from the foothills of the Drakensberg in the early twentieth century for a prominent banker, it featured alcoves with wood framed small pane windows, a large patio that surrounded the house on three sides and a Spanish style tiled roof with generous overhanging eaves that made for deep dark and cool shadows in the heat of the day.

A sweeping circular driveway leads up to the main building situated fifty yards from the road below while a broad staircase led up to the imposing solid stinkwood front door where the visitor's approach would be monitored by the impersonal eye of a CCTV camera. Why, in that sub-tropical climate, the house would feature two chimneys, was a mystery possibly explained by the architect's sense of aesthetic beauty.

Mounted to the side of the one was a high radio/television mast that seemed equally incongruous seeing the close proximity of local broadcasting stations and the wide international cover they provided.

A large satellite receiving dish placed on the slope of the roof pointed north.

Stables and a carriage house had been converted to garages and were located on the far side of a brick paved courtyard. The whole surrounded by two acres of lawns, tropical shrubs and trees. Eight foot high white faced brick walls could do with a new coat of whitewash but the double strands of high voltage wire mounted on top looked well maintained and the casual observer would be inclined to heed the warning signs placed at regular intervals on that perimeter wall.

Double steel gates were electronically operated under the watchful eye of yet another CCTV camera.

A small plaque next to the gate said Phoenix Executive Solutions.

It took four minutes and thirty five seconds after pressing the buzzer next to the gate's intercom for the heavy doors to swing open and allow the panel van from the Thekwini Municipality Water and Sanitation Department to roll on through. The man in the passenger seat made a careful note of the time interval in a small notebook he returned to a pocket of his blue worker's overalls.

He produced a mobile phone and appeared to be speaking into it. In reality he was taking rapid sequence photos of the layout of the place. As they approached the steps where a man was waiting for them he stowed it away. 'One of these days,' his companion said, 'All this shit will be obsolete. We'll have mini remote controlled drones to do all the surveying.'

The man did not step up to the van, waited for both of them to get out, the expression on his bearded face wary, the hand clutching something in a pocket of his lightweight bush jacket very still. A professional the driver noted with approval. Definitely the right address. He liked that, hated working with amateurs, they were dangerously unpredictable.

'What's this about a water leak?' the man asked, still blocking their way. 'We haven't had any problem here.' The voice was gruff, the accent unmistakeably Afrikaner.

'This *is* 135 Ridge Road?' Harry Dance asked, frowning as he scratched his head while peering through half moon glasses at a clipboard stacked with paperwork.

Hesitating, the man nodded. *Ja*, but I told the lady who phoned there's no problem here, so why don't...'

'Sorry, sir,' Harry interrupted, 'But there's a major water leak somewhere in the neighbourhood and the engineers down at central think it's right here. That's why they phoned to let you know we're coming to inspect.' Selena, Harry thought with a suppressed smile, doing her no nonsense long suffering municipal secretary's voice with easy aplomb.

'There's also the question of the possible leak from the sanitation sink,' the hitherto silent black man lumping the heavy looking case of plumbing tools said, looking at Harry, 'The contamination Mr Matthee mentioned this morning...'

'What's the boy say?'

Ignoring the racist slur Harry explained that E coli (he hoped he pronounced that right) had been isolated from a drinking water specimen taken from the neighbourhood. 'Now, sir, if you wouldn't mind showing us to your water meter and then we'll have to check all taps in the house and take water samples.

'What's in that case?' the man who gave the name of "Smit" said, pointing to the heavy metal box Vusi had dumped on the ground. Harry's indignant explanation that it was their tools met with no joy and Vusi was forced to open the lid while Smit peered over the contents. Satisfied that no assault weapons or bazookas were hidden amongst the assorted spanners, washers and pipes the man relented and led the way to the water meter situated at a corner of the front garden. On the way over Harry counted two cars, both Land Cruisers, parked in the garages while a small red Volkswagen Golf was parked at back in the shade of a large jacaranda tree. No other sign of people about, the house shuttered and quiet.

No dogs, unless they were tied up at back which Harry thought unlikely.

Walking three paces behind and softly cursing as he lugged the heavy metal toolbox, Vusi also took in the surroundings, knowing they would compare notes afterwards.

It took two minutes for Harry to check the readings on the meter, carefully recording his findings on an official looking page which, on closer inspection, would have proved to be from an Excel program with a suitable Thekwini label skilfully applied courtesy of Selena's computer skills.

'All seems OK here,' Harry said climbing to his feet with a grunt while putting a hand to his lower back, stretching and muttering something about it killing him. 'Now let's check the taps.'

'And the toilets too,' Vusi reminded him as Smit led them back to the house.

As they approached the front door swung open to reveal a second man, younger than the first, who was dressed in a singlet and shorts, rubber flip flops on his feet. The logo on the top said Welcome to St Lucia, the wary look behind the shades said let's make this quick. Harry had him for about early thirties, the tattoo on the forearm said Parachute Battalion, the jagged scar on the thigh shrapnel. As he waved them inside he never turned his back and Harry reckoned there would be a 9 millimetre tucked in his belt.

Pausing for a moment to allow his eyes to adjust to the cool darkness Harry took in the modern Ikea furnishings and the large tapestry on the wall. To the side an open archway led to a reception area where a secretary was typing away, sparing them barely a glance.

Several comfortable easy chairs, magazines on occasional tables and a small bar in a corner. All tasteful, all expensive, the whole hinting at the hand of a decorator.

No customers. Harry reckoned most of the business deals would be done in the executive suites of international hotels. This place was more a HQ to plan and run operations from. The radio room – the range of equipment he glanced through a door left ajar suggested no less – also featured a control centre of sorts judging by the flickering monitor screens showing different views of the house and surroundings.

Four bedrooms, each with en-suite bathroom and a large dining room with an impressive yellow wood table that seated twelve with ease. At Harry's guess it would serve as a conference room. All sparsely but tastefully furnished. The odd antique blending in rather nicely with more modern pieces.

Very few pictures on the walls, certainly nothing to hint at the kind of far flung hellholes where the employees of Phoenix Executive Solutions would ply their deadly trade.

Nothing to make the international businessmen who would be the typical client nervous or bring on a sudden attack of guilt or conscience.

Taking their time, an impatient Smit breathing down their necks, Harry and Vusi inspected each and every water outlet and toilet, putting on a show of taking samples amidst much muted muttering and significant nodding. Harry thankful neither of the two occupants seemed to have the slightest background knowledge of plumbing which would have quickly rumbled their little charade.

All the time making careful mental notes of the layout and the kind of security in place. Two bedrooms had signs of occupancy and Harry guessed the two men so far encountered lived on the premises, the posters and photos of combat scenarios a no-brainer and a final affirmation of the kind of business Phoenix was into.

Various other rooms were of little interest until they reached the study. A sign on the door said Private and at an unseen cue from Harry, Vusi who had been following close behind stumbled and sprawled across the narrow corridor temporarily blocking a cursing Smit. It gave Harry the chance to open the door before the man could stop him.

It was a surprisingly large room, oak panelled and furnished in richly coloured tapestry and large padded armchairs facing an ornately carved oak desk. The walls were lined with bookshelves bearing leather bound volumes and, more to Harry's interest, was the large safe in a corner.

The diamonds, if they really existed, *had* to be in that safe.

'Come out of there! Can't you read?!' A livid Smit was manhandling a still crouching Vusi out of his way as he angrily waved at Harry to leave the room, brusquely pulling the door shut behind him. 'No fucking tap in there, you idiot!'

Evidently deciding that he had tolerated this nonsense long enough he announced they had now seen everything and it was time to take their silly little tool set and get in their funny little van and get the hell off the property.

Minutes later, driving down Ridge Road and heading for their hotel Harry and Vusi compared notes. 'Nice touch,' Vusi said 'the false teeth giving you that lisp, the half glasses you peer over and the stuff Selena rubbed into your skin to give you that weather beaten look. Doubt whether your own mother would have recognised you.'

'Let's not forget the dirty fingernails and the smelly overalls,' Harry said before adding, 'They might not have recognised me but I did make the older one who called himself Smit.'

Vusi's raised eyebrows said oh?

'Heywood, Jack Heywood. At least that was his name when last our paths crossed on a Recce training camp more than twenty years ago. A hard man.'

'Think he recognised you?'

Harry shook his head, 'No. We wouldn't have left that house if he had.'

Vusi nodded; as usual Harry had been right in taking the precaution of their elaborate disguises for the reconnaissance of the place. But then, he had learned over time, all these erstwhile mercenaries and special forces types had crossed paths at some stage or another. 'Only two of them living there, right?'

'Check. The general had said four but at a guess two have disappeared already, now that there's a chance of the police taking an interest. The secretary still being there means it's an ongoing project, Phoenix's mercenaries running contracts out there and money coming in. She'd work office hours though, I suspect the little red Golf parked around the back is hers.'

'Electrically wired walls, heavy remote controlled gates, electronic surveillance.' Vusi counted the security features on his fingers.

'But only two men,' Harry said, no-one monitoring those screens. And no dogs, a mistake that.'

Vusi nodded, 'Still, there would be an alarm system. What about arms?'

'Both were carrying but handguns only. I suspect they pick up the hardware in the areas where the contracts are, get it from arms dealers over there.'

'In other words, people like us.' They both chuckled at that one. 'Still,' Harry said, 'you never can tell. There may well be an AK47 or two in that house.'

Temporarily stuck in traffic at the bottom of Smith street they sat in silence for a while, both men mulling over the details of Harry's latest crazy plan. As the light finally changed to green it was Vusi was spoke, 'When do we go?'

'With the boss dead I reckon they're about to jump ship at any moment, probably waiting for whoever else is out on a job to return so they can split the spoils. I reckon we go now.'

Vusi nodded. 'Let's hope we can get the stooges to take the bait,' he added as he fished out his mobile phone, dialled a number from memory.

'There's that,' Harry admitted.

Tsotsi was hanging around a street corner not far from Mama Tembu's *shebeen* when the call came. Digging out the new mobile phone Harry had given him he glanced at the caller ID, said hello. It was Vusi.

'Are you in position?'

'*Yebo,* I can see the *shebeen* from here. She is inside there.'

'Good. Do you remember what we agreed, what you must tell her?'

'I'm not stupid!' the young man protested, 'I'll tell her just like Boss Harry told me to.'

Vusi sighed, sooner or later he would have to start rehabilitating the little gangster, 'Good. Go now.' With that he hung up and turned to Harry. 'What now?'

'Now we wait.'

It was cool inside the bar, cool and dark. Pausing for a moment to let his eyes adjust to the light, Tsotsi picked out the towering figure of the Nigerian where he was propping up the counter across the room. A survey of the room showed that the schoolboys were not at their usual table, at a guess still at school. Not being much of a school attendee himself. Tsotsi didn't know, shrugged it off as unimportant. Striding up to the tall bodyguard he announced that he wanted to see Mama Tembu, had something important to tell her.

The Nigerian stared down at him incredulously, 'What could you possibly have that she would be interested in?'

'Knowledge,' the street urchin said proudly, raising himself to his full height that had him reach almost to the man's navel. 'I know plenty,' he added, 'where *big* money is sitting. Just waiting for someone to pick it up!'

'Nonsense!' The Nigerian laughed, waving Tsotsi away only to curse loudly as the latter made a break for the door of Mama Tembu's office. Alarmed by the loud bashing at her door accompanied by audible blows and the wailing protests of a youngster, the lady yanked open the door to stare with incredulity at the two standing there. 'What the hell?'

'Sorry, boss. He's very quick. I'll throw him out.'

He had Tsotsi by the scruff of his neck and was dragging the kicking and shouting youngster away when a sharp command from Mama Tembu had him halt. 'What did you just say?' She was addressing Tsotsi who angrily shook himself free from the bouncer's grip.

'Mr Naidoo,' he replied angrily. 'I know where he hid his money.'

The tableau remained freeze framed for a moment then Mama Tembu motioned for the young man to step into her office, ordering the Nigerian to fetch her a whisky, Tsotsi indicating a beer wouldn't hurt either. At a stare from both parties he reluctantly changed the order to a Coke.

Inside the office she waved him to a visitor's chair. 'Tell me more,' she said in a voice she hoped sounded friendly and reassuring.

Twenty minutes later, having sent the young informant back into the bar with instructions to give him a meal, she phoned Mr Tammany.

At that moment the Minister of Customs and Immigration was sitting in his office contemplating his future. A future that suddenly seemed already behind him. Not only had the lucrative deal with the Chinese fallen through but he was now being blackmailed by some shady Customs official in Mozambique and there was the lingering unease that Mr Heidmann could have taken out some insurance against the kind of event that had befallen his late business partner.

Only too aware that the President had the habit of changing his appointees frequently, each close associate getting a chance at the feeding trough of nepotism and corruption, his own chance of enriching himself was now all but over. No doubt someone had already "bought" his job and notice would be delivered at any moment. With a sigh he picked up the phone. 'Yes?'

'It's Tembu. Are you on a secure line?'

Tammany groaned, 'I told you I don't have the money right now. just give me another...'

'Shut up and listen. I have information about where a cool few million dollars, US dollars, is sitting just waiting to be collected. Money that idiot Naidoo got from the Chinese. It's right here, in a house in Berea with only a single guard looking after the place.'

'Naidoo?'

'Oh for God's sake! I know it was you who had him killed just like I know you were behind the killing of that white businessman, Heidmann. It doesn't matter, what matters is we can get our hands on that money!'

'How do you know this?' Tammany had got up from his desk to move to the window, on the way checking that his office door was closed,

'A boy I know happened to be one of the ones taken by Naidoo and the Chinese. While held prisoner he overheard a conversation between Naidoo and a Chinese woman about the payment.'

'Tell me more...' Tammany said as he lit a cigarette, aware that his pulse was quickening. This could be his way out.

He listened for a long time in silence as Mama Tembu carefully laid out the plan, finally asking why she was sharing this with him. 'I've checked out the house,' came the ready reply. 'At a guess it will have elaborate security measures and, as I've said, a guard on duty. The best way in is with a search warrant and what goes with it.'

'A search warrant?! On what premise?'

'You *are* the Minister of Customs and Immigartion, dear brother-in-law. I'm sure you'll think of something. Besides, isn't one of your brothers a local judge?'

22
CHAPTER

Jamie Watson grinned in delight as Selena peered around the door to enquire how her favourite wildlife photographer was doing.

'Come into my parlour, you pretty woman,' he said, holding out both arms to be rewarded with a hug and a kiss. 'Harry too! And bearing gifts! Is that champagne I see before me?'

A smiling Harry closed the door of the private hospital suite behind him and set about opening the bottle of Cinzano Spumante, a personal favourite. A still weak Jamie had cleared space on a visitor's chair for Selena, a stack of magazines being unceremoniously relegated to the carpet.

'The nurse told us you've made a speedy recovery and should be out of here soon. The ironic thing, of course, is that it was the fast action of Colonel Ehlers that saved your life, giving you that anti-venom.'

The young man, pale against the white of the hospital sheets, grimaced as he reached for the glass of bubbly Harry was holding out. 'Probably the only time in his whole life he helped another human being. What happened to him, anyway?'

'Killed by a lion,' Harry said. 'Happens all the time in Africa.'

Jamie thought this over for a few seconds, decided it wasn't worth pursuing and asked about the children.

'Currently still on the ship in Maputo Harbour,' Selena said, 'while we arrange to bring them back and find a more permanent home for them. We have arranged for them to be properly clothed and fed and Harry feels they are at present better off there than being brought back to Durban prematurely.'

'They are street kids,' Harry explained, 'runaways all with the exception of Lukas, Vusi's son. Without some proper measures they'll be back on the streets in a flash.'

'Vusi...?'

'The black man you photographed climbing out of the truck. Our associate.'

Watson nodded and accepted a refill of the champagne. 'Thanks for returning my photographs and notes. The editor is planning to break the story in a special edition this Friday. Should cause quite a stir.' A thought made him sit upright in the bed, carefully set the glass down on the side table. 'You said something about making arrangements for these kids?'

Harry nodded as he pulled up a chair. 'We've done some research since we last saw you, at least Selena did. Tell him, darling.'

'At the last government survey in 1993 there were at least 9,000 homeless, runaway, black children in South Africa. Virtually all were boys with a median age of 13 to 15 years. Some as young as seven. Sixty percent of them estimated to be HIV infected. The country is estimated to have more than a million AIDS orphans, a significant source of these street kids...'

'And most seen as criminals by the public,' Jamie added.

'At the last census there were ten thousand white children in state-registered subsidized children's homes with no government facilities provided for black children. If we consider that in South Africa the black population outnumber the whites by about five to one, it follows that there are fifty thousand black children out there right now desperately needing our help. *Fifty thousand!*'

'In the research for my story I looked into all that,' Jamie said, 'what you've said is sadly true. Little has changed for the black street kids in the New South Africa but there is an increasing number of private charities stepping up. The YMCA has been helping for going on a century, now. It's the *need* that's so overwhelming.'

'What puzzles me,' Harry said, 'is why they're all boys. Virtually no female street kids.'

'In the African culture girls are from an early age placed in the role of looking after younger siblings and greater effort is made to keep them in the family. Sadly this is not the case for the boys who all too often are simply seen as a burden and dispensable. In the squatter camps and black townships alcoholism, poverty, abuse, are all factors in the disintegration of families. By the time they run away eighty percent of these boys will have suffered physical, sexual or emotional abuse. Many have no concept of time, don't know how old they are. They can only tell you how many Christmases they've been on the street. Then there's the glue sniffing ...'

'The horror...' Selena said softly as an exhausted Jamie leaned back against the cushions, a thin film of sweat on his brow testimony to the fact that the paralysing effect of the poison hadn't quite relinquished its grip as yet.

They sat there in silence for a while as the young man's laboured breathing slowly returned to normal. It was Harry who finally spoke, his voice flat, something in his eyes the young man hadn't noticed before. Regret perhaps? But about what? 'We, Selena and I, have decided to do something about all that, a new start for us.'

'It will cost money,' Jamie said wistfully, 'lots of it.'

'I reckon we have that covered,' Harry said. He did not elaborate, thought it better the young man did not know too much about their modus operandi. He was, after all, a reporter.

'Ever wonder what happens when, after a long day in the field, those three clear notes sound on the hunt master's bugle, Jamie? Ha, la, li! The end of the hunt, end of the day's killing, time for the hunters to come home. But what then? What comes after?'

They watched as Harry reached for Selena's hand and something she saw in his expression brought the hint of a sad smile to her lips. She thought of how at the end of the Great War the remnants of a generation, a lost generation, came home to find all wars lost, all gods dead. Nothing left to believe in....

Noticing Jamie's quizzical look she shook her head, 'Nothing. Just lost in thought there for a moment.'

But Harry, lost in his own world – a world of yesterdays and the fool's dusty death – didn't notice. '... they tell stories, Jamie, that's what old hunters do. Sit around a camp fire and tell each other lies...'

He smiled and squeezed his wife's hand to let her know he was OK. 'I want to tell my story, Jamie. A kind of cleansing of the soul. And I want you to hear it and, if you will, write it. But first, before we sit down for that chat, there's a matter of unfinished business.'

And with that he rose to bid a pensive Jamie Watson a speedy recovery and for the journalist to wonder what he had just been told. And what that look in the eyes of an ever enigmatic Harry Dance signified. No regrets, he decided, that wasn't the look. *Resolve.* That was it. Or perhaps hope?

The raid went down at ten to midnight the next day. A police patrol car, lights flashing, pulled up at the gates of Hlangana, two uniformed policemen stepping up to the intercom. Seated in the back was Tammany and next to him, dressed in a black pants suit and looking tense, was Mama Tembu. The second car, an unmarked prowler, spilled out Detective Sergeant Gericke, a burly black plainclothes cop with a shaved head and the Nigerian who looked out of place in a striped Adidas tracksuit and trainers.

Sitting in the van parked fifty yards further along the road and in the cover of the deep shadow cast by a giant marula tree Harry studied the approach with interest. Selena was in the driver's seat with Vusi at back. All were dressed in green overalls adorned with reflecting white strips and the red logos on the chest and back said paramedics.

Where the side panels on the van had recently indicated Thekwini Water and Sanitation Dept it now read Ambulance in bold red against the white the vehicle had since been re-painted in. Appropriate red and white roof mounted flashing lights completed the picture. Ever the stickler for detail, Harry had even scrounged a siren from a local scrap yard. He reckoned it would be good for the getaway.

They had been parked there since eight that evening, taking turns to rest in the back while they waited for the call from Tsotsi who had been keeping surveillance on Mama Tembu. The shebeen queen never left the premises of her business before the crack of dawn and Harry figured any departure before then could only mean the game was on. For good measure he had Piet Niemand, through his many contacts, keep an eye on the movements of the minister.

When the big man phoned Harry with the news a search warrant had been issued for a raid on Number 135 Ridge Road, also known as Hlangana, it was all the confirmation they needed. After pacifying Niemand who was enraged by "that snake, Gericke," being part of the enemy camp all along, Harry had persuaded him to take up his pre-arranged position at the back of the property, notify them of any attempt by the target to escape along that route.

Under their overalls all were wearing Kevlar vests, even Niemand had reluctantly agreed to take one, muttering that it was for "pussies" and that he had never needed one to date. In each of the bulky black canvas paramedic holdalls was a snub nosed Heckler and Koch machine pistol with spare clip and several stun grenades as well as tear gas canisters and a gas mask. In addition Harry carried his Beretta while Vusi was similarly armed, Selena taking comfort from the Taser in a side pocket of her overalls.

A lifetime of experience in this kind of venture had taught Harry that an adequate medical kit should always be part of the equipment and a well stocked such bag was stored in the back. It *was*, after all, an ambulance.

At their final rehearsal Piet Niemand had expressed great interest at where the hell Harry had managed to get hold of the kind of hardware – he referred to it as "highly illegal weapons" – he now saw displayed along with several other suspect items. Harry's explanation that, in an earlier life, he may or may not have been a sort of weapons supplier and thus had contacts, was met with a grunt of disapproval.

In a muted display of scorn Niemand turned down the offer of a machine pistol, stating that his trusty police issue nine millimetre had always done the job quite nicely, thank you.

Inside the house Smit, dressed only in a pair of gym shorts, was staring at the video screen with mounting incredulity. Jesus Christ! Just another two days before the rest of the team returned from that contract in Baghdad with the big pay packet and now this!

'Jerry!' he shouted over his shoulder at the other man who had emerged from his own room, rubbing his eyes. 'It's the fucking cops! I'll hold them off, open the safe, the keys are in the general's desk, top left side drawer. Get the strongbox and ...'

He fell silent as the police prowler reversed and then accelerated, the car's re-enforced steel bull bar taking the gates clean off their hinges as the vehicle crashed through in a mass of tangled steel and smashing glass from the headlights. Momentarily stunned Smit watched as the two vehicles raced on to screech to a halt at the steps to the front door. Numbly reaching for the AK 47 his young compatriot held out he was finally spurred into action as the figure of Mama Tembu and Tammany alighted in the glare of the motion activated security lights.

'This is no fucking raid! It's the money they're after.' He shouted as the first of the uniformed policemen hammered at the front door, ordering the occupants to come out with their hands raised.

In the light he could see both cops were wearing body armour, one hefting a twelve bore pump action shotgun, the other a handgun. Fanning out further back two others, both in civilian dress, had handguns.

'Take this, you bastards!' Smit shouted and fired a long burst at the front door, the noise deafening in the enclosed space of the front hall. The nearest cop went down in a hail of splintered wood, flying glass and a pink mist of blood, the second man staggering back under the impact of the bullets slamming into his protective vest.

There was a moment's silence as the firing stopped, Smit scanning the monitor screen only to see it go black as Gericke shot out the camera.

Switching off the hallway lights to leave the front of the house in darkness he moved to an alcove window and carefully peered around the shelter of the heavy drapes. The body of one cop lay sprawled over the steps with the other back at the car and getting something from the trunk. The two unknown males were crouched behind their car and he could see both had guns. Tembu and Tammany had disappeared from view and at a guess had moved around the side of the house. In confirmation he heard the tinkling of breaking glass as a window somewhere at back was smashed, followed quickly by two rapid fire gunshots.

'Jerry!' he shouted over his shoulder, 'watch out!'

'I got the fat one!' came the answering call, 'the other one has ducked out of sight.'

Turning his attention back to what was happening outside the front door he was in time to see the uniformed cop lift a rocket launcher from the boot, line it up at the front door. Jesus! What kind of cops were these!?

Desperately diving for the cover of the reception desk he was too late as a huge fireball took out the front door and a large chunk of the hallway's back wall, the explosion deafening followed by the crackle and pop of an instant fire. Stunned by the blast and with blood rushing in his ears Smit could see the blurred images of figures stumbling over the rubble, his shell shocked mind unable to register their sounds. There was something wrong with his left arm and as he gazed down he could see it was at an angle and with the white glistening of a protruding bone.

Training took over. These men were not about to take prisoners.

Neither was he.

Rolling onto his back and fighting off a sea of pain he raised the AK 47 and fired a short burst, cutting the figure of the last man inside almost in half. Then, with a superhuman show of sheer grit, he climbed to his feet and set off in pursuit of the rest.

One hundred yards away Harry Dance listened to the static over the police channel. Routine chatter, nothing about a shooting in Berea. So far so good. Picking up his mobile he dialled Piet Niemand's number. He knew the other man would be monitoring the police radio channels as arranged but all their team's communications would be by the more secure personal phones. Once they went into action they would revert to their personal short wave two way radios.

'Sounds like all hell has broken loose inside there,' the big man growled.

'We stick to the plan,' Harry said. 'You monitor the police radio, if any units respond forestall them at the front using your official lights etc. Tell them a armed response team is on the way. Any sign of someone coming out the back way?'

'Nope.'

'OK.'

'When do we go in?'

Harry glanced across at Selena who was studying him with that old mocking smile, the one that said sure you're up to this, big boy? Behind her he could just make out Vusi's silent questioning stare.

'No time like now,' Harry said, bracing himself as Selena slammed the van into gear and floored the accelerator.

Inside the study, working in a frenzied haste, Jerry had the safe open and was staring at its crowded contents in bewilderment. As a junior member of the organisation he had never been present when it had been opened but knew it was where the cash was stored. What confronted him was stacks of US hundred dollar notes, in ten thousand dollar bundles, a multitude of other currencies reflecting the countries Phoenix conducted business in and a number of files and sealed official looking manila envelopes. On a lower rack some small arms and ammunition clips, a handful of well thumbed passports.

And a large black steel strongbox. No key but it opened to his feverish touch.

Jerry Bridges had once seen a movie where such a box was opened. The cinema goer never got to see what its contents was, just the golden glow that suffused the enraptured faces of the men who stared down at it.

The glow from the box was not a golden one; more the dazzling multicoloured light from a thousand twinkling stars. All winking and enticing and saying all yours, buddy.

Diamonds. More than he ever imagined could be together in one enclosed space.

Seconds earlier he had heard the explosion from the front of the house but reckoned it was Smittie tossing one of the grenades he always seemed to have close. But now he could hear the sound of heavy boots in the corridor – his mate was barefoot – and an urgent whispering. Slamming the box shut, he turned just in time to see a cop in a blood spattered uniform lunge into view, raising a submachine gun. The two men fired simultaneously, Jerry hitting the policeman in the neck as the other man's burst took him across the belly and spun him into a corner from where, as he lay dying, he could just make out the fast blurring shape of the strongbox and all it represented.

So close. So close...

From where she was standing immediately outside the shattered window Tammany had climbed through before he got shot, Mama Tembu considered her options. There was little doubt there was serious money inside that house, those men – by now it was clear there were at least two of them – were guarding something big. Uncle Cecil was dead, she could see that from there, his fat torso a mess of congealing blood and spilled guts, glazed eyes staring unseeingly at nothing at all. Standing motionless she listened. There was a momentary lull in the fire fight and she reckoned, with a little luck...

A sudden noise made her turn, raising the gun in her hand only to lower it as she recognised her Nigerian bodyguard. 'Lovelace,' she whispered urgently, 'I want to take what's in that house. You lead the way.' Grabbing him by the arm to push him through the window she hesitated as an ambulance with screaming siren and flashing lights screeched to a halt at the front of the house, paramedics shouting at each other as they came running.

The Nigerian was already inside the room and moving cautiously with the aid of a flashlight he held at arm's length next to his handgun like he'd seen them do in the movies, Tembu about to follow when a voice behind her brought her up short.

'You don't learn, do you? Drop the gun.'

Standing quite still, her back to the voice, the gun suddenly heavy in her sweat lined palm, Mama Tembu said, 'It's *you*, isn't it? That bitch who Tasered me.'

'Bitch is such a strong word,' Selena said softly. 'I prefer "lady."'

'I suppose you've got a gun?'

Selena smiled, 'You never can tell.'

'*Bitch!*' Tembu snarled and whirled, raising the automatic in one smooth movement as Selena shot her twice, through the heart, a tight double tap grouping she thought Harry would have approved of.

Methodically moving through the rooms starting from the front of the house, covering one another as each room was cleared in turn, Harry and Vusi heard the shots from the side of the house and seconds later Selena's reassuring voice came over the small personal two way radios they were now using. Mama Tembu was dead, she said, but her bodyguard was somewhere inside the house.

She was wrong; realising his employer was lying dead in a flower bed the man decided this job was for suckers and, moving to a window in a vacant and seemingly undisturbed room directly across the corridor, slid open a window and quickly faded away into the night.

'Go back to the van and wait there, keep the engine running.' Harry wanted to add they were coming out soon but then he didn't know, did he? He checked whether Niemand was still in position and cursed when there was no reply from the big man's radio. There was no time to worry about that now and with Vusi close behind he entered the next room.

Smit was sitting with his back against the wall, a blood smear indicating where he had slid down. The eyes dark pools in a face gone deadly white.

The slump of his body suggested he hadn't much left to give. 'Harry Dance,' he said with a tired shake of the head. 'I should have recognised you the other day.' Glancing down at where his right hand rested on the carpet he reached for the AK 47 lying there.

'Don't,' Harry said, shaking his head. 'You can still be saved. Why do it?'

'It's a living,' the wounded man replied, the smile ghastly.

'Dying isn't much of a living.'

Stepping over the shards of broken glass and shattered furniture Harry picked up the rifle, motioned Smit to remain still and followed Vusi into the next room.

At that moment, crouching at the back door they had forced, Detective Sergeant Gericke and the black detective who went by the name of Duncan Cele, were in muted but heated discussion. The issue was who was to be the point man. Being of senior rank Gericke thought it should be Cele, who disagreed. Things came to a head when Cele decided that this whole dangerous business was a criminal affair and that he no longer wanted part of it. With that he turned to walk away and Gericke shot him in the back.

Nobody was going to walk away. Raising his police issue R4 assault rifle he started down the corridor leading to the front of the house where the firing had come from, all the while cursing that they had not had the foresight to bring radios. Then again, it was supposed to be a walk in the park, wasn't it?

Instinctively he knew that bastard, Harry Dance, had to be behind the whole thing.

Harry and Vusi were paused outside the door to the study when the command brought them up short. 'Stand quite still!'

Turning they saw Gericke at the end of the corridor, the barrel of his assault rifle pointed straight at them. No chance. Both men knew they would be cut down long before they could bring their own weapons to bear.

'Where's the big prize, Dance?'

'In there,' Harry motioned his head towards the open study door, careful to keep his hands raised.

'What's it anyway?' Gericke asked, moving steadily closer, the barrel never wavering.

'The stuff dreams are made of,' Harry said with a sad smile. It seemed like a lifetime ago when he had uttered that phrase gazing down at a doomsday device the size of a football. Another time, another place.

'Diamonds,' he said softly, seeing the other man's puzzled expression. There seemed little point in being evasive.

Gericke nodded. 'It makes sense.' He raised the rifle, 'So long, Dance.'

The single shot was loud in that confined space, Harry thought there was even an echo somewhere down the corridor. Frozen they watched the expression on Gericke's face turn to one of baffled surprise, the man lowering his head to stare dumbfounded at the growing red stain on his belly. Vusi staring with alarm at where the fast travelling bullet had torn a hole through the sleeve of his jacket.

Seemingly in slow motion Gericke sank to his knees, lips mouthing a protest that never made it into words. Then, with a sigh, he toppled face down onto the floor, the rifle clattering down beside him.

'I hate crooked cops,' Piet Niemand said as he stepped into the pooled light of the overhead hallway chandelier. In his hand was a smoking .38 Special.

'Shooting a cop,' Harry said, 'that's a serious business.' He nodded in the direction of the other man's gun. 'They'll trace that firearm to you.'

The big man shook his head as he bent down to check the fallen man's pulse and, finding none, straightening up with a grunt. 'Throwaway back up piece,' he said staring down at the gun with a frown. 'Unregistered and untraceable. Never leave home without it. Jeez, don't you guys watch TV?'

There was a crackle of static as Selena's voice came on their radios. 'We're on the police radios now. Armed robbery in progress, Ridge Road. All units.'

There was no time to waste, obviously an alarm had been triggered or possibly a neighbour had phoned in deciding the gunfire was more than the usual for a weeknight in Durban.

'Piet! To the front gates, block them with your car. Vusi, help me drag the strongbox over to that window, the damn thing's bloody heavy, I reckon there might even be gold bars at the bottom. Then get Selena to bring the van around to the side and we'll load it. Move!'

Seconds later, having lifted the box through the window with Vusi outside and dragging it across the porch to the idling ambulance that now had all its lights flashing, Harry found himself alone. Hastily shovelling into a canvas bag the stacks of cash he became aware of a second person in the room. Turning he found himself face to face with Smit, the wounded man's expression a mask of pain, in his hand an automatic was pointed down as he struggled to raise it. 'Seems like old times, Harry,' he said with a weary attempt at a smile.

'Yes,' Harry said simply, part of his brain registering the sound of nearing sirens.

'I had to come back...' Smit said, raising the gun.

'I know,' Harry said and shot him. Just one bullet. He knew it was enough, the man had been all but dead already. As he watched the broken body crumple to the ground he was suddenly filled with a deep and unnerving sadness. Old memories. How many more times would he find himself here?

With renewed focus he zipped up the bag and ran for the window, half dragging the heavy weight behind him. Then he was climbing through and Vusi was helping him and they were in the back of the ambulance and heading for the gate.

As they careered through the ruined gates, swinging left up Ridge Road and away from the fast approaching sirens, Piet Niemand's Camry slotted into their wake with a screech of tyres and the protesting howl of an over revved engine.

They had made it! Against all the odds, they had made it! Glancing through the rear windows he could see the first of the patrol cars, lights flashing coming over the rise in the distance and he gave the signal for Selena to switch off their own. No sense in drawing attention now.

'Better to split up,' Niemand came over the radio, 'I'll head downtown to pick up Tsotsi as planned and meet you back at base.'

'Roger. You're fading in and out of range. Go back to the phones,' Harry replied.

They were headed for the safe house in Umhlanga, a few miles north of Durban, a rambling old two storey set well back in an overgrown garden with, most importantly, a large double garage where they had done the work on the van. Harry had decided it too risky to travel far with the goods, going to ground early being a safer option.

At that hour the streets were all but deserted.

Inside the van a party atmosphere had broken out, the adrenalin levels still way up there and the tension of the raid fast ebbing. Incredible! They had never done anything quite like this before! All that planning, the umpteen times they had done the drill, Harry as always insisting everyone knew their role...

'Slow down!' Harry shouted across from the back of the van where he was struggling to secure the heavy sliding box. 'We don't need a traffic cop pulling us over. Or...' He was going to add "accident." Not now that they were this close.

'Police cars coming this way, Harry! I can see their lights.'

'Damn! Must be units coming in from Umhlanga.' Thinking quickly, Harry instructed Selena to turn off the highway, take a little used road that, just beyond the mouth of the river, turned inland in the direction of nearby hills passing through a series of squatter camps along the way.

The road was little more than a track, nominally surfaced but with all attempts at maintenance long abandoned. As they bumped along Harry waited until they rounded a small bend then instructed Selena to pull up in the shadow of a large tree and douse the lights. They sat like that in complete silence for what seemed like minutes, each aware of the other's breathing as they listened to the sounds of the sirens fading in the distance.

Finally Harry decided it was safe to proceed. 'Safer to stay on this road,' he said, 'it will join up somewhere ahead with a main road that will take us to the house. Keep it slow!'

But, with the imminent danger gone, the spirits of elation and flooding relief quickly returned and as Selena took the first of the tight turns climbing up the hills she was joining a jubilant Vusi in the first strains of The Gambler.

'You've got to know when to hold 'em. Know when to fold 'em...'

They were leaving the last of the squatter camps behind now, the incessant barking of endless stray dogs fading into the night and Harry rested his back against the side of the vehicle having found a pillow to sit on. He was starting to feel tired, old wounds from too many tight scrapes with the devil taking their toll, especially the omnipresent pain in the shoulder, the legacy of that time he was dangling from the guard rail of an icebreaker and thinking this is it.

Maybe he was getting post traumatic stress disorder, at least that's what he thought the term was. So many of his comrades seemed to labour under that diagnosis. Too many battles, too many dead faces...

'... *You never count your money, when you're sitting at the table...*'

Harry was jerked from his reverie by a shout from the front and a violent swerve as, coming around a sharp bend, Selena was confronted by a milling herd of goats dead ahead. Skidding on the unsurfaced road the van hit a large pothole, swung violently to one side, then toppled slowly onto its side, the rear half dangling over a steep drop.

Scrambling painfully onto his hands and knees, Harry could see that, restrained by their seatbelts, the others were unscathed and struggling to undo the buckles. The impact had shifted both steel box and heavy canvas satchel to the rear end of the van and, as his eyes adjusted to the gloom, Harry could see through the rear windows that there was a distant hill, sharply outlined against the night sky.

The hill was rocking. Slowly, up and down.

'Everyone OK?'

Answering monosyllables from the front indicated they were, although there was blood on the side of Vusi's face where he would have bashed it in the rollover.

'We're balanced on the edge of a drop, I'm not sure how far down it goes,' Harry said, 'Stay up front while I take a look through the rear windows.'

With that he started moving gingerly to where he could make out the metal box and the heavy canvas bag lying next to the doors. A sharp pain in his side made him pause for breath, taking the time to clear some of the myriad small objects that had spilled from the shelving that represented their efforts at creating a plausible ambulance scenario. As he did so he glanced at the rear windows again and was alarmed to see more of the valley below; in fact moonlight glistening on a winding river. At the same moment there was an ominous creak of strained metal and a small but definite movement under his feet.

Jesus! They were balanced on the edge of the knife, a thousand feet drop below! Any further weight shift towards that box and bag was liable to tip them over. 'Nobody move! Don't come back here. Vusi, see if you can kick out the windscreen, then climb out onto the hood, shift your weight forwards. Take Selena with you.'

He was sweating now, old body aches clamouring for attention which he firmly pushed out of his mind. Glancing at his objectives he gauged the distance at no more than six feet away. So close! Yet he knew it was a bridge too far. To his rear he could hear Vusi grunt as he repeatedly kicked at the windscreen, after a few seconds announcing that it was giving way.

His violent jerking action was starting to rock the van and at a cautioning from Selena he slowed down. 'What do you think, Harry?' she called while keeping an anxious eye on what Vusi was doing as he carefully folded the shattered glass outwards. 'Think you can reach it?'

Ignoring the question Harry asked if there was any rope in their kit, something he could throw over the items as a loop, draw them towards him.

There wasn't.

Vusi was crawling out onto the vehicle's stubby nose now, struggling to keep his grip on the slippery metal. 'For God's sake, don't get off!' Harry shouted as there was another deep groan from under the van followed by the sound of dislodged rocks careering down the cliff face.

Moving forwards to where his back was now against the driver's seat, Harry forced himself to think clearly. One option was to all climb onto the hood then, at a signal, all jump onto the road together and most likely watch the van, and their hard earned prize, tumble down into that ravine. Harry filed that one away under last resort.

Maybe Selena, whose slight frame couldn't possibly weigh more than what, 130 pounds, could swap places with him, make that trip and retrieve the canvas bag at least?

Smiling wryly to himself Harry knew he couldn't fool himself. He couldn't do that to his woman. Not in a thousand years. There *had* to be another way!?

There was a new sound in their confined space and it took Harry a few seconds to realise it was static from the radio, still tuned to the police frequency. 'What's it say?' he shouted over his shoulder at Selena who had also climbed out to join Vusi on the front end of the van.

'It says the clock is ticking, they're mounting a helicopter search at first light. They're looking for an ambulance, someone must have seen us.'

They still had time, the choppers wouldn't fly before dawn which was some hours away. 'Have you tried getting hold of Piet? He could drag us back onto the road.'

No phone reception,' Selena shouted, 'And we're out of range of our personal radios.'

Harry stared gloomily at the two items resting a few feet away, yet seemingly a mile away. Tired, his mind was beginning to wander, thoughts of Tsoti and Lukas and the other kids, all the plans they had for buying them that better life while placing themselves, finally, into the semblance of a normal life. Angrily he shook his head to clear his mind. This isn't you, Harry, *think*! Think outside the square, that's what you're good at.

Outside the square. That was it! Through a nebula of fatigue options were slowly taking shape and with that came a surge of energy pumping adrenalin. They still had the police radio as a means of communication and Piet was monitoring it, wasn't he? It would be easy for the man to drag them back onto the road. Be a problem however, if regular police units responded, arriving first...

He would have to give Niemand their location of course; a problem there. Then, secondly, he'd have to ensure the big cop knew it was a message aimed at him personally...

The answer, when it came to him, was so simple he laughed softly, shaking his head. It made the other two glance back at him uncertainly. Selena asking if he was OK?

'Nobody move!' he shouted over his shoulder. 'I've got a brilliant plan...'

There was a moment's silence from the front, Selena and Vusi exchanging glances, the black man still precariously balanced on the van's hood.

'How?' he shouted, 'we grow wings and fly outta here?' Adding, after a second, 'For God's sake, Harry, tell me you've got something for this bastard's going *down*!'

'The police radio! We send out a distress signal identifying ourselves as a police van involved in an accident and needing a tow out,' Harry shouted between helpless bouts of laughter, the sudden movement enough to rock the van, an ominous screeching sound cutting him short. Shifting right up to the front while casting an anxious eye at the vehicle's rear windows, he explained. 'Then we *become* Detective Captain Piet Niemand. Responding to our own distress signal...'

There was a moment's silence as this was digested. 'And Niemand, realising it's us, tells the others to back off, he's handling it,' Vusi added. 'It's so dumb it might just work!'

'Thank you,' Harry said, 'now pass me that mike. If I'm not mistaken we passed an all night fast food joint on the way up here. I'm starting to feel hungry. A hot coffee wouldn't be bad either, maybe some eggs on toast, pancakes with...'

THE END

www.ingramcontent.com/pod-product-compliance
Lightning Source LLC
Chambersburg PA
CBHW021324190726
48288CB00003B/952